Joyce
Happy Birthday

Mike

ALL I WANT FOR CHRISTMAS

michael i bresner

iUniverse, Inc.
Bloomington

All I Want for Christmas

iUniverse books may be ordered through booksellers or by contacting:

*iUniverse
1663 Liberty Drive
Bloomington, IN 47403
www.iuniverse.com
1-800-Authors (1-800-288-4677)*

*ISBN: 978-1-4759-6314-4 (sc)
ISBN: 978-1-4759-6315-1 (e)
ISBN: 978-1-4759-6316-8 (hc)*

Library of Congress Control Number: 2012921857

Printed in the United States of America

iUniverse rev. date: 01/3/2013

Acknowledgments

To my wife, Barbara,
who never complained when I woke in the middle
of the night to scribble another chapter.

Any many thanks to members of my critique groups and mentors:
Dick Towers, Sandra O'Connell, Janice Walker,
George Hess, Marissa Foix, Jeffrey Jacobs,
George Moore, and Susan Jordan.

DECEMBER 11th

chapter 1

He shifted his weight from one knee to another and then back again. The movements were not an attempt to combat the falling temperature—he was used to this extreme cold—but rather it was the anticipation of the event that he hoped would soon occur.

Crouched behind a high mound of snow, he watched the polar bear devour the freshly killed seal. It had taken more than twenty minutes to simply sneak up on the bear, to get within thirty yards without being detected and attacked. Now, waiting for the right time to act was taking an eternity. The bear's meal had been small, so he assumed the massive predator would soon be searching for additional nourishment. However, to the concealed spectator's surprise, the bear started to play with the carcass. It used its front paws to push the remains back and forth over the ice until the seal accidentally slid into the hole through which it had recently emerged. Only seconds passed before an icy slush engulfed what was left. It would be a short time more until solid ice would provide a permanent tomb.

The witness to this activity remained still and hidden. He rested one knee on the edge of a burlap sack he'd laid on the ground and readied himself to act should the animal detect his presence. He admired the Arctic's most efficient killing machine. Here was an animal that showed no fear, for there was nothing in this environment that offered any real natural threat. The bear was the top of the food chain. Death from a bear was usually quick and decisive—a rapid blow from the animal was enough to crush any opponent. The observer envied its efficiency.

The animal lumbered around the hole watching what was left of its meal bob up and down on the surface of the underlying glassy black water. The bear appeared tired, and the onlooker surmised it probably wanted to burrow into a protective snowdrift to rest, but he also knew the requirement to fulfill its hunger was more important than its need for sleep. A new hunt for food would soon commence.

A shift in the wind's direction carried an unfamiliar scent to the bear. It rose onto its hind legs to investigate; but when it saw the small figure stand, it lurched forward, landing on all four legs, and began to give chase.

The distance between the two adversaries rapidly diminished, and just before the bear launched its final charge, it encountered still another scent. It paused its attack to identify the odor. Unlike the first, this one was familiar—the scent of fresh blood.

The bear approached in steady, measured strides; its quarry remained immobile and continued to face his attacker. The animal's front legs swung out to the side, and its huge paws folded toward the body until, just as they were set down, they flicked forward. The arc of the longer back legs seemed to nudge the front ones forward. The wedged-shaped animal was not afraid of its next meal, but it was confused. Rarely would something this small dare to turn and fight.

Its prey kept eye contact.

The bear couldn't detect any fear in this small two-legged

creature, one that moved sideways and even slightly forward, but never backpedaled.

The enormous animal was only a few yards from its next meal when the figure threw the blood-scented sack. The hunter moved its head to easily dodge the bundle, which sailed harmlessly by. Striking the hard packed snow, the bag's drawstring broke, and the sack opened to allow a strong odor to stream out. The bear's front paw swiped at the cloth covering, and its sharp claws easily ripped through the flimsy material.

The now destroyed sack offered up its contents of a severed body: torso, arms, legs and a mutilated head.

The bear was too engrossed with its new meal to see the figure fleeing to safety across the snowy landscape.

DECEMBER 18TH

chapter 2

"Yes, I am concerned. It's been a week since he was last seen." Amak, the village's elected mayor, defacto law enforcement officer, part-time toy manufacturer, and unsuccessful labor organizer, was an unexpected visitor to Knute Brulog's home.

"Maybe Norved just took off," Mr. Brulog replied.

Trying to fight the cold, Amak paused to rub his hands together. "No, Knute. We searched his home, and he seemed to have left all his belongings in place. He even had food set aside for an evening meal."

Like most of the villagers, Knute was only slightly concerned. This time of year, it was common for someone to suddenly decide to abandon the village and return to their birthplace.

"Anyway," Amak said, "I'm just going around again, asking everyone if they remember anything that might shed a light on Norved's disappearance." He paused and glanced at Mrs. Brulog who was busy preparing the food. He hoped for an invitation to share the morning's meal, but none was voiced. Disappointed, he walked to the door and continued, "I'm sure he'll turn up sooner or later."

A blast of frigid air greeted Amak when he opened the door.

He hesitated at the opening, not wishing to leave the warmth of the house, but, realizing he must, he stepped into the cold.

Mrs. Brulog had added nothing to the conversation between her husband and Amak. She had silently stood by the sink readying and packing her husband's lunch, but as soon as the door closed, she spoke. "Isn't it odd that all of Norved's belongings were left behind? Do you think something bad has happened to him? I don't know; it doesn't sound right about him going missing. I just don't know."

Her husband seemed preoccupied and did not answer.

The day began the same as yesterday, dark and bitter cold, but Knute thought this day seemed a bit darker and a bit colder. The blackness was not going away and there would be no sun burning through. That great globe was vacationing on the other side of the earth and would not return for months.

The delicate crystals of frost united to create an opaque blanket on the window. Using the long, curved nail on his little sixth finger, he scraped a circle large enough to view the thermometer attached outside. The light from within the house passed through the circle and created a beam that illuminated the column of quivering mercury.

"Minus thirty-eight already. It's getting colder every day."

"Why complain?" his wife questioned. "You know as well as I do that last week's milder temperature was a fluke."

"The cold may be normal, but nobody says I have to like it. I'm the one who has to drag my tired body to the workshop every day, and when I arrive, there's no guarantee they'll have the heat turned up. I might as well be working outside."

He tried not to argue, it was typical of their relationship that if they disagreed about anything, especially work, they simply avoided the subject. The anger that had arisen so rapidly when he looked at the thermometer retreated just as quickly when he turned and looked

8

at his wife calmly working at the sink. He watched as she shuffled back and forth between the sink and the stove.

The cottage was one of the smallest in a village of small homes. The largest of the three rooms, twenty by twenty feet, included the kitchen area, a dinner table with three wooden chairs, a worktable and two stuffed lounge chairs. The stuffing in both was in desperate need of replacement. An unmatched patchwork of worn cloth covered the chairs, the latest piece of fabric obtained from a shirt recently discarded. It was an accumulation of furniture that would have remained unsold and unclaimed at the end of a daylong flea market.

She absentmindedly looked up towards the broken clock on the wall but assumed the time was nearing for him to leave and that she should serve breakfast. A small pot of meat and barley soup in a large blackened pot simmered on top of the stove. The aroma from the morning meal easily overpowered all other smells in the small cottage.

He lumbered to the kitchen table, sat down, and watched as she ladled out two bowls of the same soup they had eaten for the past three days. He hoped that today would finally deplete this, her favorite meal. His tolerance for the monotony of the weather and of the menu had grown thin.

His wife also had to go to work. He knew this. During this season, their boss expected everybody in the village to work. Mrs. Brulog, too, had to suffer the cold, but she chose to be the stoic, never complaining aloud. He thought of this but decided his work was far more demanding and stressful. Thus rationalizing, he again felt he had the right to voice his anger. "Damn it all!"

They had been married long enough for her to understand his moods, so she ignored the comment and changed the subject in an attempt to arrest his rising frustration and rage. "By the way, when are you going to fix the clock?" she asked with a smile. "You're the great handyman. Maybe you've some mystical ability to know the exact time without a clock, but I don't."

"I'm really sorry. Really I am," he answered. "You know I don't have a spare minute right now." Guilt replaced his anger. "After the holiday, I promise, I'll get to everything that needs repair."

"Only the clock is broken," she said, almost apologizing for the fact that they owned little else, and that, more than anything, kept breakdowns rare. "Anyway, who cares what time it is? Nothing ever changes here. There's nothing that can't wait."

"Nothing but work, and I have to get going," he replied. He gazed at the window hoping that, somehow in the few minutes since he had last looked, the weather might have changed.

She gathered some crackers from a ceramic cookie jar meant to look like a laughing Santa Claus and carried them and the two bowls of soup to the table. He delayed eating until she sat, placed the napkin on her lap, and took her first spoonful. They finished the meal quickly, without speaking, but there was no silence. The wind had increased and howled steadily. A groan from outside that sounded like a voice in pain interrupted his thoughts of work. In unison, he and his wife asked each other, "What did you say?"

"I thought you said something, honey."

"I thought I heard you asking me something," he replied.

A muffled creak on the roof drew their attention. They looked at the ceiling, again acting in unison.

"Just the wind," he said.

"But the voice?"

"Just the wind," he repeated. "Nothing more."

Staring at the ceiling, she stood, and slowly backing away from the origin of the noise, she bumped into her husband's chair. She turned to apologize and noted that he still was staring at the ceiling.

The room was in shadows except for an area surrounding the

nearby workbench. There, the husband had long ago suspended two bare light bulbs from long electric wires looped then hung from the thick, wooden rafters.

Wherever his wife stepped, a small cloud of dirt mushroomed into the air; but even these inert particles seemed cold, and they soon floated down to huddle in neat piles.

"I have to first drop off some things in Tooten before going to work. Nothing like taking an extra hike in the cold. Of course, then I get to travel two more miles back to the workshop. Gosh forbid they'd give me a sled and some dogs to make life any easier." He looked at his wife as he continued. "If I reach my quota, maybe they'll let me come home at the end of the scheduled shift. If so, we'll play cards and talk some before bedtime."

"That would be nice if you could," she remarked skeptically. Both knew that he couldn't. During the last few days of the holiday season, there was no upper limit to the work quota. Reach one level of production and someone immediately raised the demands. No, he wouldn't be home early. She walked over to him and lovingly squeezed his hand.

They gathered the toys from around the room and the workbench, and while he held a cloth sack open below the edge of the old pine table, she carefully began to slide the toys in. As she pushed a small, squirrel-shaped clock into the bag, it bounced off the lip of the sack and tumbled to the floor. The tick-tocking continued uninterrupted. He quickly stooped to pick up his craft and carefully examined each section. "Just my luck," he said wearily. "Part of the tail is scratched and chipped off." The veneer of dust, although thick, had not been enough to prevent the damage.

"Can you fix it?" she asked softly, annoyed with herself for adding to his woes.

He realized he was looking for sympathy when he deserved none and told her all he had to do to repair the damage was to apply a

11

little paint. He placed the clock gently on top of the rest of the toys in the sack, tugged at the two drawstrings to close the opening, and tied a double knot to assure it would not come loose—nothing must fall out on his way to work.

His wife walked to the front door and removed his bulky wool coat from the wooden wall peg. "Button up honey," she chided as she handed it to him. "This time of the year would be a horrible time to get sick."

They both turned when they heard a thud against the door. "Who's there?" his wife questioned. No one answered. She assumed it was the wind dislodging a chunk of snow from the roof but again questioned aloud if anyone was at the door—she didn't want anyone left standing out in the cold. Again, nobody answered. Even the howling from the wind seemed to abate.

"Great day to have to walk to work," her husband again complained.

He took the coat from his wife, slipped it on, and felt immediate warmth from the new covering. Although he knew that pleasurable feeling would quickly disappear once outside, he had no alternative to this second-hand garment since his bearskin and seal hide parka had literally fallen apart last month. The coat sleeves, although shortened, were still an inch or so too long for his stubby arms; and once the coat was on, he always found it difficult to use his hands for any intricate task.

"Dear, I put my hat and gloves on the mantel to dry. Would you please get them for me?" He watched as the dust followed her feet like a vapor trail dragged along by a highflying jet. "Did you pack my lunch?"

"Yes," she replied and pointed to the other side of the room.

They arrived at the sink simultaneously. He took the gloves from his wife and put them on deliberately, not wanting to accidentally poke a finger through the thin material. Like a mother dressing her youngest son, his wife pulled a tassel cap onto his head. She tugged it further down to ensure the cap protected his pointed ears against the outside cold. He, in turn, did not struggle against her help, but was engrossed with wedging his gloved, right hand under the handle of the lunch box embossed with a picture of last year's teen idol. The snug fit would guarantee he would not lose his grasp. He walked to the center of the room, grabbed the cord dangling from the sack with his stronger left hand, and swung the heavy bulk up and over his shoulder. He did not anticipate its full weight and staggered back a few steps until regaining his balance.

"Well I'm off to deliver the toys," and he added mockingly, "Ho! Ho! Ho!"

"Now that's the attitude you need," she replied and stood on her toes to gently kiss his cheek. "Why don't you wear a scarf to protect your neck? Let me get it for you," she volunteered. "You'll catch your death if you are not dressed properly."

"Don't bother," he protested softly. "I'll just pull the collar up if I need to. See you later." He wanted to hug her, but both his arms were occupied, so he instead smiled as she opened the front door.

chapter 3

The last flakes from the early morning snowfall fell gently to the already white ground. The unbroken carpet stretched in all directions, interrupted not by colors but by shades. The villagers considered color a treasured luxury in the Arctic vastness. The monotony of the boundless, desolate landscape was deceptive. It was a frozen, but not a dead, world. Although difficult to locate, life forms did exist. In an environment that was so hostile, all species became hunters. Thus, when the circle was completed, the hunters often found themselves victims.

As he did most every day, Knute stepped into this frozen, lonely world. His eyes adjusted to the darkness, and straining to see across the open field, he viewed the twinkling of the lights from the village center and the workshop. His broad, flat shoes prevented him from sinking into the new powdery snow as he began the trudge to the neighboring village, Tooten.

A gust of raw wind greeted him as he rounded the front of the cottage. The blowing, frozen snow struck him full face, and even his long, unkempt beard offered little protection from the burning stings that the crystals produced. He turned his back to the needle-like flakes and waited for the tempest to ebb. After a minute without any change in the wind's force, he decided to abandon the planned route across the open area. He chose instead a longer path that would take him through the mounds of ice and snow at the perimeter of the flat terrain. These natural barriers would provide the protection he desired.

The white walls of snow reflected the scant available light and made it easier for him to negotiate the small and large crevices in the ice-covered ground. The trek was familiar and his concentration was not required to contemplate each step. Instead, he thought about going on vacation after the holiday. Maybe they would visit his wife's family. They had not seen each other for more than a year. With less available craftsmen than last year, the work this year was frantic. Even so, he was one of the fortunate ones. With his seniority, he was able to choose the section he wished to toil in, and thus each season, he was able to select a different group of toys to design or assemble. He pitied those forced to assemble the same item each year.

If it were only the boredom of the same job, it might not be so bad, but coupled with the boredom of the Arctic environment, the rate of workers quitting the shop increased each year. Amak was right. Maybe they should have voted for and tried to force unionization in order to help working conditions. But he already had his security. He was one of the lucky ones, and anyway, change was next to impossible in this eternally icy kingdom.

A chunk of falling ice started a minor avalanche of balls of snow to cascade down the mound lining the path. The dull thuds they produced when they struck the ground partially camouflaged the sounds of something rapidly moving away.

"Hi, ho. Anybody there?"

His only answer was the Arctic wind blowing through the canyon of ice and snow. His left arm tired from carrying the heavy sack, and he swung the weight from his shoulder to the ground. By stretching his arm and repeatedly opening and closing his fist, the numb sensation that had crept into his stressed muscles began to subside. He reached down, pulled on the cord securing the sack and found the knot had worked loose. He extracted his other hand from the lunch box and removed his gloves in order to retie the knot. In the few seconds it took to perform the task, his exposed fingers began to feel the effects of the bitter cold. He rubbed his hands together, replaced his gloves, and rubbed the now protected hands again. The pain, which had been evolving, disappeared a minute later.

The heaps of snow lining the twisting path were more than fifteen feet high in this area, and he could no longer see his home behind him nor the village ahead. Realizing he was more than halfway to Tooten and that he had left early enough to arrive on time, he decided to lean against the adjacent wall of white and rest a while longer.

The wind must have tired, too, as it suddenly stopped. For a brief moment, he again thought he heard loose snow crushed beneath footsteps. Mystified and alarmed, he remembered Amak's concern with Norved's disappearance. If he hadn't deserted the village, what could have happened? *Maybe he had fallen into an ice crevasse, or worse yet, maybe a polar bear had attacked and killed him.* Accidents, even fatal ones, occurred on a regular basis, but a polar bear mauling was rare. It was odd for a bear to roam this far north during December, but it had happened before. Perhaps it was foraging for scraps of food in the village. The toymaker remembered all of this and worried.

His ears flared out to trap any sounds but heard none. He tried to recall and identify the noise he had just heard. No two feet striking the ground were exactly the same. No two men, no two animals created the same sounds. The loudness, the rhythm of their gait was a fingerprint for each individual creature, but there were no longer any sounds to analyze.

His eyes widened in an attempt to view the top of the mound of snow. There is nothing any animal fears more than the unknown. The hair on the back of his neck stood on end, and he felt the thumping of his heart increase in speed and intensity. He would have felt safe with a companion, but he was alone.

A large piece of loose, frozen snow fell and struck his shoulder. The unexpected sensation changed the fear into panic. He quickly turned to see what had battered him and slipped on an icy patch that had formed beneath his feet. As he tumbled to the ground, his head hit a projection on the side of the snow bank. He began losing consciousness even as he fell, but instead of propelling him further into the abyss of senselessness, the contact his head made with the path below actually jolted his awareness. The cold on the back of his exposed neck awakened him even more.

For an instant, everything felt oddly peaceful. His fear no longer present.

Instinctively, he did not attempt to rise. Other than his head, nothing really hurt, but when he looked at his limbs, he saw the lower portion of his left leg jointed and bent where no joint should have been. He thought not of future inconveniences caused by the fracture but of the time off from work because of the disability. Time off that would last well past the seasonal rush. His dazed mind envisioned the confines of his comfortable, warm bed. Broken bones need not be all that bad.

The wind picked up and made a snarling sound. The noise, not the temperature, made him shiver. It took only a moment for him to realize the wind did not create the noise, but that it was coming from an object atop the canyon wall. And although he tried to focus, his blurred vision was limited to five or six feet.

The sound changed to a sickly, murderous howl as a blur descended from the heights above him. He knew the action was progressing rapidly, but the scene presented itself like a series of time-lapse photographs. The blur entered his focal range, and the encasing white walls of ice and snow illuminated the first frame of a discernible image. Twelve hairy toes with razor-sharp talons stood poised above his head ready to strike. He turned his head to the side as his perception of the events returned to normal speed. The scream he now heard was not coming from the attacker but from his own throat. The object had landed on his neck, and a slicing, burning pain began to spread. He reached for the painful area of skin with his hand and felt not skin but the raw, warm surface of exposed muscle. Holding his hand close to his eyes, he could see the reddish-brown color of his own blood. Clots were already freezing on the webbings between his fingers. From the corner of his eye, he could see a fountain of blood pulsating into the air above his neck. Aware that a major artery must have been severed, he tried to utilize his hand as a tourniquet around his neck.

He used his free arm to prop himself up, and he attempted to locate the attacking bear's position. His eyes stopped searching when he spied a pool of dark snow still steaming from the heat of the blood pouring from his wound. In shock and oddly detached from the danger, he watched the river of blood showering onto the snow, first melting the cold surface, then overcome by the frigid temperature, turning into a frozen red patch on the sterile white ground.

A gurgling noise, followed by laughter, intensified behind him. He twisted to see the animal he knew was going to kill him. A mouth disproportionately large to the small face that surrounded it greeted him. The mouth maintained the smile possessed from its previous laughter, but as it slowly, tauntingly approached, an expression of hatred replaced the smile. Saliva overflowed the sharp, pointed lower canines. The prison of teeth held the portion of meat that had recently been part of Knute's neck.

It was not a bear that had attacked—he knew that now. The darkness that was enveloping him prevented the victim from identifying his killer.

The mouth opened more and lunged for the already wounded, exposed neck. In the blackness of impending death, the mangled body felt the teeth sink into the skin, clamp shut, and then pull back. Knute once again attempted to scream, but the voice box was no longer there, and the last sound he heard was a hissing as the air escaped through the hole in his neck.

chapter 4

The bear cub slipped as it tried to climb the hummock and jagged ice ridges. His mother had been leading him on this circular excursion for well over an hour and the pangs of hunger now overtook the cramping muscle aches in his legs. It was unusual that the two bears weren't comfortably curled in a snow den, but a loud thumping noise had startled the mother. She had pulled her son closer and listened intently for additional sounds, but none presented. Drifting back to sleep had been easy, but soon after she closed her eyes, a rumbling awoke both. Fully alert, the mother had feared that the ice floe might be cleaving and decided to vacate their temporary winter quarters.

The cub opened his mouth to broadcast a growl of discontent, but a flurry of snow blew into his face and the irritation initiated a series of quick sneezes. There was no need for any signal from her cub. The mother knew he was hungry, and hopefully, for her own increasing hunger, he was tiring too. She knew she could find any number of seals' breathing holes in the ice floes, but she also knew any attempt to stalk and kill a seal would be impossible if accompanied by her son. It was certain that no seal would surface if there were a noise. Absolute stealth was needed to obtain food, and her cub had yet to learn all of the lessons of the hunt.

Months earlier it would not have been necessary to leave their natural ice cave on the floe. Then, she still had a store of food in her body and her new son, still blind and hairless, was content to suckle the warm milk from her nipples. Nestled and curled inside the confines formed by her legs and underside, he had obtained the warmth needed to survive the icebox he was born into. The weeks had passed and the cub's fur had lost its yellow tint; within the next month it had developed into the thick, creamy white coat of his mother. The milk no longer satiated him, and the meat of seals, young walruses, and pieces of stranded whales that his mother brought him now supplemented his diet.

He was definitely tiring now and would soon topple to the ground. While he slept, his mother hoped to leave and make the kill alone, without the noise of wasted motions. Sensing his fatigue, she quickened their walking pace as they approached a sheltering crevice in a small mound of ice.

She waited until he caught up to her and with a gentle push from her giant paw, nudged the cub through the opening. A second nudge pushed him gratefully to the ground, where he collapsed with a soft whimper. She stood by her young pupil until he fell into a deep, needed sleep. Knowing he might panic if he awoke alone in this barren, white landscape, she turned to hurry back to the seal's breathing hole.

A foreign scent drifted into her nostrils. Poised for danger, she stood silent, listening for a sound that might accompany the odor. None did. Lifting her five-hundred and fifty pound frame onto her back feet, her head now over seven feet above the ground; she searched for a clue to the nasal intrusion. She stretched her long neck for a better view but did not see anything extraordinary against the continuous arctic white. The smell was gone now, and she settled back to support her body on all four padded feet.

A prowling arctic fox might blend well into the monotone of the surrounding vista, but she would easily see the slate blue and brown varieties. Still, it remained possible one was present and burrowed into a loose pile of snow. Certainly, the small, three-foot-long fox was not a threat to the mother bear and probably not to her cub. The young polar bear's worst natural enemy was another polar bear. A hungry male bear often showed no hesitation in making one of its own kind, even one of its own offspring, its next meal. Quelling one's hunger and not the perpetuation of the species was the prime motivator to those in constant search for food.

Crouched by the breathing hole, the mother bear used her sharp claws to enlarge the small opening. She quickly finished the task and positioned herself to remain as motionless as the surrounding frozen scene. The Arctic is the ideal place to learn patience. Her breath joined with the frigid polar air forming a vapor that dispelled in an invisible breeze. She tried to slow her chest movements so that the whispers of her own breathing would not interfere with her attempts to hear the popping bubbles when the seal exhaled near the surface. The hole in the ice meant the seal would have an opportunity to obtain the life-requiring oxygen. The bear would strive to make this the site of the seal's last breath. Now, in early winter, the sun was well below the horizon, and at this time of day, the clear winter sky achieved only a dusk-like haziness. The bear realized it would be difficult to see the seal's bubbles, but tried to place herself in the best possible position for the kill.

Only the animals changed in the colorless Arctic desert. For more than one million years, the snow and ice blanketed the area. Survival was always difficult and adaptation to the environment made this survival somewhat easier. The bear's white coat, the pad of fur on the soles of her feet, her layers of fat, her ability to swim great distances, to run up to twenty-five miles per hour, her tolerance of the loneliness—all through evolutionary changes—allowed the polar bear to exist in this desolate region of cold.

The mother had been sitting at the hole more than twenty minutes and she began to worry about the cub left behind in the temporary den. She could wait only a few minutes longer before forced to return to check on her son; then if he awoke, there would be no chance of food again until tomorrow. That too would be a valuable lesson taught. She sniffed the air again, trying to remember and identify the strange odor she detected before, but no scent lingered.

Popping bubbles interrupted her thoughts. Her eyes opened wide and her pupils dilated to take in as much light as possible. Again, she heard the bubbles breaking at the water's surface, but this time she was also able to see them. The muscles in her front legs tensed and she slowly raised her right paw a few inches above the ice floor.

Like the tip of a periscope, a nose breached the surface of the water but quickly retreated from view. The bear remained silent, knowing that any sound, any movement, would warn the seal of its presence. Bubbles again popped and the nose appeared once more, this time followed by the top of a head and two large, watery black eyes. The head had emerged facing away from the side of the hole where the bear waited, and as the seal's body turned to take in the full vista, its webbed flipper propelled the head a few more inches above the water.

The few inches were enough—the massive right front paw whipped against the side of the seal's head, instantly crushing it. Retracing the arc of her swing, the paw stopped above the seal's limp body and scooped it out of the water before it had time to sink.

She laid the one-and-one-half-foot long ringed seal on the icy table adjacent to its breathing hole. There was no playing with the catch. The hunter did not pause to rest. She pushed the seal once or twice to corroborate its death and then seized it with her teeth. The bear's canines easily pierced the thick skin and fixed firmly in the underlying fatty layer.

The mother hastily loped back to her sleeping cub. Approaching, she again paused to check for any strange odor or disturbance in the scene around her. The mild scent from her catch masked any other smell and the stillness of the landscape seemed unchanged.

She dropped the seal unceremoniously in front of her cub's nose, and the combination of noise and smell immediately woke the sleeping youngster. He still did not understand how these meals mysteriously appeared after he fell asleep, but his hunger did not allow time for contemplation. Still lying on the icy bed, he stretched all four legs, rubbed his eyes, and stood.

Using a front paw to pin down the seal, the cub bit into the meaty underbelly and began his meal. His teeth not yet dulled by the abrasion of crunching through bones allowed the sharp cusps to easily penetrate, rip, and cut the meat into sections readily swallowed. As famished as he had been, only a few small mouthfuls were enough to diminish his hunger. He stepped back from the meal, licked his paws clean, and rubbed his nose on the floor. His mother, who had waited patiently, now approached the partially eaten seal and used the same technique of pinning and biting to remove the remaining meat and fat from the carcass.

For both mother and son, a self-cleaning and preening process continued for another few minutes.

The mother stood and used her long nails to rake the opening in the icy crevice, wide enough to accommodate both bodies. She backed into the now larger cave-like space, collapsed into a ball, and gently pulled the cub towards her warm body. Curled and intertwined, the two quickly fell into a deep, contented sleep.

A slow, continuous shaking of the underlying ground woke the mother. The sensation caused by the breaking of the floating ice mass was common in the Arctic. Her son could already swim; that was not her fear, but he might be caught in the crushing grip of colliding ice masses. It was better to move rapidly away from the rumbling warning sounds.

She roused her son, then, not too gently, shoved him through the opening of their icy bedroom. The blowing snow had diminished the size of the hole, and the cub's face, then body, dilated the exit as he passed through. The mother paused to lick some fresh, powdery snow to quench her thirst. She used her paw to enlarge the opening even more, and with the increased view, she was able to glimpse her son pacing in circles in front of the icy overhang.

Her immense body had not completely cleared the portal when the smell attacked her nostrils. It was the same odor she detected before, but now much stronger. She hurried out to reach her son—her defenses distracted by her maternal instincts.

A howl resonated from above and behind. She turned in time to see a figure dropping from the roof atop the snow mound. A mouth with disproportionately large teeth preceded a small form. The figure landed on her back before she could react. In a single continuous motion, she tried to dislodge her attacker by twisting and then standing on her rear feet, but the intense pain from the sharp teeth entering her fur-covered neck caused her to collapse back onto the ground.

Lying on her side, she could see her young son rearing on his hind feet but remaining a distance from the danger. He was just mimicking the stance he had seen his mother take many times before when confronted with possible danger. Never, though, had there been any real threat. Nothing had ever dared attack the massive polar bear. He had no idea what he could do to aid his mother. That lesson had never been taught.

The teeth would not release their vice-like grip on her neck. She tried to turn her head to see her attacker but couldn't without inflicting even more pain. The blood was rapidly draining from her wound, and with each heartbeat, more blood pumped to the ground. The attacker's weight shifted and she felt the teeth retract from the wound—perhaps there would now be a chance to escape.

She heard, before she saw, the steel blade cross in front of her face and enter her side. One of her larger ribs blocked deep penetration of the knife and there was little additional damage. The blade was withdrawn and again thrust into her side. This time, after hitting a rib, it slid off and punctured first her left lung and then her heart.

Her son knew that she was dead. The expression of death does not change. The seal's face had the same appearance of frozen fear when his mother had brought it home. Still, he did not know what to do. He lay, curled up whimpering, looking at his mother and her killer.

The attacker pulled the long, straight blade from the carcass, knelt astride the inanimate mass, and emitted a howl that echoed against the surrounding icy rises. Moving rapidly, he sliced, then hacked through the ankle area of all four of the polar bear's feet. Once freed from their ligament and tendon attachments the feet dropped to the snow where he picked them up and tossed them into a sack. "Sorry, sonny, I need mother's feet for a project planned later in the day."

He stood to leave and smiled when he saw the young cub gazing on the murder scene. Without food, the killer knew the cub wouldn't survive more than a few days. He also knew the cub was too young to have learned the hunting skills necessary to obtain any food.

Extending the blade in front of him, he approached the terrified cub. When the bear made no movement to protect itself, he grabbed its neck and dragged it to its mother. Pushing the cub's head towards his mother's carcass, he bent his own head backward to face the heavens and laughed.

DECEMBER 19th

chapter 5

"Don't worry, Mrs. Brulog, I'm sure your husband will turn up. We're all certain nothing bad has happened." Small white, bursts of vapor accompanied the words exiting Amak's mouth. He watched to see any indication whether she believed the unlikely possibility that his utterance was true, but all she did was cross her arms against her chest. Amak wasn't sure if she did this to guard against the cold or the possible truth about her husband's disappearance. "Now, if we could go over everything that occurred right before Knute left yesterday morning."

Mrs. Brulog stared at the group of villagers mingling in front of the workshop. They huddled in groups of three and four, speaking in subdued voices, anxiously discussing the mysterious disappearance of another of their own. No matter who or how many times somebody told her that everything would work out for the best, she was still convinced something bad had happened. She was equally convinced that everyone thought her husband was just another worker who suddenly decided to quit his job and abandon the village. Certainly, such acts were commonplace during this time of year. Most times, it was one of the older individuals, like Knute; but unlike her husband, it was usually one who no longer could tolerate the hectic pace required during the Christmas season.

Amak turned and glanced at the clusters of onlookers, and he knew the rest of the villagers assumed that tomorrow, or at the very most, in another week, word would filter back that someone had seen Mr. Brulog in one of the nearby villages. But like Mrs. Brulog, he had his own doubts. Last week Neved had also disappeared, and although his parents were from a village only a day's walk away, no word ever returned that anyone had seen him. When questioned by Amak, the missing worker's girlfriend could not think of any reason for his disappearance. They had not fought, and as far as she knew, all was well at work. His belongings remained untouched in the cottage he shared with another friend. The puzzle remained unsolved, and Amak's only annoyance was because the untoward event would further disturb his daily routine.

Amak interrupted Mrs. Brulog's reflections and again inquired if she might have forgotten to tell him anything about Knute's disappearance.

She turned to face her inquisitor. "There's nothing to forget," she insisted. "Knute left home yesterday morning. He went to Tooten to deliver some presents for the workers to complete, and then he planned to return to begin his shift at the workshop. He was carrying a sack of toys he'd brought home to repair—to repair on his own time, I might add. No one asked him to do that, but he always did more than was asked." She again stared, past Amak, beyond the village, into the blackness of the sky. "That's all that happened. He never returned home. When I returned from my job, he wasn't there, and eight hours later he still hadn't come home."

"Could he have returned and left again while you were at work, Mrs. Brulog?"

She ground her teeth and took a deep breath. The intake of the frigid air elicited a series of barking coughs. She looked at Amak through squinted eyes and replied loudly, "No! No food was eaten. The bed wasn't messed. Nothing in the cottage changed from the time I left. I've already told you—he never returned!"

Amak judged that additional questioning would not yield any helpful information. "Mrs. Brulog, I want you to go home." He placed his hand on her shoulder. It was more of a command than a sympathetic gesture. "I'll send one of the other women with you. I think it would be best if you wait there in case Knute returns. I'm sure everything will be all right." He realized he was being redundant, but deemed the reassurance was expected. "I'm in the process of putting together some search parties and they'll be leaving any minute now."

The temperature continued to drop, and in a futile attempt to close off the cold, she crossed her tattered shawl over the front of her cloth coat. She was docile now. The questioning, the temperature, and her anxieties had extracted their toll. Earlier, when alone and having the time to think about her missing husband, she actually hoped he had abandoned her. The only other likely alternative was far more dreadful.

"Thank you, Amak. I'm sorry I raised my voice before." She shuffled her feet and alternated her gaze between the ground and the sky. "My husband always had kind words to say about you. Back when others voiced their opposition in your attempt to organize the workers, my Knute said he felt that you were doing it because you believed it would be in their best interests. You know he voted for your plan. He said you were fair and that you honestly cared."

"I am sorry we lost that vote, Mrs. Brulog. I'm sure if the referendum had passed, everyone would be happier today. Anyway, he'll have another chance to correct the naysayers' poor judgment on next year's ballot. I won't give up."

"I won't either, Amak. I'm sure Knute will be home before long."

He had already started turning away. "I'm sure he will, Mrs. Brulog."

Amak made the necessary arrangements with two of the village's women to accompany Mrs. Brulog home. Unlike himself, she wouldn't be accustomed to the solitude, and no one should be compelled to be alone in this desolate place. Until yesterday, she had a constant, supportive companion. Someone to discuss the day's activities, both good and bad. Someone to embrace in bed. Until recently, Amak had chosen to isolate himself from the responsibility of any permanent relationship. Her isolation, however, was suddenly thrust upon her, and even the strongest could be destroyed by a sudden lack of companionship.

Amak had only a minimal kinship with Knute before the union organizational meetings began last year, and even though Knute was one of the few to voice his agreement that a union was in the workers' best interests, a personal relationship had never developed. Amak had expressed his gratitude to Knute for helping to shoulder the verbal attacks against the plan, but the two rarely saw one another outside the workshop.

Amak actually had thought he had a chance in his previous attempt to organize the workers. Then the boss appeared at one of the meetings, and with his usual persuasive oration, he had swayed the vote. The final tally wasn't even close. What little discussion that had followed didn't surprise Amak. The babbling of the workers, who had then explained to the boss that they couldn't understand how the issue had even come this far, was upsetting. But Amak was accustomed to it. They had been working under the same conditions and with the same work expectations their entire lives—the same as their parents and their parents' parents. No one expected the workers to express original ideas. They only had to perform their assigned tasks and meet their quotas. "After all," the boss had reminded them, "the timely culmination of your work is the important outcome. And remember, you're all responsible for its success."

The workers' actions and speeches had not bothered Amak that night. What did, however, was watching the boss slip into his bulky red costume before delivering the speech and once again stifle any free thought the workers might have had. Here in a land perpetually covered in white, it was the ultimate snow job. The speech never changed. "How can we think of changing the way we work? To change would be selfish. We all work for the good of others. We don't expect additional rewards more than we now have. No one here, including me, has any perks. What's there to gain by organizing and protesting?" And so forth and so forth.

The worker's heads dropped and Amak knew the battle was lost. Even so, a few continued to agree with his ideas. His closest friend, Erog, was one and, clandestinely, so did one of the boss's nephews. The fight would continue.

Amak returned to the staging area to be certain the members of the search party knew their orders. One missing individual was enough for today. There was an obvious loss of morale whenever someone left the village by choice and, worse yet, if the villagers thought the lack of return was not voluntary. Production at the workshop decreased; sickouts increased and when the workers returned, their loss of concentration produced mistakes; irritability between villagers bred fights; restlessness, apprehension, and anxieties were sure to increase. Unlike the boss whose only worry was production numbers, Amak's concern was that he was obliged to continue the appearance that he had everything under control.

Although he was the tallest person present, Amak chose to stand on a mound of snow to ensure those in the back of the group could hear and see him. He was less than five feet tall, but standing erect always made him appear taller. He had no facial hair, but he did have a bushy, singular eyebrow that extended from one eye to the other.

The hair on top of his head was thick, coal black, and worn in a short ponytail. His barrel chest was a consequence of genetics and physical conditioning, both of which he prided himself on.

"I don't want any of your wives waking me tonight. You're all intelligent enough to know that you must search only in pairs. No individual heroics. Should any of you find anything, anything at all, both members of the team come back right away and report to me.

"I spoke with Knute's wife and she doesn't think he just abandoned the village, but just in case, two of you search the path back to his parents' village. I think he came from Vibron. Does anybody here know for sure?"

A voice was raised from the middle of the group that Vibron was indeed Knute's native village, and since he, too, was from there, the volunteer would lead a team in that direction. Another voice said that Knute also lived for a short time in Tooten and he would search there.

"Just what are you planning to do while we freeze our asses off?"

Amak's lips tightened into a thin line, and he glared at Danat for a few seconds before he answered. "That's none of your damn business. What's your reason you don't want to help find Knute? Do you have something more important to do?"

"You know what, that's none of your damn business. And you know what else—I think I'll be staying here just to see how you can screw up an already screwed-up situation."

Those listening to the conversation were well aware of the hatred and the distrust between the two, but they also knew Knute would remain missing if the pissing contest continued. One of the members of the group interrupted the combatants. "Enough of this bull. Let's get started with the search."

Amak and Danat took steps toward each other but stopped short of any contact. Eventually, Danat turned and walked away; and after assigning the rest of the group to different search patterns, Amak waited until the last man melted into the sunless vista.

It was time to inform the illustrious leader of his latest inconvenience.

chapter 6

I t seemed appropriate that his lordship's cottage was on a rise, not a towering one, but one that elevated his home above every other structure in the village. The home was large, not because it housed such an important person, but because a smaller one would place undue physical restraints on its inhabitants. Amak never complained that his superior ever abused his authority by demanding lavish, materialistic luxuries. Aside from the greater square footage of his home, there were only two other perks, neither of which any villager regarded as a luxury. The first was a storeroom used to protect foodstuffs from roaming polar bears or any other predators. The workers did not eat as often or as much as their boss—they could exist on one-third his consumption—so they had no reason for their own storage sheds. When they had a successful hunt, they ate their quarry and only their quarry until only a carcass remained. Soups, stews, and meats were prepared to last days.

A short wave radio was the second perquisite. It kept the boss abreast of any world events that could require an alteration in product quantities or product destinations. Events taking place anywhere outside the circle of the surrounding villages was of little concern to the workers; they were resigned to the fact that nothing could possibly occur that might affect them outside the workshop.

As he approached the house, Amak could smell the afternoon meal. (Odors travel better in the cold Arctic air.) He guessed today's meal contained onions, fried potatoes, and meat. The meat probably overcooked to please its diner's taste.

The big guy must eat. Keep the jolly fat man happy.

A heavy black smoke curled down from the chimney, drifted into Amak's eyes, and made them water uncontrollably. If he stayed in the cold much longer, each of his eyelashes would soon be supporting its own icicle. He stopped walking for a moment and futilely attempted to rub away the irritation.

Then in a hushed tone, he reiterated the boss' mantra. "There must be no arguments in the village. Harmony must reign. Disharmony breeds discontent. Discontent breeds a reduction in production."

He slowly climbed the steps leading to the front door. A brace of large, red-and-white striped wooden candy canes flanked the oversized entrance. Originally, there had been red satin bows attached to the decorations, but the cold and wind had quickly, and without effort, destroyed them. Amak stepped between the ornamental sentinels and knocked on the door.

Working for the great Santa Claus was rarely fun. It was not all toys and games—that is except for the ones you had to make.

The year 1814 is identified as the year of the elves' salvation. During that year, Santa Claus, himself persecuted in his native Europe, sought the isolation of the Arctic for his new home. Of course, this was not the original Santa Claus. Although children tend to consider their favorite toy distributor eternal, Santa was and still is the title of the office, and as a mortal, did have a life expectancy not unlike others.

The Santa that settled in the Arctic was the sixth in a line that continues today. He left Europe an outlaw. Tried in absentia. Technically, he was accused and convicted of defying trade laws. His real crime was interfering with both the Church and State. Any act that weakened either was certain to bring about a death sentence, and this was his verdict in all but a few of the western European countries. To some, preaching that helping one another and giving free presents was a blessing. To others, it was an act of heresy or an act of treason. The clergy felt they should have the exclusive right to endear their flocks with charity. The powerful merchant guilds felt the transfer of goods required the transfer of money. As a consequence, most new years found Santa stealing away in the night, traveling to a new town or country. Each time someone discovered his home, local and state constabularies stumbled over each other to capture him and claim the substantial reward. The general populace, of course, protected him but he could never settle in one place long enough to establish the type of toy and gift production system he desired.

The alliance of Santa and the elves was beneficial to both. Before meeting, Santa had relied on the limited abilities of the inhabitants of whatever village he located in. He did not choose the village because of its workforce; he chose it because of its ability to hide him from the authorities. Toys were produced, but quality was not always the predominant feature. The expression, "It's not the gift but the thought that counts," was not without reason. Santa was often forced to leave broken toys beneath many a tree and in many mantel-hung stockings. Quantity, not quality, was the key to production.

Kris Kringle, Santa's given name, had not known of the elves' alleged skills as craftsmen and artisans when he finally settled in the Arctic. He had no choice but to ask their help. It was them or their cousins, the dwarfs, and he soon learned that dwarfs had no interest in the mundane task of making toys. The elves were finally able to supply the skills necessary to attain both the quantity and quality Santa needed.

At first, there was an equal partnership, but within a few generations the understanding was clear; Santa was the chief, the new leader. That an outlander could lead the elves never completely sat well with the entire elf population, and periodically some would rise to dispute Santa's role. Occasional minor verbal battles took place, but because the vast majority of elves enjoyed the special worldwide prestige that Santa brought, each of these very minor uprisings soon dissolved away without change in the status quo. Only the traditionalists, like Amak, continued to refuse to capitulate to this outlander. The rest were resolved to their subordinate position.

Amak wished to return to a time when the elves determined their own destiny, and if his plan worked, he would be the new "Emperor of the North."

The knock on the door interrupted Santa's inspection of the newest model of the Huggy Pudgy Teddy Bear. He placed it on top of the stack of fifteen other toys he still had to check.

"Who's there?"

"It's Mayor Amak," came a muffled reply through the thick pine doors. Amak purposely used his title whenever he was with Santa.

"The door's always open, Amak. Come on in."

Santa's home, the workshop, and a few of the other village buildings had two sets of doorknobs. For the Claus family, one was set midway up the door, the other, for use by the elves, was set much lower. The current Mrs. Claus had the lower set installed to help the elves, who before the change, had to reach for the upper doorknobs and awkwardly push against the door. Amak reached and turned the upper doorknob. A good deal of cold and a few snowflakes followed him into the house.

Santa pushed himself up from his deeply cushioned armchair.

"Amak, I haven't seen you in a couple of days. I hope nothing is wrong at the workshop."

"No, you don't have to worry." Amak noted Santa's expression of relief. "Nothing is wrong at the workshop," he added sarcastically.

"That's great." Santa dropped his glasses onto the lower ridge of his nose and peered out over them. The action was enough to make Amak feel as if he was being closely scrutinized and looked down upon. "I noticed yesterday's reports showed we're actually a little ahead of last year's production. You know what they say: 'Christmas is a coming and the geese are getting fat.'" Santa could not help but add a "Ho! Ho! Ho!"

Not so many years ago, he had been concerned that the elves couldn't fabricate the intricate parts needed for the new video games and home computers. Production went up, however, and Santa voiced the opinion that the increase was because the elves' tiny fingers actually made the work easier. That set off an argument between Santa and the then mayor, Danat, over the perceived slur. Arguments escalated to a level that prompted Santa to suggest to his workers that it might be best to elect a new mayor in order to have harmony return to the village. The elves listened and Amak was elected. Lately, however, the tension between mayor and boss seemed to be rising again.

"Santa, you don't have to worry. It's not anything that concerns production. It is, however, something that does matter. Another elf is missing."

"Damn! That makes five this year and two in the last week. Now of all times." He drummed his fingers on a nearby table. "I assume it's another case of a worker quitting and returning to his native village?"

"Actually, Santa, eight elves have left this year, and I don't know that it's a case of being homesick. I assume they left because they were disgusted with their working conditions."

"What? What did you say? I didn't understand."

Amak knew the reason for Santa's inability to understand. More than once, he had overheard Santa and other members of his species complain that elves spoke with a cadence and pitch that at times were undecipherable. They claimed anything that small couldn't possibly sound normal.

"I said eight elves, and they didn't leave because they were homesick."

"Let's not get into that discussion again, Amak." Santa leaned back and placed his fingers in a steeple configuration under his chin. "You lost your referendum. Let's be thankful you did. Could you imagine the chaos it would have created had you won? But you lost. You lost decisively. Your own elves voted you down."

"I don't think it was chaos you feared, your lordship."

Santa scowled at the sound of the provocative title but refused to allow himself to be drawn into an argument. "Well anyway, Amak, who's missing now?"

"Knute. Knute Brulog. He's been putting toys together for you for over ten years, and I doubt very much he suddenly got homesick and left. Maybe bored, maybe fed up with the conditions, but not homesick. I know Knute, and he's a good worker and a good husband. His home is here." Amak was annoyed that Santa always assumed that it was some inherent weakness in the workers' temperament that prompted them to leave. "I think something happened to him."

"Why would you even think that? He's lived in the Arctic his entire life. I'm sure he knows its dangers and how to avoid them."

"Well for one thing, there've been polar bear sightings during the past weeks, and they have to be damn hungry to come this close to the village. We've had to kill a few in the past months when they're this near. You'd think even dumb bears would learn the limits of their wanderings, but when they're hungry, they're dangerous."

"I think you're jumping to conclusions, Amak."

"I don't know if you remember that my assistant, Norved, disappeared last week. That certainly might be related to a bear attack. All of his belongings are still here, and no one has reported seeing him at any other village."

"Enough about bear attacks. So what have you done to find Brulog?" Santa asked.

"Same as always. I organized search parties to fan out and sent others to his old village just in case." As he spoke, it bothered Amak that his order to search Knute's old villages might make Santa think that he was agreeing with the assessment that the elf had deserted.

Santa's slight smile confirmed he realized his small victory, but he did not pursue or gloat over Amak's admission. He also realized and was distressed that the formation of the search parties would deplete the number of elves available for the workshop.

"He'll turn up, and as always, Mayor Amak, you are to be commended on doing your job so well."

Both men turned when they heard a door open. They watched Mrs. Claus leave the confines of her bedroom to join her husband. She had been sitting at her sewing machine, laboring the last hour to mend defects in quilts produced at the workshop. The workers called it laboring. Mrs. Claus, however, did not voice any complaint. She enjoyed the activity.

"Amak, hello. How are you?" Not waiting for an answer, she turned toward her husband. "I'm not interrupting shoptalk, am I? Production is good, isn't it?"

"Honey, another elf is missing," Santa announced.

"Dear me. Who is it this time? Didn't you just tell me yesterday that seven of the workers have left this year?"

"Eight, Mrs. Claus."

"Really that many, Amak?"

"That many and I'm not so sure whether anyone can say they all just up and left."

"What do you mean by that?"

"I mean there's evidence that Norved, and maybe this last worker, may have met some misfortune."

"Who did you say was missing?"

"Knute Brulog."

"He's one of the old timers isn't he? Don't he and his wife live in that isolated cottage at the other side of the village?"

"Yes, that's where they live." Mrs. Claus' effort to know all she could about the workers and their families always impressed Amak.

"Kris, maybe I should stay with her until we hear something or Knute returns." It was not often that anyone heard her refer to him by anything other than Mr. Claus or Santa.

Again impressed with Mrs. Claus' concern, Amak turned to her. "Thanks for your offer, but somebody's already with Mrs. Brulog."

"Well maybe I'll get some food together and bring it over."

Santa walked across the room to his wife and draped his arm over her shoulder. "Okay, Honey, why don't you prepare whatever you want to take, and I'll walk you partway there. I think I'd better go to the workshop and make sure this disappearance doesn't hurt morale and production. I think a pep talk is in order. Just let me get my red suit on and then we'll go."

"A pep talk! Santa, words won't help! What you need is to change working conditions!"

"Now, Amak," interrupted Mrs. Claus, "Mr. Claus knows what's best for his village."

A rapid, heavy knock on the door prevented Amak's answer.

"Come in!" Santa shouted.

An elf and a blast of cold air entered at the same time.

"We found Knute. At least what's left of him."

43

chapter 7

"**S**anta, I don't want to hear anymore." Mrs. Claus turned to leave the room. "When you're done talking about Knute, I need to check on Rudolph."

Santa, Amak, and the elf that brought the news about Knute remained mute until the door to the Claus' bedroom closed.

"I told you Knute didn't run off." Amak took a step toward Santa. "I told you there was more to it."

Santa held out his arm, palm forward, a dual signal for Amak to stop approaching and for him to stop his assertions that he was right. "Enough, Amak, we don't know what happened. Maybe he was in the process of deserting the village before the attack took place. Maybe he was dead before something discovered the corpse and decided it was an easy meal."

Now Santa took a step forward. "It didn't have to be a bear. If Knute was already dead, a fox could have easily inflicted the damage."

Neither the mayor nor his boss gave in. Eventually, Amak told Santa he would form a small party to bring Knute to the village. Santa agreed, "But don't bring the remains anywhere near the workshop. Morale is already low and we don't need anything that might affect production. I have to first check on some things and then go to the workshop."

Neither Santa nor his wife spoke as they walked. Neither wanted to discuss the possibilities of what happened to Knute.

The corral, which encircled the reindeer, resembled any corral found on any farm or ranch that needed a means to arrest an animal's desire to roam free. The posts and railing were wood, which, like the rest of the wood in Santa's village, had to be arduously delivered from an outpost one hundred miles away. And although it was quite far, it was still the closest source. A large shed that housed Santa's one-of-a-kind sleigh, its auxiliary equipment, and the reindeer feed blocked the open end of the U-shaped fenced-in area. Steaming piles of freshly deposited manure decorated the one-hundred-by-one-hundred-foot exercise area.

Peter, at work at the distant end of the corral, was Santa's recent appointee as caretaker/trainer of the reindeer and custodian of the enclosure. He was a second-generation inhabitant of Santa's village. His father, who toiled in the workshop more than twenty years, used his seniority to cajole Santa into giving his fifteen-year-old son the job. He was relieved his son need not join him on the assembly line. Like many of his generation, he didn't give Peter a traditional Inuit or Scandinavian name. They wanted their children to have a better life. A name change might have been only symbolic, but doing so told the siblings that they weren't imprisoned by the culture of their forbearers. The offspring's given name depended on the proximity of the parent's native village to a French- or an English-speaking region.

Peter had just completed digging a sixteen-inch-deep hole into the ice and positioning a new post—the old one having been snapped by a blow from a reindeer's hoofs. He had next packed snow into the hole to provide the initial support to the post and was now pouring water over the snow and adjacent ground. In a few hours, the frozen mixture would achieve sufficient strength.

Reindeer that have the ability to fly were once as plentiful as the bison on the American plains, but like these very distant cousins, humans hunted this unique subspecies of the common deer into near extinction. They butchered and ate the reindeer meat; fashioned ropes, clothing, and blankets from the hides; burned the fat for heat; and fashioned the remaining bones into utensils, ornaments, and weapons.

Santa maintained a small herd of about thirty of these special reindeer scattered in the surrounding elf villages. He kept about half as many in his own village. The elves who cared for those reindeer outside Santa's private stock carefully bred them to ensure there was a constant source of animals available to power Santa's sleigh through the air. Each year Santa toured these breeding pens and chose the hardiest reindeer to bring back to his village. Those reindeer not chosen to pull the sleigh were kept as replacements, each pampered as if it were one of the revered nine.

It is widely misconstrued that reindeer that fly can launch themselves into the air whenever they so choose. Much like the annual period when deer rut, these reindeer have a three-to-four week period during which they can actually fly. Luckily, for Santa this natural event coincides with the Christmas season. During this window of time, a long leather tether attached to one of their hind legs restrained the reindeer—wood fences do not keep in flying reindeer.

Both reindeer and caribou differ from other members of the deer family by having large, deeply cleft hoofs that support them in both the deep snow and the soft, spongy tundra of the south. Caribou stand from six to eight feet and weigh up to seven hundred pounds, while reindeer normally stand and weigh much less. But Santa had no choice when it came to selecting one or the other to pull his sleigh—caribou can't fly. On the ground, a reindeer can pull a fully loaded sled over and through the snow at a rate of twelve to fifteen miles per hour and continue to endure this task for hours. No one has ever clocked their speed in the air.

Rudolph was unique among the unique. The names of the other reindeer were interchangeable. Dasher, Dancer, Prancer, Vixen, Comet, Cupid, Donner, and Blitzen were names arbitrarily given to the reindeer each year by Santa. Donner could just as easily be called Blitzen on any succeeding year. However, Rudolph was always Rudolph. He was bred for the characteristics needed to be the leader: size, strength, intelligence, and, of course, a shiny red nose that seemed to glow at night.

In an attempt to avoid spooking the reindeer, Santa and his wife gingerly approached the corral. For the same reason, they spoke in quiet, monotonous voices. Most of the reindeer already could, if left untethered, fly across the twenty-thousand-square-foot expanse. Others were only capable of hovering for a prolonged second or two over their launch area.

Santa exchanged waves with Peter and continued into the shed through a side door, while Mrs. Claus approached the corner of the corral where Rudolph stood. As usual, Rudolph had segregated himself from the other reindeer. It was not, as legend had it, that the other reindeer shunned him. Animals may not be able to display arrogance, but Rudolph flaunted a good impression. The special treatment he had received since birth had eventually conditioned his attitude towards his fellow fliers. And while his compatriots seemed to appreciate their coddled lifestyles, Rudolph seemed to expect it.

He was not yet fully able to fly, but that did not stop him from practicing his takeoffs by bending his hind legs and leaping up and forward, only to return to the ground just a few feet away.

Rudolph turned towards the approaching shape, and through

the combination of familiar odors and the sight of an upright two-legged animal, he seemed to recognize Mrs. Claus. He hurried to the fence and meekly draped his head over the upper rail. The act was rewarded when his visitor reached into her coat and pulled out two large carrots.

"Rudolph, my baby," she murmured softly. "How are you today? I see you're practicing for the big night." If the reindeer understood, he gave no indication. He was too engrossed with finishing the first of the carrots offered him. She alternately stroked his forelock and jowl. The other reindeer smelled the food, but they knew better than to expect their share; their regular feeding time was still hours away and there would be no special treats, just the usual grain. Still the faint odor that drifted across the open area excited them, and they pranced and leaped, enough so, that Peter pressed his lips into a tight line to indicate his annoyance with Mrs. Claus for causing the commotion. The new fence post was still not secure, and he did not want any of the reindeer to accidentally batter it.

Mrs. Claus wrapped her arms around Rudolph's neck and gave him a tight hug. "You're looking stronger every day, my beautiful boy." Rudolph twisted his restrained head searching for the second carrot his nose told him was near. "I guess my Rudolph wants his other carrot?" She released her grip and offered the additional treat while she continued the stroking and endearing babble.

Santa was pleased there was an adequate supply of feed grain stored in the shed. His choice of replacing the older, infirmed Erog with the more nimble and enthusiastic Peter was already paying dividends. While Erog had proven that he could improvise when new problems arose, few problems needed improvisation. But Peter was better able to formulate the mechanics to obtain a continuous supply of grain hauled to the village. Santa felt Erog mirrored Amak. Both were obstinate when it came to modernization. Peter, schooled in a Norwegian village, was comfortable with the changes needed to keep pace with a world the majority of which wasn't perpetually covered with snow. The reindeer, especially Rudolph, seemed healthier and stronger this year. Santa was certain it was the feed mixture Peter had ordered and was happy to supply his caretaker with extra sleds and dog teams for transport— although Peter had gone as far as suggesting delivery by helicopter or plane. Here Santa had drawn the line.

Content that there wouldn't be a problem with this season's grain supply, Santa went to the far side of the shed to inspect the harnesses. He had to admit that Erog had performed well when he cut and bound the long leather strips to create the needed configuration. It was unfortunate that Peter's and Erog's personalities and values clashed. They would have formed an impressive team. One of them had to go, however, and Santa had decided that Peter was more valuable and less confrontational.

Santa's sleigh was red, of course, with simple green wreaths painted on the sides and the back. Each year, a team of land-bound reindeer pulled the sleigh south to have a fresh coat of color applied; the temperature was never warm enough in the village to allow for the proper application and setting of the paint. It was enormous as far as sleighs go, measuring eighteen feet from front to back and seven feet across. There was a simple wooden plank spanning the front that Santa used as a seat. Peter had promised to fabricate a more comfortable cushioned chair to replace the plank before the yearly flight. He also promised Mrs. Claus that he would attach a seat belt after Santa told her he'd almost been bounced out of the sleigh when it hit some violent aerial turbulence last year.

The sleigh's capacity was large, but certainly not large enough to carry all the toys that Santa delivered on Christmas Eve. How then was this task accomplished? Only Santa knew and he even kept the secret from his wife. The elves speculated that it involved magic.

Others assumed that Santa had worldwide distribution centers, ones that stored the toys until he picked them up along the way. But Santa would not tell. Only his successor would know the answer to the riddle.

Before leaving, Santa checked the sleigh's runners to ensure the metal bolts were securely fastened to the underbelly. He was surprised to find that two of the fastenings, where the metal supporting struts joined, were loose. He would have to remind Peter to correct the problem.

All else seemed in order, and Santa shut the door behind him and walked around the shed to join his wife.

The noise of the snow crunched beneath her husband's weight caused her to turn her head. "I want you to talk to Peter about Rudolph. If you could have seen the way he just devoured his carrots, you'd know he's not getting enough grain." She gave the reindeer another hug and spoke into his ear. "Don't worry. Santa will take care of it. He'll make sure you get more food."

Santa extended his hand to his wife, but she wouldn't release her hold on her charge. Something had changed this year. She had cared for the reindeer before, but this year her attachment to Rudolph was obsessive and intense. Santa felt that maybe this season he had concentrated too much on the workshop's activities. Maybe, he thought, he should let the production take care of itself, or at least delegate some of the responsibilities to Amak. But he knew he couldn't do that. Once he delegated even a little of his authority there was the danger that all would be lost. Centuries and generations of unilateral leadership could end. Tradition mandated that the institute of Santa Claus remain unaltered.

He silently watched her caress Rudolph and recollected her recent complaints. He remembered her increasing criticism of the cold. She had even suggested a vacation after the holiday. "I miss a daily sunrise and sunset. Let's go somewhere where the sun is shining and where we wouldn't have to wear three layers of clothes each time we stepped outside."

Lately, she began to complain of mysterious pains and headaches, difficulty breathing, and an increased pounding of her heart. Foods seemed to disagree with her more and more, and oftentimes she could tolerate only a bland soup for days on end. Last week he came back from the workshop to find her crying, but when he asked what was wrong, she could not honestly give him an answer.

There was recent, frequent minor bickering. These never escalated into arguments—he would not let that happen. Santa never attempted to discuss their disagreements; instead, he found it easier to claim that he had to leave to check on things at the workshop. He rationalized his actions, what she referred to his indifferences, by convincing himself that he had no way of knowing what he was supposed to do. Their socialization with others of their own kind ended many years ago. How was he expected to know how to react to situations and behavior that had only recently appeared?

Maybe he would agree to a vacation, but right now, he did not have the luxury or the time to think about it.

"You're out here every day pampering the heck out of him."

"Please just talk to Peter and make sure Rudolph gets his additional grain." She repeated it, but this time speaking into the reindeer's ear hoping he would realize that any additional food received would be because she had insisted upon it.

"He'll be too fat to fly if you keep this up."

Her eyes widened and her voice rose. "He won't be too fat to fly! Don't you worry about Rudolph. Just worry about the production at your workshop. There wasn't any problem last year when I cared for him and there won't be a problem this year. Just tell Peter to give him an extra ration of grain."

Santa was concerned that the tone of the conversation was

escalating to a level he wanted to avoid. He moved closer and gave her a peck on the cheek. "We'll talk about this later. For now, please just calm yourself."

"Don't patronize me! I'm not one of your elves!"

Santa looked across the corral to see if Peter heard these last remarks, but the young elf appeared engrossed with fixing the railing and had either not heard, was not at all concerned, or chose not to display his concern.

"Rudolph is not your child. The only reason he should get any special attention at all is that he's a reindeer that can fly."

She chose not to reply. The fact was that she did treat Rudolph like the children she had lost, and when he led the sleigh into the sky on Christmas Eve, her eyes filled with tears, like any proud mother watching her son walk down the aisle to receive his diploma.

Rudolph was her child. When his shiny red nose identified him at birth as a potential lead reindeer, Mrs. Claus had pleaded with and finally had convinced her husband that he should raise the newborn at the main village, and that she should be his primary caregiver. At times, especially when Santa was busy with Christmas activities, Rudolph was her salvation. They had lost one of their children at a young age to an illness that easily could have been treated if they had lived in proximity to an urban area. But they lived in a village in the middle of the Arctic, and their child and Mrs. Claus had paid the price for their isolation.

She was never close to her nephews, Matthew and Nels, and they reciprocated with their own indifference to her. The elves in the village, although appreciating her genuine concern for their overall welfare, still considered her an outsider, what they referred to as an outlander.

Santa watched as Rudolph again nuzzled his benefactor. He wondered whether the reindeer really was reciprocating his wife's affection or whether he'd learned early on that such acts usually brought additional culinary treats. Minutes passed before Rudolph concluded no food was forthcoming. He pulled his head from Santa's wife's embrace and moved to the center of the corral, far enough away from all the others so that he could again be left to practice his takeoffs.

Santa accompanied his wife back to their home, and while he changed into his red uniform, she gathered some food to take to the Brulogs. Together they walked the short distance to the workshop where they parted, he to provide a morale-boosting speech to the elves working inside and she to begin the trip across the field to the now widowed Mrs. Brulog.

chapter 8

Four elves had been transporting toys from an outlying hamlet back to the main village. With world demand for new toys increasing each year, the workshop was no longer able to produce the required inventory, so Santa had set up a network of minor workshops in seven nearby areas. Of course, Amak said this division of labor was not designed to decrease the load in the workshop. Santa could easily have insisted that the structure be enlarged, but by not doing so, he was able to increase and maintain his influence and control of the region. More importantly, Amak said it would divide the total workforce into ineffectual smaller bargaining groups.

The elves had not heard of Knute's disappearance, but the dark blemish his body made on the eternal white carpet, drew them towards this site. White was the norm in this environment and any other color required immediate investigation. Coming upon the body, they first assumed a worker had deserted the village and had frozen to death in the recent cold wave, but then they overturned the body and saw the evidence of the bear's brutality. Maybe, they thought, they had interrupted the bear's meal and had scared him off, but no one had seen it leave. There was no explanation for the outcome they now saw. They decided that two elves would stay to guard their dead companion while the remaining two would take the other sled and continue on to the village for help.

The two elves left behind to guard Knute's remains initially tried to warm themselves by crawling between the stacks of toys secured atop on the sled, but the temperature continued to fall and soon they were compelled to use some of the toys to fuel a fire. The sled was more than a quarter empty now. In minutes, the blaze consumed weeks of labor, but survival was paramount. They could have built an ice shelter at first, but Santa's village was only fifteen to twenty minutes away by sled, and they thought help would return sooner than this. One of the elves threw a toy boat into the dwindling fire, and the flames quickly consumed their new nourishment and belched sparks into the air.

They had constructed the fire to lie between themselves and the corpse allowing the flames to convey an illusion that the body was receiving a fiery Viking burial. A shifting wind forced them to turn away from the blowing snow and gray smoke. The fire had given them a sense of security, a barrier protecting them from the mutilated corpse, but now with their backs turned, there was an ominous feeling that any moment the corpse would spring upon them much the same way they thought the bear had sprung upon Knute.

They were accustomed to death in the Arctic, but the death they knew was usually a simple, almost aseptic one. Animals were shot or trapped for food and clothing but certainly never mutilated. Elves died, too, but rarely violently. The immobilizing cold of the land routinely ended the lives of a few elves each year. Age and, more commonly now, outlander diseases killed a few more. Some elves were lost to roaming bears and occasionally to packs of starving wolves, but rarely was anybody subjected to viewing the victim's remains. Any kill made in this barren land was for survival, and the victor disposed of the loser by eating, not mutilating, and leaving the carcass.

It was this unnatural act that bothered the two elves safeguarding what was left of one of their own species. The bear that had killed Knute did not kill to protect itself; certainly, Knute was not hunting it. It had not killed for food—the remains were testimony to that. It had seemingly killed for the joy of it, and the bear was still alive to kill again.

The only sled left in the village was that brought in by the elves with the news of Knute's discovery. All of the others were with the search parties. Amak knew the dogs could not return to the trail without some rest, so he and a few other elves decided to set out on foot.

The wind was gusting, and whenever the intensity decreased, the walkers unconsciously quickened their pace before the next air blast slowed them again.

At first, there wasn't any conversation, but eventually in pairs, they spoke of what they would find; the description of the corpse had been hideous. Conversations soon changed and the elves questioned the reason a bear had left its prey without consuming it. After a short time, all conversations again stopped. There would be no answers until they reached their destination, and wasting energy by talking would not make it come any faster.

The troop looked like Bedouins, heads bowed, trekking through a desert. They transformed from a single file procession to multiple small groupings and returned to single file with the cessation of conversations, but Amak had always maintained the lead.

The polarized membrane covering elves' eyes enabled them to translate the limited glow from the ever-darkening sky into sufficient light to illuminate the landscape. Only Amak, among the procession, did not stumble nor slacken the pace. When not performing his duties at the village, he alone used his free time to exercise, to relearn past survival methods. The past was Amak's future.

Shifting ice floes produced a loud rumbling cloaking Danat's approach. "Hey, Amak, I guess you figure to walk us into the ground. What's your rush? He's dead you know. No point in killing us too."

"Shut up, you idiot. He was one of us."

"But still he's dead and he won't know if we get there in ten minutes or four hours. You of all people should remember the old ways. There was no sentiment then. The old, those who could not work or hunt were left behind, alone on the ice floes. This land doesn't allow these burdens any right to cling to life. Pity is still a dangerous luxury."

"But Knute is dead. He is not a burden. He won't eat your share of food. He won't come into your cottage asking for shelter or clothes. He won't ask to share your woman."

"No, he won't ask for or take my woman. You already did that, Amak." Both stopped to face each other. "Let's see now. First, you took over my job as Workshop Supervisor, then my job as Mayor of the village, and then you decided I hadn't given you enough, so you took my wife. By the way, how is the tramp? She hasn't talked to me in months."

Amak turned away and resumed the trip. "I told you to shut up, Danat. It's interfering with your walking. We both know you have trouble doing two things at the same time. Too much mental stress for you."

"Amak and the Great Claus. You claim you're against his authority and yet you want to control. You want to unionize the elves, but you want to be in charge of the union. No one benefits in that plan except you. Just the leader would change. You and Santa are interchangeable, and I can't stand either of you."

"What's really bothering you, Danat? Is it the fact that most everyone hates your guts? That everyone finally figured out what an idiot you are? That it wasn't me that took Loti away but that Loti ran away from you. She tried to be your wife, your type of wife, but slavery has never existed in the Arctic, even though you thought it should. We need each other, all of us, to survive this icebox. At least in the old days, the old and infirmed knew enough to sit out on the ice to help Death take them, but you're too stupid." The rest of the elves started to gather close. "You continue to remain a parasite on our tribe. The food that passes through your big mouth would be better put to use to feed one of the dogs. At least he would wag his tail in appreciation."

"One of these days you are going to find something sharp shoved up your ass, Amak, and it won't be Loti's tongue."

Amak turned to punch his adversary but Marjac's shout that he spied smoke ahead interrupted the potential fight.

"Is that all you found?" Amak scanned the scene. "Have you touched or changed anything since you first found Knute?"

"Now he's the great detective. How many hats do you want to wear?"

"Shut up, Danat! Shut up right now and get the hell out of my sight!"

Danat did not move. He remained still as an ice sculpture. Amak chose to ignore him and turned to question the two elves who had found and then guarded the mangled body.

"Well, we didn't think there was any mystery to be solved. It's obvious a bear did this. What kind of evidence or signs would you expect to find? There's Knute. You can see the condition he's in. Something chewed off half of his neck. When you check him out, you'll see teeth marks on his shoulder and puncture marks through his clothes. The ground all around him is frozen so you can't tell if he put up a fight. There is no sign that there was any rolling around in loose snow. The blood is only around the body, so death must have been pretty fast. The way we figure it, the polar bear was either waiting for him, hidden in a blind crevice, or stalked him until it felt it had the opportunity to attack."

Danat interrupted. "Maybe it jumped him from above, from atop the ridge."

"Bears don't jump on their victims from atop heights. Bears don't know fear. They walk right up to their victims, face to face, and kill them," Amak replied.

"Well I'm going up there anyway, on top of the hummock, and look for paw prints."

"That's a good place for you, Danat. Just keep out of everybody's way." Amak joined the group that now formed a wide circle around Knute's remains. No one had yet attempted to investigate the body. It was not just the odor of death pushing them back—it was Death itself.

The body was on its side and except for the left leg that protruded at an unnatural, reversed right angle, it seemed in repose. It appeared that Knute was resting on a red blanket, but it was blanket of frozen blood. Amak approached the corpse cautiously, pausing to search for any clue as to why the bear had attacked. He bent down and touched the outstretched leg. Its gross angle bothered him. Taking hold of the thigh with one hand and the ankle with his other, he attempted to straighten the limb. It did not bend however. It might have been that the leg had frozen into this position. It might have not have straightened because the bones were impacted on each other, or it might have been that rigor mortis had set in. Whatever the cause, the leg would not move.

Amak rolled the corpse over. It was a clumsy effort because of the leg. He was somewhat surprised that touching the dead man did not bother him, but his first view of Knute's head and neck did. The left side of what remained of Knute's neck appeared everted. The ragged edges of the wound intertwined with the underlying internal mucosal lining of the throat. Knute's left ear and left cheek were missing, replaced by another hole that opened into the underlying sinus, which made the void seem even larger. The bone around the eye had been destroyed and the soft orbit hung downward from a frozen pedicle of muscle and nerve tissue. Teeth protruded in all directions through what tissue was left on the side of the face and gave the appearance that a deformed second mouth had grown.

Amak looked for other wounds but could find none. As he again turned the body over, the dangling eye brushed the packed snow below and the suspended stalk of frozen tissue snapped, allowing the eye to roll towards Amak's foot. As if being attacked by a fierce opponent, fear pushed Amak backwards causing him to stumble and fall on his side. The eye continued to roll on the smooth ice and came to rest next to Amak's own face. The detached orbit's stare bore right through him. A horrified Amak tried to push himself away and stand, but again the glass-like terrain caused him to slip, this time with his elbow landing on and crushing the cycloptic globe.

Nausea and revulsion replaced his fear as Amak used his gloved hand to swat off the frozen remains of Knute's eye. The fluid in the eye had already frozen, so what remained resembled a splintered, colored ice ball. Amak's movements were so rapid and jerky that an intense muscle spasm developed in his right chest and spread down his arm. He arose slower now, finished brushing off his elbow, and kneaded his spastic muscles through the overlaying coat. He achieved only partial relief and to support his aching, weakened arm he tucked it into his coat pocket.

His companions had been watching the examination of the corpse and now looked away not wishing to embarrass the elf who preached the traditional ways, ways that demanded an individual not demonstrate fear. But they knew that this was a different kind of fear.

Amak also looked away from his companions. He boldly returned to Knute to begin a new examination of the ripped clothes and puncture wounds on the shoulder and the front of the coat. These, he surmised were made by the bear's teeth. He was uncertain what exactly he was looking for, nothing seemed unusual, but he and all those present had seen only the results of bear attacks against seals or the occasional sled dog. The mysterious reason for this attack added to the horror of the corpse.

Amak ended his investigation of the body and systematically examined the ground beginning with the area closest to Knute. There was no evidence of a great struggle, although nothing in the Arctic would be expected to combat a polar bear one-on-one. Once a bear overtook his prey, the end was swift. There was never a prolonged fight, just the inevitable death. Amak's scrutiny stopped when he sighted a series of depressions in the snow, but when he walked to the spot and bent to more closely examine the marks, he was unable to discover any definite pattern. He continued his search, and near the area where the elves stood, he thought he spied another depression beneath one of the scattered toys. As Amak neared, the outline began to take the more definitive shape of a paw print. The print, however, seemed unnaturally small for a polar bear, at least for a bear that would have been big enough to kill Knute. Moving the toy aside, Amak was now sure it was a print, only a partial print, but even so, it appeared unnatural. He studied it for a moment and then called out to another member of his party.

"Sponson, come over here. I want you to help me cut out this print. We'll bring it back to the village to show Erog. Maybe he can help us identify it."

The elf withdrew his snow knife from its sheath and within five minutes, he had cut and extracted a block of ice one foot by one foot

61

by one-half foot. Framed on the face of the block of ice was the print that Amak felt required further inspection. They carefully placed the piece of ice back onto the ground.

Amak turned towards the others. "All right, let's get Knute wrapped in something and tie him on the sled. Make a sling for the ice block and two of us will carry it back."

"Don't you think we should leave the body alone?" Marjac interrupted Amak. "It would give Dr. Skeen a chance to examine him."

"This isn't Yellow Knife. We don't have a medical examiner." Amak looked at the gaping wound in Knute's neck. "I think we can agree that the cause of death wasn't a suicide."

"Shouldn't we determine if the corpse's stiffness is due to rigor mortis and not the cold?"

Shivering in the frigid cold, Amak decided he had finally discovered the village idiot. Marjac melted to the back of the group.

The elves carefully redistributed the remaining toys onto the sled to make room for the corpse and then laced a tarpaulin of bear hides over the mangled body and multicolored toys. It made an odd holiday package to be unwrapped back at Santa's Village. There would be no happy faces, however, when this present was received.

"Sponson, you and your brother ride the sled back and the rest of us will follow on foot. When you arrive at the village, bring the sled directly over to the storage shed. Don't let anybody touch anything. Don't let anyone see the body—especially not Knute's wife. Say nothing. We'll be there as soon as we can."

"Do you want us to tell Santa?"

"No, I told you, say nothing!"

Amak supervised the loading of the ice block onto a bearskin sling. Mikel held up one end of the sling while Amak grabbed the other end. They picked up their bundle and in unison began the walk home.

"Hold it, Amak! There's something on the top of the hummock I think you should see."

"Danat, what's bothering you now?"

"I just told you. Hell, you've wasted enough time down here. What I've found is important and I found it where you smugly insisted my search would be a waste of time."

Amak's flesh tightened and his eyes widened. "Danat, don't push me!" Seething, he continued, "Mikel, let's put the paw print down for a minute while I deal with the imbecile." Amak rocked onto his toes trying to stretch his four-foot six-inch frame. The hunter was appraising his prey, readying to strike, but Danat turned and walked away.

"Follow me if you're not afraid to be proved wrong. I told you to search above. I found some prints that prove the bear attack came from atop the hummock. He probably pounced on Knute before he ever saw it. You say that bears don't attack that way, but the prints above prove otherwise."

The short climb took an inordinate amount of time because of repeated slips on the icy surface. Reaching the top, Danat's beaming, smiling face met Amak. Danat pointed down to a group of depressions at the edge of the precipice. These were definite polar bear tracks, not like the confusing print found below, but prints made by a bear's two rear and one front paw. The wind had not had time enough to destroy their definition, and their size indicated a female probably made them. Danat had been right. The attacker obviously had watched the elf walk beneath, then when directly below, had leaped upon his victim. Without acknowledging Danat's correct assessment, Amak called to the elves below to join him and help excise these new prints.

They decided not to carry the three ice blocks back down the slope. A fall of either elf or cargo was certain on such a trip. Instead, they fastened each block with a cradle made from rope and slowly lowered each to the path below. The remaining members of the search party gathered around the prints and uniformly agreed that these were definitely polar bear tracks and that Danat's scenario of the kill had to be correct.

The murder of one of their own, not for food, but seemingly for the pleasure of it frightened those present. They alternately stared at the prints and the corpse now lying in state on the sled. Elves anticipated and were accustomed to a life made up of a series of monotonous events, and because of this, even mildly unusual occurrences provoked feelings of apprehension well beyond a normal cause and effect. This event was shattering.

Mikel and Amak had just picked up the original slab of ice when Danat approached. "Let's see your print, Amak," Danat demanded as he pulled back the folded edge of the sling. He stroked the impression in the ice and the warmth from his hand started to melt the edges of the print. As rapidly as his fingers left the surface of the ice, the cold quickly refroze the lines, but in slightly new locations and altered patterns.

"Leave it alone, Danat. You can see it back at the village."

"I'll look when I want to look and nobody, certainly not you, will tell me differently!"

"Don't touch it, you fool!" Several globs of saliva exploded from his mouth causing Danat to duck to let them pass.

"I'm not a fool," Danat whispered. A smile fixed on his face and for the moment, everyone felt a crisis had passed. Danat stepped closer, broadening his smile even more, and then suddenly lunged at the ill-prepared Amak. The ice block slid off the sling and first struck Amak's chest before it and Amak fell to the ground. The impact, although not great, was enough to explode the ice into multiple, unrecognizable pieces.

Danat dropped knees first onto Amak's chest and a cloud of vapor burst out as expelled air escaped the mayor's mouth and nose. He grabbed Amak by the beard and used his hold to repeatedly slam his adversary's head against the hard ground. Amak's eyes glazed over. He had no strength to combat his attacker. Blood oozed from his scalp as the pounding intensified. In between the jolts of pain when his head struck the ground, he could hear Danat's snarls. It reminded him of the noise the sled dogs made when Peter was late with their expected meals.

Two elves rushed over, tackled Danat, and a new fight developed between the three. Eventually, two more elves entered the fray to help to control the enraged Danat. They dragged him a short distance from the still supine Amak and held Danat seated against the icy wall of the hummock. The rage diminished as he watched the other elves worrying over their leader. Danat laughed at Amak's attempt to stand, and with each slippery, sliding step Amak took, his laughter grew. Still somewhat dazed, Amak approached his secured foe.

"You ass! Can't you accept that you're not in charge anymore? Can't you see you are worthless to the village?" With joyous accuracy, Amak punctuated the last sentence with a sharp kick to the side of Danat's unprotected face shattering two already decayed molars and sending the pieces mixed with fresh blood into the air. Danat collapsed from his jailers' holds.

Amak smiled at his fallen combatant, looked to the sky, and howled.

DECEMBER 20ᵀᴴ

chapter 9

"Did you see the body yet?"

Erog continued working and did not look up. Few people ever bothered with him so he ignored the question assuming it was directed at someone else in the noisy room. There were eight other elves working in the building, all busy with their tasks, but not so busy that it interfered with a steady stream of conversation. The smallness of the room only intensified the cacophony of sounds from the hammering and the electric tools.

Amak repeated his inquiry. "Erog, did you see the body yet?"

Before he could answer, one of the other elves asked Amak about Knute. The subject had been the major source of conversation this afternoon. All work stopped as the workers paused to hear Amak's reply. He explained that they'd found Knute's body and that a bear had apparently killed him.

"Are you going to form a hunting party to track and kill the bear?"

"This is not the time to pull additional elves from production for a search unlikely to succeed," he replied.

A third elf mockingly asked when the video tape replay of Amak's fight with Danat would air.

"First we'd have to get television," another interjected. Amak just rolled his eyes and ambled closer to Erog while the others continued to deride the lack of outlander conveniences.

"Did you see the body yet?" Amak leaned against a large bin piled high with broken toys—toys needing minor repairs to be ready for Christmas delivery.

This time Erog replied. "Yes, I did. Horrible wasn't it?"

"I don't understand why a bear would attack like that."

"There could've been lots of reasons. First of all, Knute may have been stalking the bear, attempting to kill it, and the hunter unfortunately became the victim."

"No, he was on his way to Tooten to deliver some toys to be gift boxed. According to his wife, he had no weapon, just the bag of toys he had brought home."

Erog put forth another possibility. "Well, maybe the bear was with her cub and the mother felt threatened."

"That's a possibility, although I can't imagine a bear being afraid of an elf."

"Bears aren't invincible, Amak. None of us are, especially in this wilderness. Hey, maybe the bear just felt like killing something. Hell, I know I've felt that way some days. I've heard of a bear that attacked a group of elves who were minding their own business, just sledding home. No reason, it just attacked. Then again, maybe Knute just surprised the bear and it attacked."

"No, I doubt that. All evidence seems to indicate the bear waited atop an adjacent hummock and leaped upon Knute as he passed by."

"Evidence. What kind of evidence?"

"Well, that asshole Danat found bear prints in the area."

Erog chuckled when he heard Amak's opinion of Danat. He had no use for Danat either. It was not that the two of them had any major arguments, actually not even a small one, but like Amak, he often expressed his opinion that Danat was a leech on their village. "I heard you had some trouble with Danat. How the hell did you let that idiot provoke you into a fight?"

"Erog, we don't all have your patience—the patience that arrives with years of practice."

"Not that patient and certainly not that old. In case you forgot, you're a year older than me. To be honest with you, I've considered kicking his ass a few times, but I was afraid my cane would slip out from under me and I'd be the one lying flat on the ground. Anyway, what went on between you two?"

"Nothing new. Same old stuff. First, he tried to buck my authority. Next, he baited me with talk about Loti. Then he flaunted his arrogance in front of everyone present. Finally, he busted the print I was going to bring back for you to look at."

"Busted it? I saw those three prints; there were two rear bear prints and one front right one. From the size and depth of the depressions, I'd say the bear was about seven feet in length and weighed about six hundred pounds. Not much else you can expect to tell from the prints."

"That wasn't the print I was talking about."

Erog looked puzzled. "There was more? I thought, I mean, someone told me you found only three prints at the edge of the hummock. Where else did you find one?"

"Close to Knute's body."

"Another bear print?"

"That's just it, Erog, it was a portion of a print, at least it looked like a print, but there was something odd about it. I don't know, maybe it wasn't a bear print. That's what I wanted you to tell me. Anyway all that's academic now since Danat broke the ice block."

"Couldn't you bring the pieces in? There might've been some way to identify what you found."

"No, by the time Danat and I finished rolling around on it, there wasn't too much more than small, ice cubes left."

"Did you look around for other prints?"

"No, I wasn't in any mood. Actually, I was still a little groggy from getting my head smashed against the ground. I was hoping to get back there tomorrow and check the scene again."

Erog pushed himself up and hobbled toward his coat draped over another chair. "Why don't I take a sled over there now? You're not up to it and if you wait till tomorrow, the weather may destroy any other evidence worth investigating."

"I appreciate the offer. The only problem is I sent the remaining sleds to call in the other search teams. I couldn't expect you to travel." Amak smiled and continued, "Even with your cane it would take at least half the afternoon for you to walk there."

Erog's scowl told Amak he did not appreciate the attempt at humor. His need for a cane was an annoyance to be sure, but it represented more. In a region where mobility meant the ability to escape, where escape meant life, this inability to move without the cane symbolized his reliance on others. Arctic society required mutual aid to survive, they offered it as needed, but it wasn't always appreciated or accepted. Amak knew Erog felt the cane both requested and demanded charity. No one in the community wanted to be a burden to others. The immediate area surrounding Santa's village functioned like an outlander's society, but not far from here, traditional customs still prevailed. These were areas where the old and sick were still left on the ice floes to die. In the Arctic, as in other places, food and shelter equated with survival, but in a region where both were hard to come by, these two necessities weren't wasted on those who couldn't help replenish either. Amak had confided to Loti that he thought his friend Erog was afraid others felt he no longer could contribute.

Sensing his mistake Amak continued, "How about you and me

leaving early tomorrow and we'll search the area together? Your eyes are still the sharpest around. If anyone could find something, you should."

Erog seemed pleased. "All right, Amak. I'll take you up on it."

"Good, I'll get the sled ready in the morning and pick you up at six o'clock in front of the workshop. In the meantime, if you wouldn't mind, how about doing a thorough examination of Knute's body? Maybe you'll find something I missed."

"What about Knute's wife? Has she seen the corpse yet?"

"No, she hasn't. I told her what happened and that I thought it best she didn't view the body, but she said she wanted to anyway. She insisted. She can be a real tough lady. Still, I wanted to have somebody with her when she came. Of all people, Mrs. Claus volunteered to help and said they'd view the body tomorrow morning. She surprises me sometimes, Mrs. Claus I mean. She surprised me this morning when she knew who the Brulogs were and where they lived. There are times I've the impression that she cares more about the people's well-being than whether or not they meet her husband's quotas."

"Don't go soft on me, Amak. She's as bad as Santa. In a way she may be worse because she does nothing to try to change him."

"Well anyway, Erog, do me a favor, check out the body, and don't forget I'll pick you up at six."

"By the way, Amak, if you should see Loti, ask her to drop by. I want to show her the ankle bracelet I'm working on for her. Tell her that I should be here for another hour or two."

"She told me about it. Let's see what it looks like."

Erog reached under his workbench and opened a drawer. He carefully removed a small white cardboard box. He opened it revealing a square of cotton, which when lifted, exposed a gold ankle bracelet. Amak reached out his hand to take the box, but Erog drew it away, allowing Amak to look but not to touch. The bracelet was a series of intricately hand-carved shapes of Arctic animals: polar bears, seals, reindeer, caribou, foxes—all majestically posed.

"Erog, it's unbelievable. How did you carve something this delicate? She'll love it."

"Loti saw a similar one I made for Unata last year and has been hounding me to make her one for Christmas. I hope she likes it."

"I'm sure she will. Maybe I'll go see her now. She should be finishing teaching her class soon, and I'll give her your message." He turned to leave, but paused in mid-stride. "She really likes you, Erog. She talks about you all the time." He hoped this trivial information might somehow brighten Erog's day. "See you tomorrow morning."

"See you then."

Amak pushed against the door to make sure it had closed tightly. A steady twenty-miles-per hour wind kicked the snow into the air and he wanted to prevent any unnecessary cold from entering the building. Amak had no real friends. He didn't allow himself that luxury. To have a friend required sacrifices and compromises, and he wanted to be free to disagree—sometimes intensely and totally—with anyone and at anytime he chose. Erog was the one inhabitant of Santa's Village who most often agreed with his own ideals, traditional values being the utmost of these ideals, and this made Erog as close as anyone that he could call a friend.

Amak often felt a great sympathy for his comrade. Erog's infirmities frequently prevented him from performing tasks he might easily excel in, much more so than many of the other elves in the village. He isolated himself from the others, and except for Amak and Loti, he rarely disclosed his thoughts to anyone else. Lately, he'd obviously extended this isolation to include his wife, Unata. The tension between the two had escalated to a level that all conversations ended in arguments.

Erog found it increasingly difficult to travel without the use of mechanical support. He had to have special oversized shoes to encase his swollen feet and even those were not wide enough. Perhaps it was self-consciousness, but he refused to make new, even larger shoes because he said he already felt like a circus clown and that all he needed was a big red nose like Rudolph's to complete the costume.

Of course to him, and unfortunately he feared to the others, using a cane represented debilitation. It was a visible sign that he was evolving into a parasitic relationship with the villagers. For that reason, he minimized using it. He could not use an ordinary cane, the single pole either stuck in soft, new unpacked snow or slid across old, ice-like snow. He tried using the kind of three-legged walking stick that outlander stroke victims used, but the width of the base interfered with his smaller stature and he often tripped over one of its legs. Lately, he used a cane that he designed and fabricated from spare toy parts. It had a single candy cane shaped pole and handle, but the base had a broad flat disk to prevent it from sinking into the soft snow and cleats to prevent it from sliding on the ice. He also customized the shape of the handle so a gloved hand could firmly grasp and securely hold on. Still, whenever possible, he tried not to use the cane, and on most short journeys within the village, Erog would slowly and carefully negotiate the path between his point of departure and his destination without the use of his prosthetic crutch.

It was not difficult for Amak to remember the mobile Erog. He and his wife were relatively new arrivals at the Village, having come only two years ago. During those earlier times, Erog was more active and more vocal in expressing his displeasure with Santa, even more so than Amak. Often Erog would protest the evils of Santa's so-called progress and how it was destroying the tribe—as he called his fellow workers. At times, Amak thought there were two Erogs: one who spoke with monosyllabic words and the other, a philosopher

75

who expressed concepts even Amak had difficulty understanding. Eventually Erog's ardor cooled, as did most things in this icebox environment. Erog settled down to a steady shift in the workshop and volunteered to give up most of his free time in order to care for Santa's reindeer.

His wife, Unata, worked a full day at the food center. Amak could not think of anyone who had anything nice to say about her. At best, the villagers were polite and mentioned how she rarely missed work and never had asked for vacation time to visit her native village and family. He wondered why she chose to isolate herself from the others. Conversations with her were usually reported as abbreviated as "yes" and "no" and anything more than this usually raised eyebrows in surprise.

Erog and Unata were one of the few married couples never to have had children. Maybe this was the source of their dispositions. Family meant a better chance for survival as one aged. Children, not friends, would be expected to care for you when you became infirm. Maybe, Amak thought, the couple was afraid that they were about to be left out on the ice.

chapter 10

A mak lumbered to the other end of the village. Still wobbly whenever a gust of wind blew, he had to plant his feet and brace himself to prevent a fall. The schoolhouse, the village's second largest structure, was set in an area as far from the workshop as possible. The workers had specifically chosen this site so the children were less apt to see their parents' daily trudge to the factory.

Most wanted a better life for their offspring. That was why they insisted the children attend some type of formal school. The workers wanted their progeny exposed to the histories and the ways of the more affluent and comfortable outlanders. Not all, however, were against their children embracing the traditional mores, but they wanted to make sure the children could make an intelligent choice between the two societies.

The parents weren't ashamed of their jobs; most were actually proud that they made the toys Santa Claus distributed each year. There was even one year when they secretly signed their creations in inconspicuous places. Santa found out, however, and quickly chided them for their hubris.

"How do you expect the children to react when they see evidence that somewhere, someone made the toys? How are they to believe that the toys didn't just mystically appear under the tree each Christmas morning just because they were good during the year? Well, darn, you might as well stick a price tag and a return policy on the toys too!"

The signatures came off and were never applied again, but a little of the elves' pride came off too.

Whispers began how Santa only took his stand against the signatures because he alone wanted credit for the happiness the toys brought. The climate of discontent continued for a few more years, and it was then that Amak felt the time was right for unionization and decentralization. But he had miscalculated the power and respect Santa still held. For their part, the elves did absorb some of what Amak had said, and when they built the new schoolhouse last year, they placed it in a new location. Many hoped their children wouldn't see any rationale to labor in the workshop, but would instead leave the village to begin their own families.

A small, cluttered vestibule greeted Amak when he entered the schoolhouse. The long but narrow room served two purposes: it provided some insulation between the actual schoolroom and the outside cold when the door opened, and it was the area where the children and visitors hung their coats, hats, and any other outerwear.

Amak noted only a few of the hooks were occupied. Most garments lay strewn on the floor. Small puddles of water on the floor were testament that even though the room was not heated, it was still warmer than the outside, and the ice and snow that clung to the clothing was melting. There were a few traditional Arctic coats made from caribou and reindeer skins, but most were modern commercial coats of polyester filled with down and hoods lined with imitation furs. Amak unbuttoned but kept on his caribou coat.

He negotiated the maze of clothes on the floor and opened the inner door to enter the single schoolroom. Loti, used to stragglers entering at all times, did not glance to see who had entered but instead continued with her class lesson.

The room was perfectly square. Small, freestanding wood-burning stoves located on either side of the entranceway quickly tempered any blasts of colder air that entered the heated room. A furnace powered by the school's own generator heated the classroom, but the heat produced could never really keep pace with the outside temperatures, and some of the students still wore their coats.

There were six rows of seven desks, each neatly aligned and all facing forward to the teacher's desk. Because parents expected their children to attend only three years of school—graduation when they attained twelve years of age—there was no need to divide the class into sections based on student age. Teachers based their lectures on the three-year cycle, so no matter when a student began his education, in three years he would have heard it all. Although there were forty-two desks available, only half were filled. There was enough room for additional desks but none were ever needed. The builders of the schoolhouses had assumed the outlying villages would want their sons and daughters to attend the school, but few did, and even the number of students from Santa's village decreased as more and more families with school age children left.

Amak retreated to one of the rear corners of the room. He stood, silently watching Loti proceed with her lesson. He was not listening to her words, but was instead marveling at her appearance. She was beautiful by any standard. An elf, a native Inuit, or outlander, never agreed on much, but all would agree that Loti was bewitching.

He struggled against the intense heat radiating from the nearby stove, and shifting his weight from foot to foot, he tried to settle into a comfortable position. At the same time, he pulled at the collar of his sweater to allow cooler air in against his chest. He now regretted not removing his heavy coat before he had entered the classroom.

michael i bresner

Even with a height not significantly greater than the average female elf, Loti seemed tall. Maybe because she was thinner than most or maybe because she always stood erect. Her almond-shaped eyes and her high cheekbones were the gift from her distant Asian ancestors. The thick, straight, coal-black hair fell half-way down her back, and although it was both time consuming and difficult to stuff the hair into a hat or hood before braving the outside cold, she refused to cut it to a more practical length. She wore the typical plain brown woolen leggings, but her atypical sweater was a kaleidoscope of colors and graphic shapes.

Loti had arrived in the village just short of three years ago. All considered it an honor to be a teacher, but to be the teacher in Santa's village was the extreme triumph. The illustrious Santa had asked her to move here. He had seen and heard her teach at a village some seventy-five miles to the south. He had gone there trying to convince the inhabitants to join his network of toymakers. That part of the mission had failed, but he did return with a new teacher.

Less than three years of teaching meant Loti had yet to repeat her lectures. The boredom associated with repetition had yet to establish itself. Outwardly, her life outside the school also appeared enjoyable. She was a respected villager. Even the older elves came to her for advice. Some of the younger single males came to see her for other reasons, but except for her brief marriage to Danat and her current relation with Amak, Loti tended to avoid relationships.

Like the other men in the village, even the married ones, Amak had thrown secretive glances at the schoolteacher, but initially there was little conversation between the two. Beauty sometimes has a way of intimidating many. It suppressed any intimacy—you can look but you had better not touch. Danat had no such trouble, and he certainly did not lack self-confidence. Soon after Loti's arrival in the village, they were an "item" and within months, they married. The loud arguments began soon after, and the gossip surrounding

80

the bruises that repeatedly appeared on Loti's face followed. Divorce in this area of the Arctic was simple—one or the other participant in the marriage simply proclaimed the marriage was over. You left with what you brought. Afterward, when questioned as to why she married in the first place, Loti replied, "It was the loneliness."

Loneliness may have also been the reason Loti did not feel that an extended time span was needed or appropriate before casually socializing with other men. Eventually, Amak overcame his awe and found convenient excuses to join activities that were sure to involve Loti. Later he'd wonder whether the initial impetus to start a relationship might have been in part due to his long-standing hatred of Danat. He had found an obvious way to antagonize and aggravate him. Whatever the reason, Loti and Amak soon became lovers. They both gained from the relationship. Her loneliness abated and he found a friendly adversary to argue his theme of traditional ways.

In most ways, Loti represented civilization's, the outlander's, ways. She taught survival to her students, but not survival against the cold, but survival in the changing society around them. Amak argued that to admit that society was changing fueled the change. "Teach your students how to hunt bear and seal, not how to hunt for a job in the South." In the end, Loti laughed at his dogmatic ideas and the evening usually ended in an enthusiastic romp in bed.

Amak's foot slipped in the puddle that formed from the melting snow dripping from his boot. As he reached out for a support, his elbow smacked loudly against the wall. The noise attracted Loti's attention. She smiled broadly, the way she always smiled when genuinely happy, but kept on with her history lecture.

"Does anyone here know why the outlanders call our land the Arctic?"

No hand rose, but then, none was expected.

"Well, I guess I'll have to tell you," she continued. "Long ago in ancient Greece . . . Do you all know where Greece is?"

This time a few hands rose and Loti went to the world map hanging on the sidewall to show the country's location to the remainder of the students. An impromptu geography lesson continued for a few minutes until Loti returned to the front of the room and to her explanation of the origin of the word, Arctic.

"The ancient Greeks were great sailors. They used the stars to navigate to their many distant trading ports. What the outlanders call the Big Dipper is a constellation of stars that is part of a still larger constellation of stars, one in which the ancients imagined an outline of a bear. That heavenly arrangement, the outlanders now call Ursa Major, is a translation of the name Great Bear. It was the Greeks, however, who gave our area its outlander name. The Greek word for bear was 'arktos.' The Great Bear was always in the northern sky, so whenever the sailors traveled to the North, they traveled to the land of the bear, the 'arktikos.'"

It was a lesson the students would probably never forget. Loti's lessons always were informative and interesting and never boring. History, geography, mythology all rolled into a story the young elves would retain.

"Why not tell the rest of the story, Miss Loti?"

The students turned to see who had spoken. Loti rolled her eyes in mock disgust anticipating the problem ahead.

"Why not tell the whole story, teacher? Why not tell how the bears, the 'arktos,' entered the heavens?"

In unison again, twenty-one small heads turned to face Miss Loti.

"I'm sorry, Mayor Amak. I don't know where the bears came from. The bears like all the other stellar constellations were figments of people's imagination. One might easily assume that the ancients could have seen a pig in the sky, and then we might live in an area called 'Pigland.'"

The class burst into laughter. They were proud of their teacher. She did not retreat before a question posed by the village's illustrious leader.

Amak also smiled but only briefly. "You rely too much on outlander history and myths. It is our land, however, and perhaps we should spend more time discussing our history, our myths." The conversation was beginning to take on a more serious tone. Even the students detected the change. The history lesson had ended. It was now a subtle debate between cultures, Loti's and Amak's.

She gave him what could only be called an affectionate smile. "Mayor Amak, why don't we postpone your tale for another day? Class time is almost over for today."

One of the older students interrupted his teacher. "Mr. Mayor, what were you going to talk about?"

"I was going to tell you how the bears traveled to the heavens."

Before any other student expressed interest, Loti again reminded Amak that there was no time. She instructed the children to gather their clothes and books and said her goodbyes to each one as they left.

"Damn it, Amak, this is a school house! These children are here to learn. Your myths have no business here."

"These children don't need to know where the name Arctic came from. They need to know where we came from."

"That's what I am teaching them. It's their history I'm teaching, not your bullshit."

Amak's laughter echoed in the room. The vulgarity from such a petite thing seemed incongruous to him, and although he had heard her use profanities many times before, it shocked him each time. It wasn't that he was a chauvinist—women of the Arctic had to work as hard as men or there would be no chance for survival, but Loti could not be categorized as such a typical woman.

"Don't you laugh at me, you faggot." Additional laughter ensued and her agitation with her lover intensified. "By the way, I understand you got your head beat in by Danat."

The laughter stopped. "That sure made the rounds fast enough. Who told you about it?"

"Oh, I heard some of the children talking."

"Well, just to keep the record straight, they carried him back, not me."

"Yes, after you kicked him in the face. Real fair fight. I also heard you let out with one of your famous war whoops when it was over."

"It wasn't a whoop. It was a howl and I always do it after a victory."

Now Loti smiled. "Actually, I wish I could have watched." Loti grabbed for Amak and pulled him to her. Their kiss lasted a long time and before it was over, they had things on their minds other than lectures and fights. Loti asked Amak if he had time to walk her home, and he replied with a second shorter kiss.

She tucked her arm under Amak's, both to steady herself while walking on the slippery snow-packed path and to display her affection. Loti understood that the demonstration of emotion, or actually the lack of any emotion, was one thing the men of the Arctic and outlanders had in common. The comparison of women differed, however. Unlike outlander women, exhibitions of emotion typically embarrassed Arctic women.

A slip on the raised lip of a footprint in the snow interrupted her thoughts, but her secure anchor to Amak prevented a fall.

"Tell me, Amak, I also heard you think it may not have been a polar bear that killed Knute."

"No, I'm sure it was a bear. Nothing else could have caused the mutilation I saw, but there was an odd shaped print near the scene, and I was going to show it to Erog…"

Loti stopped walking and faced Amak. "How is Erog? I haven't seen him for a couple of days."

"Okay, I guess. Oh, I almost forgot, he asked me to tell you to stop by the shed. He wants to show you some jewelry he's working on."

"Was it my anklet? Did you see it? How does it look?" Loti was so animated when she spoke, she almost fell again. "Erog had promised to make me something special, but even so, I didn't think he would start it until after Christmas." The fact that he had placed her present before those assigned by Santa seemed to excite her even more. Erog was a special friend.

She had spent many evenings listening to Erog and Amak sometimes agree, sometimes argue about how to achieve independence from Santa. In the beginning, Erog had simply listened to Amak's diatribes. He sat in stony silence, never offering an opinion or expressing a thought. Loti had watched him intently. She did not think that he remained silent out of respect or due to a feeling of inferiority. Indeed at times, he seemed more intense than Amak. He spoke on occasion, but something kept him from uttering that first word. The silence worried Loti—silence often meant secrecy.

Loti never stopped to realize that she, too, was closemouthed during these gatherings. It was only when she first challenged one of Amak's statements that Erog's incommunicative attitude also ended. He now had a compatriot. The autocracy ended and an enjoyable discussion group of three was born.

More often than not, Loti teamed with Erog against Amak, but when the subject of "tradition" cropped up, the sides changed and Amak and Erog were in full agreement that Santa was corrupting traditional ways. Overall, however, Loti felt she had more in common with Erog then with Amak. But power and leadership swayed and mesmerized Loti. She eventually came to the realization that as the teacher in Santa's village, she, too, was powerful and a leader, and that she did not need the false security of a companion with civil authority.

Loti's cottage differed from the village's other homes. It looked like a home rather than a storage shed. It was clean. Loti couldn't tolerate dirt on the floor and, consequently, she swept two or three times a day. It was bright. Unlike other villagers, Loti had more than one ceiling light. They were not bare bulbs dangling from wire cords, but lighting fixtures, handcrafted by one of her student's parents—crafted during the off-season, of course. Her cottage was a canvas of colors. Loti placed a collage of vivid colors everywhere: the bedspread; the small, circular carpet by the door; the tablecloth and chairs. Colors were everywhere.

Photographs covered all but a small portion of the walls. A soothing, pale green paint covered the rest. The photographs were not of individuals. There were no likenesses of herself, her family, or Amak; instead, the photographs were of distant landscapes. Not landscapes of exotic Pacific islands with palm trees and white sand— Loti knew she would and could never visit these locales. Rather, the photographer had captured scenes of forests or fields of flowers in full bloom or magnificent isolated northern Canadian lakes and Scandinavian fjords—locations where elves already lived side by side with outlanders. These were the places she yearned to visit. Not one photograph displayed snow; not a single photograph had a patch of white. The only odd thing about the photographs was that Loti had grouped all in fours. They were not related in size, color, or subject. And Loti's method was undecipherable to Amak. He had once asked her the why-of-it, but she said she just thought they looked right when displayed that way.

Books were everywhere too: on the shelves, on the kitchen table, on the night stand. There were schoolbooks, mystery and romance novels, history books, books on every subject except gardening. Loti's cottage was the village's unofficial library. Unfortunately, as Loti saw it, it was a little used library. Not many students or their parents bothered to borrow any books from this northernmost book depository.

Amak pushed aside the books on the kitchen table and allowed Loti to set the dinnerware and prepare the meal.

They sat and talked a few minutes to allow the soup to cool. Finished, Amak watched Loti attack her two-inch thick sandwich. He was not surprised that she could open her mouth wide enough to consume a significant portion of her meal. After all, elves had the ability to dislocate their jaws without physical consequences, but the gapping oral opening seemed incongruous with her petite stature. They quickly finished eating and after Loti cleaned the dishes, they settled onto the floor in front of the fire. Loti put her arm around Amak, who turned and gently kissed her cheek. The cottage was an oasis in the Arctic desert—warmth, color, happiness—rare qualities in this harsh land.

Loti usually initiated the lovemaking. She thoroughly enjoyed the physical act. They had made love many times before, and many times the act had paradoxically consummated an argument. Tonight was not one of these times. Tonight the foreplay was marked with tenderness and whispered endearments. They removed each other's clothes, not in a rush of passion, but in slow seductive stages. Lying in front of the fire, Amak rolled towards Loti. He kissed her neck tenderly and then gently caressed her breasts. His hand found its ultimate destination between her thighs and multiple stimulations awakened Loti to her first and second orgasms of the night.

They rested for a few minutes before Amak began again. This time he rolled Loti onto her stomach, straddled the back of her thighs, and started massaging her back and neck. Amak raised himself onto his knees, slipped one hand beneath her waist to lift her buttocks in the air, and began to mount her from behind.

"Don't. Please don't." Loti tried to squirm away from Amak's hold. "You know I don't like to make love like that."

Amak ignored her plea as he again attempted to gain insertion.

This time she spoke much louder. "Don't, Amak! I don't want you to do that!" She twisted away from Amak and stood. Loti was not prudish when it came to sexual acts, but she had established certain boundaries with her lovers. She didn't try to cover her naked body as she continued. "Why do you try to force me to do something that I don't want to do? Why do we always have to make you happy?"

Amak sat up at Loti's side. "Didn't I allow for your feelings? Didn't I satisfy you first? What kind of bull is that? Anyway, what's the big deal?"

Loti knew the answer; she had thought it through many times before when the same situation had arisen. "I think the only reason why you want to screw me that way is because you think your ancestors routinely used that position. You and your damn 'tradition this' . . . 'tradition that.'"

"It so happens they did screw like that and guess what? Everybody enjoyed it, including the women. I think there is a little defacto discrimination here. Just because it was favored in the past, you won't try it in the present. We're not missionaries bound to one technique."

"That's wrong, Amak, and you know it. I just don't like it, and don't say I have to try it first before I can say it. The fact remains I don't like it, and I've asked you before not to make love like that. Some might have called what just happened an attempted rape."

"That's a leap."

"Even if it wasn't an attempted rape, I've told you before that I considered it undesirable—undesirable down to the bone."

Loti remained standing, first looking down at Amak, and then turning to look into the fire to absorb its warmth. Eventually Amak stood to add another log. Loti used the opportunity to dress, and after another short discussion about nothing in particular, Amak dressed, kissed Loti on her cheek and left.

chapter 11

Loti sat close to the hearth, her arms wrapped tightly around her bent knees. The intense heat from the flames failed to stop her shaking. She stared into the fire and realized her displeasure with herself was far greater than her displeasure with Amak. They had had the same argument before, but that was the problem. *Why do I allow it to recur and recur?* She knew there were ways to stop it, assuming she wanted to. She could threaten to withhold sex if Amak insisted on his traditional ways. She could stop seeing him all together—there were other available men. But she continued to accept his verbal abuse, much the same way as she had accepted Danat's physical abuse. The sexual mechanics that Amak had wanted did not disgust her. *My God, I've made love in kinkier positions.* Instead, it was his reason for the sexual act. As far as he was concerned, traditional ways were the only ways. To him all else was profane. *He considers sex a biological function, one without any emotions.*

She shuffled to the table, sat on one of the wicker chairs, and tried to prepare next week's lesson plans, but the thought of being alone again kept interfering with her concentration. She put the lesson work aside and paged through an old *National Geographic* magazine. This time, however, the stories and photographs that she normally eagerly pored over each month could just as easily have been blank. Nothing pushed her thoughts aside.

Tears cascaded down her cheeks. The prestigious title of Santa's Village's teacher had been alluring. Loti knew no one expected her to spend a lifetime here, but she thought she would be happier and be able to tolerate the inconveniences for a longer period. Once again the feeling of loneliness swept over her and brought with it total despair. Once more, she tried to read but still could not concentrate. She stood, cleared the dinner dishes, and swept the floor, but these activities failed to alter her mood. She remembered Amak had told her that Erog had asked her to visit. Maybe the outside cold could coerce her brain with thoughts other than her current misery.

The few workers remaining in the building when Loti arrived had separated themselves from where Erog toiled. She waved to some of her students' parents and continued across the room to join her friend.

"Erog, I'm not bothering you, am I? Amak told me that you asked me to drop by."

Erog jumped up and in doing so struck his knee on the underside of the workbench. Objects scattered and fell to the floor. He stooped to pick up the crafts, but his foot tangled with the chair leg, and he and the chair crumbled to the floor.

"Real coordinated, aren't I?"

Loti reached her hand down to help him up, but Erog pushed away and continued speaking, "No, I can get up myself." Then quickly added, "But thanks anyway."

She bent down to pick up the fallen toys and noted Erog wince when he finally stood and put weight on his feet. She observed that his shoes were untied and was concerned he might trip and fall again. Still kneeling, she started to tie his shoes.

"Please don't do that, Loti."

"I'm down here already. It's no bother."

"Really, please don't tie the shoes."

"Too macho to let me help. You and Amak, what a pair you are."

"It's not that I'm macho, or that I don't appreciate your offer to help. It's just that my feet hurt and it feels better to leave the shoes untied." It was now his turn to offer a hand to help her stand. She grabbed the remaining toys from the floor and accepted his aid.

Loti's gaze riveted on the workbench. "Amak told me he saw the anklet. Am I allowed to look at it before it's done?"

"Sure you can. It's not as if it's a surprise; you already know what it looks like. It's just like Unata's." He righted the chair, sat down, pulled open the workbench drawer, and removed a small cardboard box. Before opening the container, he pulled the dangling light bulb closer to the table. The yellow haze over the box changed to a purer, whiter color. Erog slowly opened the box and lifted the protective cotton covering. The gold pieces sparkled in the light.

Loti reached to touch the anklet but hesitated above her present.

"Go ahead, you can pick it up."

"It's beautiful, Erog. It's the most beautiful piece of jewelry I've ever seen."

"It's not done yet. I still have to add pieces of gemstones. I know how much you like colors."

Loti wept as she tenderly fingered the work. "It's just so beautiful. I love it." She still didn't pick the anklet out of the box but continued to run her fingers over each piece. "The detail is remarkable. Each animal looks so real. Did you carve it?"

"Not the gold. First, I carved each piece in wax and then cast it in the gold. Don't tell anyone, especially Amak, but I swiped the gold from some watches and some of the electrical contacts in the more complex computer games. Some of the toys may not work too well this coming Christmas morning."

"It's just beautiful." She bent down, held his head between her open hands, and softly kissed him on his forehead. "Thank you, Erog, thank you very much." Erog looked away while she held him a while longer only letting go when she realized that he was embarrassed. Loti looked back to the anklet and this time picked it up to cradle it closer to the light. "Where are you going to put the stones?"

"Some will be the eyes of the animals and others will just be decorations on their bodies. It's almost done. I still have to string it together with a chain."

"You're making a chain too? I can't believe it."

"Sorry to blacken my image again. No, that's something else I'll have to swipe from the workshop. No one will miss it."

"Quite the thief. Am I going to be able to wear it without Amak arresting me for receiving stolen property?"

"Just tell everyone that you got the jewelry from a mail order catalog."

"Bullshit! You're going to get all the credit. Everyone is going to know what kind of work you can do. Besides, I don't want to take the rap for you. If anybody is going to the slammer, it's going to be you."

"At least I would get a reprieve from Unata's cooking. I could use a good meal."

Loti didn't smile but looked at him intently, "You know you can come over anytime and let me cook you a meal."

"Sounds good enough. Let me know the next time you cook for Amak and I'll eat his share."

"You don't have to wait for that asshole!"

He looked at her questionably. Was there a real problem between her and Amak or was she just tossing out words? He decided to assume nothing was going on. "Look, Amak has to be there. Someone has to talk to Unata."

Their laughter seemed forced.

Loti fondled her present a minute longer before carefully replacing it into the box. She asked if the anklet was the same as the one she had seen Unata wearing, and he replied that they were similar, but that Unata's had fewer pieces and no gemstones. He also said that this new one took three times longer to make. His reply prompted Loti to give him a second kiss. This time he did not look down, but instead looked straight into her eyes. Loti broke eye contact first. Now she was embarrassed.

"It really was my pleasure to make your present. Everyone else in the village is busy this time of year. I guess no one figures I can handle the stress. All I'm given are menial tasks that one of the children could do. It gets very frustrating and boring around here for someone with nothing to do."

Erog paused a moment. "At least a couple of weeks ago a few of the parents asked me to teach them how to use an atlatl."

"What's an atlatl?"

"It's a weapon used by hunters in the southern territories. It's used to launch spears further and more accurately than if they were tossed by hand. Even some of the children and Santa's nephew, Nels, joined in the lessons, but I have to admit few were what you could call prize students. Only Danat and a few others seemed to catch on.

"Two days of lessons and they all quit. I don't know if they thought they were good enough or if they got bored with the repetition of tossing the spears or if Santa demanded a return to the workshop for more important activities. Anyway, I was left to revisit my trivial tasks here at the shop."

"You want to know frustrating, Erog, just you try teaching. Try to teach the children how to express their thoughts. Try to get the children to be creative and use the right side of their brains. Look out the window. How many ways can you describe cold? How many ways can you describe white? White is the absence of color; it's the absence of life."

"That's not true, Loti, there are many ways to describe white. There's the white of a total whiteout in the middle of a snow squall. There're the different shades of white of the ice pack, the blue- and gray-whites. There's the stark white of a young polar bear cub trying to camouflage himself in the snow or the creamy white of its mother. Each of these whites has its own emotion and message—you just have to learn how to read it. You may not think so but white is a color. Granted on a clear day if you look out across the horizon, the landscape will seem entirely white, but if you look, if you study the landscape, you will see that it is really a patchwork of different whites, each with its own meaning. To survive, here in our land, we must learn and understand these meanings."

"You sound just like Amak, a little more philosophical maybe, but your message is the same. You make it sound like I'm a little crazy, a little strange for wanting colors on my walls and in my clothes."

"No, Loti, I'd never say you were crazy or strange. I just want you to realize that our land isn't just one boring view."

"I don't think anybody could call this land boring. Temperatures that don't rise above minus thirty degrees for weeks on end. Storms that descend on a traveler without warning. People killed by polar bears. No, this land is anything but boring."

"I take it you've heard about Knute Brulog?"

"Yes, and I also heard about Amak and Danat's fight."

"Boys will be boys."

"I bet you would have liked to have been in on it—cane or no cane."

"As I said, boys will be boys, and I'm just one of the boys, especially when it involves an opportunity to smash Danat's face. He's such an ass. I don't think he would've given me much trouble even with me tripping over my cane." Erog smiled and continued, "Although from what I heard, Amak needed all the help he could get."

"Why is it so necessary to beat someone senseless? Why not just call him an idiot, turn and walk away?"

"It's a fool that gives an enemy a second chance, and hunters learn early on never to turn their back to an enemy. If you should find yourself face-to-face with a possibly superior foe, a polar bear for instance, if you want any chance to survive, don't turn and run. Either curl up in a motionless ball and hope the bear is neither inquisitive nor hungry, or else back slowly away. Never lose eye contact with your opponent. It's not being macho; it's just being sensible."

Erog told Loti that Amak had asked him to investigate Knute's corpse, and the two of them were returning to the site of the killing to inspect the scene for any additional evidence.

A loud discourse on the other side of the room interrupted their conversation. Unata, Erog's wife, stood halfway through the doorway, her clamorous voice demanding to know where her husband was. The elves were all too happy to point to where Erog and Loti stood, and they seemed to gleefully anticipate the coming scene.

Unata's scowl intensified when she saw the two, and she didn't bother reaching them before she spoke. "Didn't you tell me you were going to be home an hour ago? It's not enough that I have to work all day in the communal kitchen feeding people who don't have any inclination to thank me, but when I come home, I have to feed you, too. At least I would expect you to be there when you tell me you would." She looked Loti straight on but continued her conversation with her husband. "What, or should I ask, who's so important that I have to eat alone?"

Erog kept his eyes on Unata as he tried to cover Loti's anklet with the piece of cotton. His hand fumbled, however, and in reaching for the box, he knocked it to the floor in front of Unata's feet.

Unata unconsciously rubbed her foot against her opposite ankle attempting to feel for the anklet Erog had given her. She couldn't detect it through her thick leggings, but she did feel it chafe against the skin. "What the hell is this? Is this for me?" She looked at Loti who immediately turned away. "Of course not. I should've known better. What's the matter, Loti, are you getting tired of Amak? Need someone new to bed?"

Erog positioned himself in between the two women. He knew Unata was capable of provoking a physical contest. "That's enough, Unata. Loti saw your anklet and asked me to make one for her. Nothing's going on."

"Loti, can't one man satisfy you longer than a few months? Are you always on the prowl for fresh meat?"

Erog raised his voice, "Unata, I said that's enough!"

The elves on the other side of the room drifted toward the trio. They guessed Unata wasn't going to stop and wondered if Erog would hit her. They seemed excited that they were eye witnessing tomorrow's gossip. Maybe Loti would hit her or Unata would hit Loti. A semi-circle of silent spectators formed.

Ignoring Erog's request, Unata continued accusing Loti of trying to break up her marriage. The verbal barrage continued unchallenged until she called Loti a whore. That was when Loti's head snapped up, her lips tightened, and she looked Unata straight in the eye.

"Just what do you think you're looking at, you slut?" The spray from Unata's mouth almost reached Loti.

"I'm just looking at your ugly face," Loti replied. "I'm just trying to figure out just how hard I have to hit you to smash in your big hairy nose." Secretly, she felt somewhat secure with Erog standing between them, and if worse came to worse, she knew she could outrun the overweight foe to the front door.

The elves viewing the confrontation laughed aloud. That, more than the remark, incited Unata even more, and she took a swing at Loti only to accidentally hit the side of Erog's head. Unprepared for the blow, Erog again found himself on the floor. Unata pressed her attack but stumbled on Erog's prone body, and she too fell to the floor. He grabbed hold of her waist as she tried to reach for Loti's legs to pull her down. The struggle continued for a minute until Unata finally tired and gave up on her attempt to stand.

Erog rolled her onto her back and pinned her arms to the ground. "Stop this crap and get the hell out of here. There wasn't any reason for you to start anything. I made a present for a friend—that's all there is to it. No perverted payment was offered, none was asked for." He released her arms and stood above her. "I think you should leave now. I'll be home soon as I can."

Unata jumped to her feet and all thought the fight was to begin anew, but instead she kicked Loti's anklet across the floor sending it flying against the wall. "There's your present, bitch. Why don't you get down on your hands and knees and earn it?" The epithets and slurs continued as Unata backed away. She kept facing Loti, threatening her with her clenched fist. It wasn't lost on Loti that Unata never once turned her back to her when she left the building.

The audience dispersed quickly, some leaving to spread the word of the argument they had just witnessed, others going back to work; after all, they still had to meet their daily quotas to keep Santa happy.

"I'm sorry, Loti. All too often Unata gets jealous for no good reason." He grinned widely. "Gee, I guess I should be flattered. I mean look at me; I'm certainly not anybody's pinup boy. Who would want a gimp like me?"

"Don't put yourself down like that, Erog. Even with the cane you're a better man than most in this village."

She walked over to where the anklet had landed, picked it up, and placed it back in the box. Handing it to Erog, she again thanked him and said that maybe he ought not give it to her but instead give it to Unata. He told her not to worry, that he would smooth things over with his wife and that he'd have the present finished in a few days, gemstones and all.

"Is she really always like this? How do you put up with it?"

He explained how Unata had never really wanted to come to Santa's Village and that it had been his idea to do so.

"Then why does she stay? How come she never visits her native village?"

"It's because she feels as a wife, her place is by her husband's side, wherever that might be."

"That doesn't make any sense. If she was so concerned about her husband, why would she make it so hard for him?"

"I know that it seems that way some of the time, but it's only because she's so miserable about being here. I guess I must take the blame for her attitude. I'm the reason she's so sad."

"I can't see how you can blame yourself." She unconsciously took hold of his hand and squeezed it twice. "Many spouses don't want to be here, but I don't know of any that walk around with a chip on their shoulder like Unata."

Each excuse he made for his wife, each time he took more of the blame, the more Loti pitied him. Here was a good man, she thought. But maybe Unata was right. If they left Santa's village, maybe things would be better. Not just for Unata but for Erog too. There was no good reason for them to stay here.

They talked a while longer. Erog showed Loti where he had planned to set the gemstones and asked if she approved. She did, but again said that it might be better for him to give the finished product to his wife. He again replied that there really wasn't any problem, that Unata would calm down in a short period, and that he'd spend some time with her when she wasn't at work. "All will be well," he insisted.

Erog straightened the workbench, put away the toys he was working on, and replaced the anklet in the drawer. They talked some more until he said he thought it best that he should join Unata at home.

DECEMBER 21st

chapter 12

The desert was bitter cold. Christmas season meant falling temperatures and this year was no different. Loti's students were always amazed to learn that the great sand deserts of the earth actually had a yearly precipitation more than their Arctic wasteland. Theirs was a desert that extended over the vastness from the tree line in the South to the geographic pole at the top of the world. The capacity of air to hold moisture decreases with cold, and Arctic air, at minus fifty degrees Fahrenheit, holds less than one-tenth of what it can at fifty degrees above zero.

The region's snowy blanket lay relatively undisturbed for years—the temperature never rising long enough for it to melt. All Arctic inhabitants knew that frozen water they couldn't melt was of no use. The snow that did fall was usually fine-grained, dry, and abrasive, much like the sand of the tropical deserts. Loti's students weren't as surprised to learn that more living organisms lived above the sand than above the ice. Even bacteria found it difficult to exist in the cold. Geologically and biologically, the Arctic certainly qualified as one of the world's great deserts.

The sled dogs sensed the trip. Already, a few had pushed through the blanket of snow that had clothed them during the night. They really didn't mind the snow. It acted as additional insulation against the dry Arctic air that seemed to pull the warmth from their bodies. Most of the dogs remained still, their tails curled over their heads shielding their faces from the wind. On others, only the nose was exposed, a black piece of coal dropped in a white mantel.

Unlike the majority of the Arctic inhabitants, the strains of dogs were no longer pure. Eskimo dogs, the Alaskan malamute and the Siberian husky were interbred for generations, but the desired genetic toughness and resiliency of all the original breeds remained.

While some of the dogs directed their barks and howls to no one in particular, the ritual remained part of their waking up process. Others directed their displeasure towards an adjacent comrade. Civilization wouldn't change these animals. Civilization in the form of snowmobiles might replace them, but it could not change them. Amak would often stand and watch the dogs, envious that they could howl whenever they wanted—without concern that this or any of their "traditional" acts would be considered either strange or undesirable.

The younger, more aggressive males pulled at their leather tethers. Parku, the most frequently used lead dog, sat patiently on his haunches watching the others. Parku's father was pure Alaskan malamute, but his mother was a homogeneous blend of Siberian husky and malamute. He had his father's size and weight, one hundred and fifteen pounds, but his mother's coloring, a black and wolf gray coat and slate blue eyes.

Most of the dogs were unnamed. These were not pets; they were work animals. No one provided them shelter even in the harshest winter. Peter, who cared for the reindeer, also inherited the task of feeding the dogs. Once a day, and sometimes less than that, he would toss each of them a piece of seal meat. Sometimes the meat was fresh, but sometimes it was frozen and then the dogs were forced to lick and gnaw at their meal for hours.

Parku and a few of the other dogs had names because Mrs. Claus decided they should. Amak had told Santa that it was ridiculous to name an animal, that if the need arose in a blizzard, he would have to eat or feed the weakest to the other dogs. It was wanton to bury a dead animal. A marauding fox or bear would soon uncover the carcass and carry it off. Giving a dog a name made the dog a companion, and the Arctic did not allow for sentimentality. They reached a compromise by allowing Mrs. Claus to name the newborn every other year. It made little difference since neither Amak nor most of the rest of the villagers ever called the dogs by their names, and Mrs. Claus rarely spent any time with the dogs, her free time consumed by her "son", Rudolph.

Sometimes an elf picked the team's leader based on the dog's intelligence, endurance, and strength. The more knowledgeable drivers allowed the team to choose its own leader based on the dog's ability to survive. After all, that was the biggest challenge to any living organism in this icebox. Convention and genetics dictated that the challenger first eliminate the pretenders through intimidation or combat. Only then could the leader be directly challenged. There wasn't extra food if you were the leader. There wasn't preferred treatment from the elves. The only reward was the ability to mate with whichever female you desired, assuming she agreed, and, if one was to believe that dogs had one, a boost to one's ego.

Parku watched Laso strain at the tether, trying to pull the attached stake out of its icy vice. Laso's paws couldn't gain an adequate grip on the slippery, packed snow, and, each time he pulled against the tether, his feet slid from beneath him. Barking and snarling at the stake did little to change his captivity. He grabbed the restraint in his mouth, pulled, and again was unsuccessful. But instead of letting go, he started to chew through the leather. No one expected the tether to withstand such an assault; it was placed as a reminder to the dogs that they were not free and to keep them from wandering off. Within minutes, Laso was free of his shackle.

His challenge for leadership did not begin with the customary ceremonial act of circling and aborted launches directed at his foe, instead the instant he was free, Laso turned and leaped at his rival. Parku met the rush with his chest and crashed to the ground. Laso rolled away from the still tethered leader enraged that he had lost any advantage of a somewhat surprise attack. The other dogs stood, and the intensity of their barking cloaked all other sounds.

Laso circled Parku looking for an unprotected path for another attack. The hair on his shoulders and neck stood on end and ropey saliva dripped off his exposed teeth. Courage can be an attribute necessary for survival, but without accompanying wisdom, courage can kill. Laso charged again, leaping for the exposed side of Parku's neck, but the instant before the attacker's teeth could grasp and tear at the vulnerable area, Parku moved his head aside and sunk his teeth into the challenger's soft neck. Death would have been quick, but the momentum of the leap pulled Laso free. His wolfen eyes glowed in the light from the nearby overhead lamp, and he again circled Parku. Blood matted and froze on his fur. Again, he leaped to strike, but this time a heavy stick swung against his side abruptly stopped his trajectory in midflight.

Laso slammed against the other dogs. He stood and spun to attack his new tormenter but not before the stick descended on him again. Two more times the stick knocked him to the ground. The third time he arose and limped back to his stake, which was still firmly secured in the ground.

Amak put the axe handle down but not out of reach, and he tied the two chewed ends of Laso's tether together. "Damn dogs! I ought to let you kill each other and just get some snowmobiles. Damn dogs aren't worth the trouble!" With that, Amak stood and kicked some loose snow into Laso's face. The other sled dogs were still barking, and it took a series of loud threats and swinging of the stick through the air to finally quiet them. The dogs knew to be careful around their masters or they, too, might suffer from a stick or a kick to their ribs or in the extreme situation—death.

There were thirty dogs in the village, but Amak decided he would need five to pull the sled today. The dogs could easily pull two or three times their weight, and the only weight other than him and the sled would be Erog. No supplies would be required on such a short trip.

He selected five harnesses from the group that hung from the wooden pegs on the side of the nearby shed and attached the first to Parku. Once Amak placed the yoke around the leader's neck there'd be little or no trouble with those that followed. The dog stood passively while Amak tightened the cinches. Parku knew no other life. He was born to pull a sled, and like most dogs, he would die in harness pulling a sled through some future Arctic storm. The dogs seemed to understand their fate and accepted it as an inevitable event. Amak next attached a twenty-foot leather backline to the harness. In turn, he would harness each dog and link a progressively shorter backline. The resulting fan-hitch allowed a wider distribution of the team's weight and allowed a wider separation of the dogs to prevent fighting. The varying lengths of the backlines prevented the dogs from attacking the back of the more forward dog. If a dog turned to fight a dog on a shorter rope, he would need the courage of facing his adversary as well as the driver's whip. The fan hitch was most frequently used in the high Arctic. Further south, the dogs were hitched in a straight line in order to better negotiate the narrow paths within the pine forests that were sometimes traveled.

Amak dragged the smallest sized of the three available wooden plank sleds toward the tethered team, attached the gangline to a steel ring, and fabricated a bridle by tying all the dogs' backlines to the same fastener. Finally, he set the snow hook to secure the sled but still left the dogs tied to their stakes to prevent further assaults.

He left the dogs fidgeting in anticipation of upcoming work and entered the small shed. A string dangling from the ceiling light gently brushed his face as he passed through the doorway, a sharp contrast to the icy snow spicules that blew outside. He pulled the string to send the electric current from the outside generator and begin its battle against the resistance established in the frigid wire. The shed did not burst into a sunrise of light, but a faint yellow glow from the dirty bulb allowed Amak to view the shed's contents.

Shelves lined the room on three sides. Caribou and polar bear skin blankets, tarpaulins, and spare wooden slats used for the sleds lay on these long wooden planks. Sled runners, whips and leather lashings hung from wall hooks. Broken and non-matched snowshoes littered one corner. Elves with their large, flat feet rarely needed the shoes, but Santa and his family often did. Amak stepped over broken sections of caribou antlers used as cross-braces for the sled runners, removed one of the four whips hanging on the wall, pulled the string to shut the light, and turned to leave.

A large object silhouetted against the outside lights startled Amak. Large objects usually meant danger to elves. In this case, however, Amak quickly deciphered the silhouette belonged to a benign shape—Santa's youngest nephew, Nels.

Santa had no children of his own, and since his brother died ten years ago, his two nephews had come to live with him. The assistance from these two genetically linked individuals helped make Santa feel more comfortable, more secure. No one could specifically point to any of his actions as being prejudiced against elves, but he certainly kept all "important" decisions within the family. Eventually, on his death, his title and its associated duties would transfer. To date, Santa gave no clue as to who would receive the title of Santa Claus, but the smart money was that Nels' brother, Matthew, would inherit the "Throne of the North." This year, Santa had sent Matthew to tour the villages to make certain the workers met their quotas, a most important job, as noted by Mrs. Claus. Santa had put Nels in charge of production at the village workshop, but everybody knew it to be a titular job, with Santa really maintaining control. Nels did not complain to his uncle; however, he did complain to Amak. If one year Santa wanted more traditional toys, Nels would comment how old fashioned, out of date Santa was and how the children would be disappointed. If another year his uncle wanted electronic games instead of dolls, Nels would come to Amak complaining how the tradition of Christmas was being bastardized by progress.

Nels entered the shed and greeted Amak. "I'm glad I caught you." He was taller than Santa by a good three inches and his weight was fast approaching his uncle's. Although currently beardless, he had grown both full and abbreviated versions. The redness of the hair that grew in made him feel silly for some reason, and he decided to keep the covering off his face until the gray and white of old age appeared. He had never completely adapted to the coldness of the Arctic. It's a myth that your blood changed to conform to the temperature and to somehow make the frigid air more tolerable. Nels had enough layers of garments on to warm four elves.

"Hello, Nels, what's up?"

Nels did not answer but posed his own question. "Where're you off to?"

"Erog and I are going to check the area where Knute was found."

"Why the continued investigation? I understood it was nothing more than a bear attack."

"I'm sure that's all it was, but I found portions of strange footprints in the area of the corpse."

"What do you mean by strange?" Nels asked. "Did Erog get to see them?"

"No, they were destroyed."

"I take it that happened during your friendly discussion with Danat?"

"Shit, who doesn't know about that?" Amak looked disgusted. "Anyway, Erog and I are going back to see if we can find any more prints."

Nels tried to replay Amak's last statement. Like his uncle, Nels sometimes had difficulty deciphering elves' high-pitched voices. The two Arctic dwellers stood silent for a second before Nels realized that Amak's last remark was not a question needing answered. Instead, he asked his own question. "Need some help? They sure don't need me here. I'd be glad to have an excuse to leave the village."

"Thanks anyway, Nels, but I really don't think we'll find anything of importance. By the way, why were you looking for me?"

"I'll tell you but first let's get out of this dungeon."

They left the shed and began the trek towards the dogs. But within the first few steps, Nels slipped and almost fell to the ground. Amak tried not to smirk for it was well known that Nels had difficulty walking on snow much less the icy surface they were now on.

Nels quickly regained his balance and spoke. "A couple of days ago, I sent a couple of elves to pick up some supplies from the outlander's village by the southeast forest region. On the way back they were attacked. They made it to a friendly village of elves but are in no shape to return by themselves. I was hoping you could send someone to pick them and the supplies up. We really need them if we are going to keep up."

"By them, do you mean the supplies or the elves that were attacked? You're starting to sound like your uncle."

"I mean the supplies."

"Since when do quotas mean so much to you?" Amak asked.

"Screw you. I noticed you didn't even ask how the elves are doing and what happened to them."

Stalemated, Amak proceeded to ask about his comrades and Nels told him when taking what they thought to be a safe shortcut through the edge of the tree line, a group of looters attacked. The fight did not begin immediately. However, the usual course of events did occur: name-calling, shoving, and then fighting. When it was over, the supplies were scattered and both elves had broken arms and one a broken leg."

Amak kicked the ground and threw his arms into the air as he shouted, "Those ugly sonsofbitches! They came down from their trees one too many times! I'm going there and crack some heads! Damn dwarfs! They're one step below monkeys!"

"Dwarfs. What makes you assume they were dwarfs? And aren't dwarfs related to elves? Aren't they pretty much the same as you?"

"They're not like elves. We're different from those assholes."

"How so?"

"They have six fingers like us but these bastards also have six toes, and more importantly, they enjoy killing for the pleasure of it."

"So, they're your distant cousins."

"Cousins! Like the Sioux and General Custer. Dwarfs hate elves almost as much as elves hate dwarfs. They never, ever have gotten along. They've fought for land and fought for food, and the elves have always won."

"Are they the reason the elves were pushed out of the forest onto the ice," needled Nels, but as he finished he realized he might have needled Amak too much.

"We were not pushed out; we pushed the dwarfs in." Amak continued to refuse that they had anything in common with elves. "Their attention span is less time than it takes me to piss. They're hyperactive, pathological liars, lacking any guilt or remorse. The dwarfs raid elf villages and murder everyone."

"But elves kill too," Nels said.

"Yes, but when we killed, we killed only warriors and then only during battle. And don't say that that was murder too. Murder is killing a member of the same species. Killing a member of an outside species is not murder and, certainly, dwarfs can't be considered to be in the same species as elves. Hell, they can't be considered anything but an evolutionary mistake!"

Still smiling Nels replied. "Sure, but now the elves make toy dolls and trains."

"Don't push it, Nels. I know you are just trying to get a rise out of me, but don't push it or I will stand up to you, eye to stomach, and punch your knee cap."

It took a moment, but Amak finally joined Nels' laughter. Nels was glad Amak had taken his taunting within the confines of their friendship. They continued walking towards the dogs that looked bewilderingly at the upright combatants. There had been shouting, anger in the voices, and just as suddenly, there was calm and laughter. No blood had been shed; the dogs could not understand this type of behavior.

Parku jumped to his feet when they approached. He snarled at Nels with a savagery that confounded Amak. "Shut up, Parku! What the hell is up your ass?" Amak turned to Nels and asked, "What's between you two?"

"Oh, it's probably because I had to use the whip on him last week when I took him on a trip. I don't think he liked it too much. I actually drew some blood. But he deserved it."

"When were you out of the village? I don't remember you leaving for any reason."

"Santa sent me on an errand. A quick back and forth excursion."

Nels bent down and helped Amak tie the dogs to the sled, leaving his friend to secure Parku. Amak then fastened the gangline to the metal hoop embedded in the front of the wooden surface. Finally, he checked the leather spreaders to make sure the lines weren't touching the dog's hindquarters and the padded collars around their necks didn't interfere with the dogs' breathing.

The dogs strained at the lines waiting for the command to "Take off!" But the trip was not quite ready to begin. Amak checked the strip of hide used to join sled parts, placed the blankets he had taken from the shed onto the planks, and again checked the snow hook so the dogs wouldn't pull too soon.

Time was passing quickly, and Amak was already late meeting Erog. He was about to leave when Nels questioned him again. "Do you think you can send someone to bring the elves home?"

"Ah! Now you have my attention. Now you show some concern for the elves. I didn't think production quotas had gotten to you yet." Their comradeship was reestablished. "I meant it when I said I think I'll go and maybe kick some dwarf-ass. I should be able to make the trip a one- or two-day excursion but I doubt I could leave before Tuesday."

"I don't think the two-day rest will bother your friends too much. Being away from Uncle's village this soon before Christmas is like getting your present early." Nels threw the last of the blankets on the sled, and then placed the whip into a holder on the side. He looked pensively to the ground, then back up to Amak. "I think my uncle is getting a little senile. I remember growing up listening to the Ho! Ho! Ho! and thinking the man was perpetually happy, but he's changed. The laughter seems forced now. He no longer seems to enjoy the work he once thrived on. He used to run up and down the aisles of the workshop cheering up the troops, as he called them. 'Work faster! Christmas Eve is almost here! Think how happy those children are going to be!' He ran up and down the aisles, and he was always smiling, patting the workers on their backs, encouraging them to work faster. 'But don't give up quality for quantity. Those children won't be happy with broken toys two days after Christmas. Make sure you do a good job.'"

Amak interrupted, "Nowadays its production quotas—full steam ahead."

"He's not quite that bad," Nels added defensively.

"Didn't he send you and Matthew to talk to that toy manufacturer who wants to pay your uncle off and take over the workshop? Hey, whose side are you on anyway?"

"I'm not on my uncle's, that's for sure, not the way he has changed. Not only did he send me to talk to Collins, but on different occasions, he travelled alone and spoke to him. But I don't agree with everything you want to change."

Amak seemed shocked. "There's no middle ground, Nels. Either with me or against me."

"That's just it. There is no middle ground and I had to choose you. Tradition is what you preach and tradition is what I want. I agree with you that my uncle needs replaced. I agree with you that I, not my brother, would be the best replacement. But I don't think your methods are necessarily the best. Unionization of the elves? That's not what I would call tradition, Amak. Machiavellian perhaps, but not traditional."

"You might be surprised but I, too, read Machiavelli. Elves can read. They can have ideals. They need not be followers. Unionization is a check against Santa going too far. Unionization of the elves is necessary."

"Would it be necessary if I were to inherit the title of 'Santa Claus'? Would I need the checks and balances? Would you trust me?"

"Of course, I would. We all would trust you, Nels, but you can't convince the elves that they need a union one day and take it away from them the next. The union would stay, but its activities would be negligible."

"Amak, you are a bull artist, but I like you anyway. As long as you stay so obvious, I have nothing to worry about." He looked down at his shorter companion and smiled. "You figure you can force Santa out, get me in, and you'd be the power behind the throne."

"Nels, you make me smarter and more devious than I ever could be. I have no ulterior motives. I just want things back the way they were."

"Whatever you say, Amak."

"What I do say is that I have to leave you now. I told you I am supposed to meet Erog. Anyway, tomorrow or the day after, I'll leave to bring the elves and their cargo back. By the way, who was it that was attacked?"

"Nice of you to ask, Mayor Amak. Sven and Hans were the victims and they're being cared for in Haulvit."

"Okay, I'll bring them back."

chapter 13

Erog stood in front of the workshop. Fully exposed to the icy wind and flying crystals, he bent his head down and turned it to one side. It did not help. The wind swirled between the buildings and changed direction as fast and as often as he changed his position. He hunched his shoulders and pulled in his neck in a futile attempt to withdraw his head into the confines of his coat's collar.

"Sorry I'm late!" an embarrassed Amak shouted as he approached with the sled. Although no command was given, the lead dog, Parku, took the initiative to stop, correctly assuming the undecipherable babble from his current master required the action. "I got caught up in a conversation with Nels and couldn't break away." Amak spoke rapidly, waving his hands in the air, and alternating grand smiles with dramatic grimaces—all done in the hope these actions would somehow distract Erog from his obvious physical discomfort caused by the tardiness. "Did you hear about Sven and Hans? They were attacked by a pack of dwarfs."

Erog's face hardened before he spoke. "When did this happen?"

"A few days ago, I guess. I have to go to Haulvit to bring them back." Amak's arms were waving again, this time not to distract, but due to his rising rage. "It's more than their sixth toe that differentiates them from us. Actually, I think they use their extra toe to hang from trees—just like their monkey fathers. They're stupid, bloodthirsty, primitive mutants."

Erog chose not to respond. He pulled his hood's drawstrings tighter to further protect his exposed face. Amak knew Erog would not complain about standing in the cold, but it was obvious he was not very comfortable and probably hadn't been while waiting for him to arrive.

"I'm really sorry I'm late. Have you been waiting long?"

"About fifteen minutes. No big deal. I could have just gone into the workshop, but it's chaotic in there and I can't take the glances from those poor souls working on the production line. I feel awkward enough socializing with them when they're not working. Just imagine how I would've felt watching them toil away. We've so little in common during this time of year. My complaints certainly don't coincide with theirs."

"Erog, we've been through this before. You know everyone understands. We all have duties in the village and you do your share. Hell, I only work on the line if there are too many elves out sick. Don't be so paranoid. Everyone likes and respects you."

"Even if that's so, which I seriously doubt, I just couldn't wait inside. I can tolerate the cold wind better than the cold stares."

Amak again apologized for being late and told Erog the details of the dwarfs' attack. Once more, he entered into a general tirade against dwarfs and elicited some subdued supporting remarks from Erog. Amak wanted to continue venting his anger, but Erog signaled the conversation's end by walking toward the sled.

"How come there aren't any emergency supplies on the sled, Amak?"

"For this short a trip? I couldn't see any need."

"You know never to assume this barren land is anything but dangerous. Much could happen, even on a short trip, and those supplies might be the difference between your life and death." Erog grinned when he continued. "Even more important—between my life and death."

"All right. We'll stop and pick up some supplies."

"Forget it, Amak," replied Erog and smiling broadly he added, "We're running late as is."

"Hell, how many times do you want me to say I was sorry? A little bit of fresh twenty-five degrees below zero air is good for you."

"What did you and Nels have to talk about?"

"He just wanted to tell me about Sven and Hans."

"As far as I'm concerned, he's a waste," Erog said as he completed his arduous journey to the sled.

"Sven? Hans?"

"No, not them. Nels is a waste."

"Why do you say that? I've told you how he's on our side," Amak replied.

"That's just it. How do you trust someone who backs the opposition against his own tribe, his own family?"

"Hey, it's not like he's planning his uncle's murder. The way we've got it planned, Santa will give up the throne on his own and Nels will be in charge."

"First of all, what about Matthew?" Erog questioned. "Everyone knows that Santa wants him to be his successor."

"Matthew couldn't lead a fart out of his own asshole. No, Nels will be in charge."

"That's my second problem. What's going to be the difference between having Nels or his uncle in charge? We're going to substitute one outlander with another. We'll still be the second class citizens in this village."

"No, that's not going to happen. Nels and I will have joint leadership. At least at first we will. But I know I can maneuver him out in a short time. He talks a good game, but he'll be history less than a year after Santa leaves."

"Amak, I hope you've thought this through. I hope once you're in charge you don't succumb to the power of the throne. I don't trust Nels. Be careful, I don't think he's as stupid and helpless as you make him out to be."

"Speaking of attacks, what's this I hear about Unata and Loti?"

Erog rolled his eyes skyward before he answered. "Didn't Loti tell you?"

"No, I haven't seen her since yesterday. Actually, I think we're in the middle of an argument. Hell, it amazes me how these women can make something out of nothing. Maybe they're bored? Maybe it's penis envy?"

"Don't let Loti hear you say that. I'm afraid if she did, you may not have a penis to envy."

"She is a tough little bitch, isn't she? Anyway, what the hell happened? Was there really a knock-down fight?"

Erog went on to describe what took place, but when asked why Unata had gotten so excited, Erog offered no explanation. Amak offered one of his own, however, "It must have been monthly madness or some other kind of hormonal imbalance." He coerced Erog to give a blow-by-blow account of the fight and laughed when it came to the part of the story when Erog took the punch to the face and fell. "I better see Loti when we get back just to make sure she's okay and see if she's still mad at me for whatever the reason."

Erog slowly climbed aboard the sled. He unfolded and pulled the blankets over himself so only a bare minimum of his face remained exposed. Amak stepped onto the platform stretched across the sled's runners, grabbed the whip from its holder, and issued the command

119

for the trip to begin. "Take off! Mush!" The dogs strained against their harness to break the inertia of the motionless sled. Like a rubber band first stretched and suddenly released, the sled jerked forward, and in the process almost slammed into the closest dog in harness.

The rider might have the whip, but on the trail, the dogs were really in charge. They would, of course, go left if so ordered, but if left was not their desired direction, no amount of either verbal or physical abuse could force them. In a blizzard, often the driver would cover himself with blankets and allow the dogs to return him safely to the village. Their sense of direction and their exquisite sense of smell enabled them to locate destinations miles away. The dogs could even smell a seal's breathing hole, and, more importantly, they could smell a polar bear at a distance well beyond visibility.

The Arctic created numerous relationships. The seal provided needed sustenance to the polar bear, the caribou and the wolf were another linked pair, and the sled dog and man still another. If the dog proved weak, it wasn't permitted to reproduce. Hardy, strong offspring, able to survive the ordeals created by the harsh environment, were thus assured. Excessive reproduction meant less food available from the scarce supplies, and then even some desirable pups would die. On a long trip, if a dog lagged or dawdled and did not seem to contribute his fair share, an elf might kill the dog—its carcass shared among the remainder of the team. Thus was the economy of the Arctic.

"Haw! Haw!" The dogs instantly acknowledged the driver's command and veered to the left. They had been on the trail for almost fifteen minutes. Except for slowing twice to detour around mounds of rough ice, the team had pulled its load at a fairly rapid pace. Parku maintained a gait that was not too fast or too taxing for his compatriots.

There was no conversation between Amak and Erog during the

trip; the cold wind and blowing snow precluded that. Each was alone with his own thoughts, but that was natural in this land.

The two riders turned to the noise of a nearby loud crack. It sounded like a rifle shot from deep within the ice, but both knew it was the sound of the edges of the ice pack pushing past each other. They were used to this and the other noises of the moving ice—the low groans and squeaks. They were always aware that the sounds could indicate the ice pan might suddenly open to the ocean below, and they and the dog team could plunge into the icy waters.

"Gee! Gee, you lazy animals!" The dogs responded by turning right. They were almost at the site of the recent tragedy. Elves, like the dogs, had a sixth sense of navigation. Even in the shadowy or black daytime of the Arctic winter, they were able to circumvent dangerous crevices in the ice and locate their destination. Even without stars to map by, they were successful in their wanderings. Closer to the magnetic North Pole a compass wouldn't have helped. The magnetic pole cannot be defined as a specific point on a map. The pole changes daily, meandering clockwise over a wide area, sometimes more than one hundred miles in a single day. Utilizing a compass close to the pole, therefore, becomes completely futile; the dial swings and jerks unpredictably due to the lack of a horizontal magnetic pull.

The sled bounced over an ice hump and Amak's hands tightened on the twin wooden handles. His grip was secure, but after another bounce, one of his feet slipped from the platform and momentarily caught in a small crevice. That was enough to jerk his other foot from its stance and Amak found himself dragged behind the sled like a fallen water skier. He tried to pull himself back onto the sled, but it was moving too fast and he could not gain the needed traction on the underlying slippery ice. His legs bounced and flailed wildly in the air and he finally admitted defeat and yelled to the dogs, "Whoa!

Stop!" The sled gradually stopped as Parku and the rest of the team slowly slackened their pace.

Erog turned in his seat, trying not to expose more of his face than was necessary. "Why are we stopping? We're not there yet."

"I just spent the last minutes of this trip being dragged behind the sled. That's why!"

"Having your troubles today, Mayor Amak?"

"Kiss off, Erog! You look damn comfortable sitting on your ass all bundled up!"

Erog laughed loudly. Each new guffaw creating a small, white vapor cloud. "Hey, I've got two bum feet. It is your moral obligation to chauffeur me around town."

"Don't get me started, you lazy sonofabitch."

Erog laughed again when Amak fell on his rear while trying to brush the snow off his boots and pants.

Five minutes later, they entered a small chasm formed by a series of moderately tall hummocks and then arrived at the site where Knute's body had been discovered. Amak jumped from the sled and set the snow hook firmly into the ground. The dogs barked their disapproval. A short trip like this was a tease, not an effort, and the dogs wished to continue.

Erog pushed aside the blankets and arduously rose from his seat. He needed his walking stick to hobble to the area in question. Amak finished tucking the blankets beneath a tarpaulin stored behind Erog's seat and joined his friend who paced the ground searching for clues.

"That's where I dug out those odd prints," Amak said pointing to a spot a few yards away. "Why don't you look around here, and I'll look on top of the hummock where Danat found the other prints."

Amak looked for an easy path to the top. The route he eventually chose was at the far end of the mount where it gradually tapered to ground level. Arriving at the top, he scanned the area carefully, but the wind had covered everything with a fresh layer of blowing snow and ice crystals, and he knew any search would be futile.

Below, Erog lost his balance as he bent down to get a closer view of the ground. He stabbed out at the icy floor with his walking stick and caught himself before falling. Twice more the same action saved him from toppling over. Amak watched sympathetically from above. He wondered if Erog had some disease that was destroying his equilibrium. He seemed to be stumbling more often. Amak hoped it was just the cold. He continued to observe his only true ally struggling to help him search for some mysterious prints that probably did not exist, concerning a strange death that probably was not that strange.

"Find anything down there?"

"No. Nothing but prints your colleagues obviously made," Erog shouted back. "I take it from the signs in the snow, that this other area is where you and Danat had your little altercation."

"Yes, it is," replied Amak as he gave up his search and started down the hill. "Why don't you look around in that area? That's exactly where I found the other prints."

The trip down was easier than the trip up, Amak having slipped only twice on the way down. Now in the gully, as he walked toward Erog, he thought he spied a lone depression in an area away from all the other traffic. "Erog, what's that over there? Is that a print?"

"What? Where?" Erog was already moving to the spot. "Where?" he asked excitedly. "Where?"

"Right in front of you. Just look a few feet in front of where you're standing."

Erog bent lower and again lost his balance. The walking stick dug into the snow pack in front of him, kicking up a small spray of snow in all directions. His fall was again prevented as the cane penetrated the loose covering snow and contacted the icy base below.

"Where? Where is it?"

"You mean where it was. Your cane just destroyed what I was looking at!"

"What was it? Was it a print?"

"No, I doubt it was anything. I couldn't see for sure, but I'm sure whatever it was, it was not a print. Don't worry about it."

"Damn. What good am I? Why did you bother bringing me along? You could have searched this small area yourself."

"Maybe so, but I probably wouldn't have known what I was looking at even if I found it. I needed your expertise."

"Don't bullshit me, Amak. I know waste when I see it, and I fit the category to a tee."

Amak argued the point some more, trying to ease his friend's mental anguish. He eventually convinced Erog to again join in the search for additional clues. Together they looked over the rest of the area but finally decided that no other clues were to be found and headed back to the sled.

The approaching crunching footsteps alerted the resting dogs, who stood and tugged at their harness in anticipation of the pull home.

Neither elf saw Danat watching from behind a nearby mound.

chapter 14

Santa's head jerked to the right as the pain knifed through his neck.

"Damn, my throat hurts!"

"You've been complaining for days now. Why don't you see Dr. Skeen?" his wife asked.

"He's not a doctor, Becky, and I don't know why everyone insists on calling him one. He's just an elf who took a couple first-aid courses and likes to read medical journals. That certainly does not qualify him to hang a shingle on his door advertising "The Doctor Is In." Just because you can boil water doesn't give you the right to call yourself a master chef."

"Kris, it's not like you're asking him to perform a heart transplant."

"Look, all I'm saying is that I don't think Skeen should pass himself off as a doctor and I don't like it when the elves are misled. Too many of them think he's capable of diagnosing and treating medical problems that are far too complex for someone who had no formal training. It wouldn't surprise me if the workers who report off sick are not really sick, or if they are, more often than not their condition will worsen after Skeen treats them. So, if you don't mind,

I refuse to see any quack. In fact, I wouldn't even trust him to treat Dasher or Donner or Blitzen. Their health is too important."

She watched him grimace when he again tried to swallow. "Nice speech. Let me feel your head." She reached over, brushed his hair away, and placed her hand on his forehead.

"Have I got a fever?"

"It's a little warm, but my hand is cold. Would you at least take some antibiotic and let me make you some chicken noodle soup?"

"All right, I'll take some penicillin until Dr. Betters, who's a real doctor I might add, arrives next week. As far as the soup is concerned, how about some pea soup with dinner instead?"

"Pea soup it is. What else would you like?"

"How about a steak? Do we have any caribou meat left?" He knew not to ask for reindeer.

"I'm pretty sure we do. I'll check the freezer later, but if there isn't any meat, you'll have to settle for fish. Anyway it's better for your cholesterol level."

"Everyone's a doctor. I can't win." This time Santa spoke with a broad smile. "By the way, Dr. Betters is coming next week, isn't he?"

"Either he'll be here or his nurse will come instead."

It surprises many that it is difficult to catch a cold, or for that measure, any infection, above the Arctic Circle. The extreme cold that makes human existence so arduous also inhibits the growth of many of the causes of common illnesses. Santa assumed this sore throat was born three weeks ago when he traveled south of the tree line. His visit to the outlander village was two-fold: first, he had to negotiate the additional shipment north of raw materials needed for the production of the often-requested electronic gadgetry; second, he met with the world's most prominent toy manufacturer.

Robert Collins was the CEO of an American conglomerate whose primary business was the manufacture and sale of mid- to high-priced toys. For years now, Collins had been approaching Santa with "a deal of a lifetime," the latest of which would have made Santa an instant multi-millionaire with a yearly half-a-million-dollar stipend and the title the Spokesman for Collins Toys. His only responsibility would be to occasionally don his famous red suit in front of a camera and read a thirty-second script espousing the thrill of receiving a present from the shelves of Collins Toys. There was also a clause that would pay Santa an additional one hundred thousand dollars if he agreed to appear at the national toy show in Las Vegas—again in uniform. Finally, there was an obligation to close the workshop. Collins promised that the elves would have the opportunity to work for him at any of his plants located around the world, and for those who didn't choose this course of action Collins would compensate with generous severance monies.

Out of courtesy, curiosity, and to satisfy his own ego, Santa had yearly meetings with Collins. Santa listened, as each year the buyout became larger and more tempting. Last year, he had seriously considered the offer. Amak's effort to unionize the elves had created animosity and tension within his work force, so much so that the preceding year was the first that Santa had really despised. His nephew, Nels, advised him to "take the money and run," but his other nephew, Matthew, and Santa's wife both successfully campaigned that he should maintain the status quo. Santa again sent word back to Collins that there would be no sale.

Collins was persistent, and at every chance, he made another offer. Santa had listened to this year's attractive pitch, but not wanting to elevate Collins hopes, he had immediately told him that he still wasn't interested. He made certain to explain that it was not a matter of more money; it was the tradition and institution of Santa Claus that prevented him from accepting any new proposal. He wouldn't be the individual that ended the reign of Santa Claus and the delivery of free presents at Christmas.

So this year Santa didn't receive millions of dollars from Collins but instead was the recipient of a virulent strain of a virus or bacteria that presented him with his current nagging, painful malady.

Santa watched his wife place her nearly finished cross-stitch project, a picture of a tumbling teddy bear and a bouncing ball, onto the small pine end table. A previously finished picture of a small bonneted child playing with a bouquet of flowers already rested on the table. She arduously extracted herself from her overstuffed chair and stood. Mrs. Claus had recently asked Santa to move it closer to the perpetual fire smoldering in the large stone hearth in order to benefit from the additional light radiating from the hot embers. The exacting task of pushing a needle through tiny holes in the mesh fabric and reading the intricate pattern was difficult even in good light, but near impossible with only a dim electric reading light. These projects usually took less than a week to complete, but with time split between filling in at the workshop for sick elves and other Christmas related tasks, her current project was nearing three weeks. The completed work was for Matthew's daughter, but she realized it didn't matter since they probably wouldn't return until after the holiday season. He and his family would be celebrating alone.

Santa was six inches taller than his wife. Her unusually short legs, combined with her short stride, made her appear to shuffle rather than walk across a room. A lack of calcium in her diet and old age combined to create a stooped appearance, evidence of progressing osteoporosis. Still, she was taller than the tallest elf by a good twelve inches.

She took her role of Santa's wife seriously. "One must look the part," she had repeated often. Her hairstyle had not changed since their wedding ceremony. Each day, she rolled and secured her snow-white hair in a bun on the crown of her head. The color of her clothes also rarely changed, red and white like her husband's. But unlike her husband, she chose to change the patterns of her clothing on a regular basis. Some days she wore stripes, some days it was checks, and on other days it was gingham, but always, when in public, it was red and white. The small round lenses always resting below the bridge of her nose enhanced the image of a benevolent matron.

Becky reached into the mass of supplies stored on the shelves above the kitchen sink, retrieved the bottle containing the penicillin and checked the expiration date. The plastic bottle had a childproof top that she always had difficulty opening, even more so since the arthritis began. "Line up the arrows, push, and twist"—a lot easier said than done. "Kris, you'll have to open this yourself. I can't get it."

Again she reached, this time to remove a plastic glass. The creamy white layer of scratches coating the inside of the glass masked the cleanliness of the object. Unsure if she had mistakenly placed a dirty glass with the clean ones, she delegated it to the sink and took another. This, too, was coated but less so. She filled the glass with water and brought it and the penicillin to her husband. Santa was still seated, but now engaged in stretching and twisting his stubby neck, hoping the movement would somehow ease the throat pain.

"Thanks, Becky. I'm sure it will help. I guess I should've taken these sooner." His fingers clamped around the antibiotic's bottle cap and easily released the cover. He started to rise from his chair and spoke, "I might as well take some extra strength aspirin also."

"I'll get them for you, Kris. Just sit back down."

"No, that's okay. I have to check the production sheets Amak dropped off."

The effects of advanced age had gained on both of them. In an environment where the frigid cold preserved most matter, the same hostile world had noticeably diminished each Santa's life expectancy. The elves and Arctic animals learned to adapt to their surroundings—not so Santa and his family.

Mrs. Claus had given birth three times. All three children had been males. That of course was welcomed, since males, like some monarchies, were required to carry on the title. One of the infants had died within a week of his birth. A second survived long enough to die in a freak accident when he fell into an ice crevice and broke his neck. The third died from an illness that could have been easily treated in any other place but Santa's Village. Now one or the other of their nephews, Nels or Matthew, would have to maintain the lineage.

Rebecca Claus had been introduced to the current Santa while both were students at the University of Rochester in upstate New York. He, of course, was attending incognito. He was not yet Santa; his father would have twelve years left to reign, but how many people would have accepted an individual who professed that his father was, and in the future he would be, Santa Claus? Not some impostor disguised in a stuffed red costume, working some street corner tolling a bell asking passersby to fill his alms kettle; nor an out-of-work, overweight, actor cradling the bottoms of children in department stores. No his father and grandfathers before were the true Santas—the true Kris Kringles.

Kris' courtship of Rebecca lasted two years. They took long walks along the tree-lined Genesee River, excursions to the wine-producing Finger Lakes region, skiing in Canada, but most of all, they spent as much time as possible being together. Rebecca Ayerst was enamored with this shy young man whose background she could never pierce. It mattered little that he evaded questions about his family and home. At first, she delighted in guessing his history and eventually assumed his father was a mobster. It added to Kris' mystique. She stopped questioning him, however, after she saw it made him uncomfortable. Neither had, nor required, many friends.

Paradoxically, their mutual desire for and enjoyment of solitude drew them together.

He finally told her the truth after an intense night of making love, and she surprised herself as well as Kris that she believed him almost at once. He did have to repeat the story twice, however. There followed none of the usual "Quit the bullshit! Who are you really?" She believed and that more than anything was the reason Kris Kringle asked Rebecca Ayerst to marry him.

Before he allowed her to answer his marriage proposal, he tried to help her visualize the life that lay ahead. He knew there could be no true description of the isolation she must endure. She, in turn, felt he was trying to discourage the marriage even as he asked her to wed. He wavered because he loved her so and felt it was cruel to ask her to join in his certain future hardships. In the end, she persuaded him to marry.

Santa's village is neither at the geographic nor the magnetic north pole. When the first Santa moved above the Arctic Circle, the workshop's location continued to change; he was still hunted by European authorities. Because his outpost needed to be near civilization's resources, it was initially located near the coastal area of Norway, close to Svalbard. Like the magnetic pole, the workshop wandered. Today it remains on a small, permanently snow-covered island in the Nunavut Territories of Canada. Transportation advances allow much of the village's required supplies to be ferried in on a regular basis.

A newspaper, actually a tabloid, article was the origin of the idea that the North Pole was the secret location of Santa's village. It must have seemed more romantic to the reporter than writing that Santa and his elves made their toys on an uncharted island in Canada. Santa saw no reason to correct the geographic mistake. He was content to have scores of tourists tracking around the North Pole in a vain search for his charitable Camelot.

Kris and Becky, as he now called her, didn't immediately move to Santa's North Pole Village. They meandered in the warmer climes of the United States and Europe for a few years, and gradually Kris directed their excursions further and further north. Residence in large cities led to moves to smaller ones, then towns, then remote villages and finally her father-in-law's home. Becky had been carefully weaned from the civilization she had known during their eight years of travel, and for the next two years, she at least had the company of her in-laws. Santa sent young Kris to distant elf villages to help coordinate production. Each trip was further away; each required more time away from Becky. This was the acknowledged method used to help a future Mrs. Claus adapt to her eventual duties and loneliness, but there really was no way that anyone could prepare her for being alone in a land where humans were not meant to live. Of course, there are people who crave solitude. They may want to live in a location without creature disturbances, but a blowing snow ramming into your face and a wind that seems to set fire to your skin leaves little time for self-evaluation.

First, her mother-in-law then her father-in-law died, and her husband was crowned with his red coat as the new Emperor of the North. The elves took an instant liking to Rebecca. They appreciated the effort she made replacing sick workers on the assembly line. The constant glut of baked goods she distributed certainly helped her popularity too. She became the consummate arbitrator, instinctively knowing when to verbally step in between Amak and Santa.

Becky's happiness abruptly ended when the children died, and she was told there could be no further chance to bear offspring. The loneliness intensified and a growing mental depression strained their relationship. Kris started to enjoy his extended trips away from the village and his wife. For her part, Rebecca began to withdraw from the extended family of elves, feeling now that she never fit in anyway.

Some years later, Kris came to Rebecca to tell her that his brother and sister-in-law had been killed by a fourteen-year-old in a robbery attempt gone bad in New York City and that his brother's two orphaned children would be coming to live with them.

It was Matthew, more than Nels, who eventually rekindled Kris and Rebecca's faltering marriage. Matthew was the eldest and as such was destined to inherit the title of Santa. He was a quick study and easily learned the mechanics of the family's polar enterprise. Although at times he would disagree with his uncle as to the need to modernize the workshop, he was devoted to the icon of Santa Claus and never suggested changing that aspect of his uncle's life.

Nels had the luck of knowing early on that he most likely would never be charged with the burden of becoming the next Santa and his personality developed accordingly. He found it easier than his brother to befriend the elves knowing he would never have the unpopular task of insisting on an increased workload. Nels never had to cope with the mantel of responsibility. He was calmer, jovial, and easier going than his brother. His attitude and ideas most often matched those of his aunt, while Matthew's most often were identified with their uncle's.

Because socializing came easier for Nels, it was he who married first, and when his two sons were born, Santa's attitude toward his two nephews slowly shifted. Everyone knew Santa would not change tradition—the eldest would remain his replacement—but everyone also knew Santa now preferred and hoped that somehow Nels might become the one to carry on.

Santa adjusted the ear extensions of his wire-rimmed glasses and began to meticulously review Amak's latest production reports. All seemed to be in order. Each succeeding day, Santa felt more confident that he could deliver the requested gifts on time.

He placed the list on the dining room table and reached for a letter atop today's newly received requests. The letter was written in Spanish from a seven-year-old Colombian boy who wanted a new soccer ball. Rebecca was fluent in four languages, while Santa was fluent in eleven but could get by in most others. This was just one of the requirements necessary for success in his occupation. He recorded the request on the master worksheet and picked up another letter. This one was from a German boy who wanted a CD player, a smart phone, and an eighteen-speed, off road bicycle. Santa only marked the bike for delivery—not every wish was fulfilled.

Matthew proved himself more clairvoyant each year. As he predicted, the new wish lists asked for far less traditional toys (dolls, trains and such) and far more electronic toys (computers and hand-held video games). The elves were accustomed to making toys, painting expressions on dolls' faces, customizing each item for each child, but now they were assemblers of toys—part A into part B—and each year the workers required additional training. Once, Nels had even suggested robotics to replace those elves who were leaving or retiring. Santa would never supplant the elves, however. He could only pray that saneness would return to the Christmas lists.

"Kris, I'm going to make a key lime pie and prepare some sandwiches to take to the Brulog's. I might stay with her for a few hours, so dinner might be a little late." Rebecca kneaded her aching, arthritic hands as she spoke.

"Don't worry, Becky. I'll probably be a little late myself. Something is usually going wrong at the workshop." He read a few more letters, shaking his head in amazement and disgust, and checked the appropriate lines on the worksheet. Next year Matthew promised to have all this computerized, maybe even with some type of scanning device. Matthew went so far as to question why not have every child stop at their local post office to fill out a preprinted computer form. His uncle assumed he was just joking.

Santa gathered the letters already tabulated and put them into a large cardboard box his wife had labeled "Christmas Wishes" and decorated with cutouts of paper snowflakes. When filled, it was unceremoniously emptied into the garbage outside the workshop or used to help start a fire in the cottage. Anyone in the village was free to use this kindling.

Santa's wide suspenders strained to hold up his heavy corduroy pants as he reached across the table. His waterproof fur-lined boots were a blessing outdoors but caused his feet to sweat as soon as he came inside. Rinsing his feet in the tub before dinner added to a growing list of daily rituals. He didn't see any reason to change into his uniform before going to the workshop. There was no need for any morale-boosting speech today and regular clothing would suffice. The first few years Santa had worn the familiar costume, Becky had to stuff the arms and stomach areas to create the corpulent illusion. After all, who ever heard of or saw an emaciated Santa. It didn't take long for Kris to naturally fill the outfit, and last year, Becky let out the seams as far as she could to accommodate his new bulk. Any additional weight gain would require a new red suit.

"Becky, thanks for volunteering to sit with Mrs. Brulog. It's a bad time of year for something like this to happen."

"Why, Kris? Is it because of a lost worker or a lost husband?"

The change in his facial expression told her that his feelings were hurt. "Come on, you know better."

She sighed and slumped back into her chair. "I'm sorry, I do know better, but why won't you tell the elves that you care?"

"Because I'm the boss first and a friend a distant second. I can't ask a friend to work as hard for as little reward as I have to ask the elves."

"You'd be surprised how much someone will punish himself for a friend," she retorted. "The elves have always been committed to their work. They've always been willing to give freely of their time, and except for a few like Amak, they never ask for time-and-a-half for overtime."

"Enough, Rebecca! I don't want to go over this again. It's just the way it has to be."

"No, it doesn't," she protested. "Change is possible."

He declined to be further drawn into the argument as he had so many times before and hoped to end the exchange by walking over and softly kissing her cheek.

She refused to be charmed but dropped the discussion anyway. "I'll start dinner before I leave. In case I am late, turn the oven down so the meat doesn't burn."

"Okay," he replied still standing above her. He bent down and kissed her again, only this time she smiled as he also gently squeezed her hand.

Santa finished gathering the remaining few toys, letters and lists and slid them all into another box—this one undecorated. He tossed the bottle of aspirin onto the pile, put on his parka and mittens, and left the house with the box under his arm.

He stepped into a quintessential Arctic day: cold, dark, and windy. The frequency of such predictable weather lulled the unintelligent into believing survival was easy. These inhabitants died young. The area around and between the house and the workshop was well illuminated with numerous mercury vapor lights mounted on three twenty-foot poles. These denuded tree trunks were the highest structures inside the Arctic Circle. The lighting was not for the elves, for they were able to see well enough without any artificial light source, but they installed the lights to ease the travels of the Kringle family. The wind increased and masked the humming produced by the synthetic suns. Santa walked rapidly past them towards the workshop, his open parka flapping as he went.

† †

Rebecca's ligaments stretched and cracked as they fought against the tightening joints. She stood, walked into the bathroom, and switched on the light. The sudden, bright glow reflected off the white tub, the white tiled walls, and white sink. Her pupils tried to help by constricting as much as they could, but they were not fast enough to prevent her sudden dizziness. Her legs buckled and she had to lean against the sink to prevent a fall. She stood, clutching the rim of the sink, waiting for her equilibrium to return. Staring into the bowl, she tried to focus on the clippings from Santa's beard, which had not been completely rinsed down the drain. It was probably hunger that weakened her so—she had not eaten lunch yet—although now with the appearance of a headache radiating from the temples and a wave of nausea, she was afraid some sinister illness might be trying to signal its arrival. She was already taking pills for congestive heart failure, arthritis, and additional medication for the beginnings of diabetes. She knew the importance of maintaining a diet with the proper amount of carbohydrates, and missing her lunch was certainly not too smart. Even so, even with her multiple medical ailments, she instinctively knew the immediate problem was not any effect of the heart disease or the diabetes, but it was the shock of the light reflecting off the white of the room. Some epileptics are susceptible to seizures when presented with blinking lights; others, like her, become dizzy and get headaches when exposed to bright stark light. "No colors outside and no colors inside," she murmured. Splashing cold water on her face helped, but shutting the light helped more.

The aroma of the key lime pie baking in the oven made her think of the Florida Keys, sunlit and hot. She was home again, in Florida, in the small town near the Everglades where she was raised. Oh how she had longed to leave the heat and the humidity. She remembered nights when even the electric fan blowing directly on her couldn't stop the sweat from saturating her bed sheets.

She could only dream about snow, for she had never seen any. How she had wanted to touch a delicate snowflake, build a snowman, and make a snow angel. She dreamed of getting away from Florida, from the sun.

The cleaning and baking done, Rebecca remembered she still had to prepare the steak for dinner and hoped there was some caribou left. Santa needed something to cheer him. She would have to check the freezer. Actually, that was a misnomer. It was colder outside than inside the small shed they used to store their perishables. The wooden walls were only there to protect the food from marauding animals. Sometimes a hungry polar bear would wander into the village in search of sustenance and rummage through the garbage left to freeze outside the cottages. On these occasions, it often became necessary to kill the animal before it attacked one of the villagers.

There was no need to lock the shed. Theft was unknown in Santa's community. Besides, a metal lock would freeze, blocking passage to even those with the proper key. Rebecca opened the door and pulled the light cord. The light, though not bright, was sufficient for her to read the labels on the stacked packages. Whenever she restocked the shelves, she made sure she placed the newest, freshest meat on the bottom of the stack. That way she would use the oldest meat first. Something seemed odd, however. She climbed onto an empty wooden crate and even then, had to stand on her tiptoes to reach the highest package. She did not remember having this much meat in the freezer. Perhaps Nels, who also used the shed, had added to the supply without telling her or Santa. She pulled the upper package off the stack and something that was lying on top, something red and round, tumbled off and sped past her eyes. She teetered on the edge of the crate before stepping down to investigate the object.

Bending closer, she gasped and had to swallow her own vomit that began to propel out of her open mouth. She screamed, stood rooted next to the fallen object, and screamed again. Santa's wife stood transfixed by Rudolph's shiny red nose lying on the floor between her feet.

DECEMBER 22ND

chapter 15

"Find him and find him now!"

Amak listened as Santa continued his outburst, but this was the fourth time Santa had repeated his demand, so Amak felt unfettered to contemplate why someone wanted to kill Rudolph, rather than who. If he could figure out the why then maybe the who could be established. As mayor, he had mastered the artistry of appearing to be interested in the conversation, hanging on every word as if it were the most important thought or opinion he had ever heard. His action had become visceral: he closed or opened his eyes as the speaker's volume changed; he provided a quizzical look or shrugged his shoulders when a sentence sounded as if it ended with a question mark; and every so often he made sure he nodded in agreement. Indeed, he had perfected the technique. His wayward thoughts were interrupted when he realized a question had been asked and a pause demanded a response.

"Who would want to scare Becky like that?" Santa repeated. "She's a wreck. She's in bed, tucked in a ball, shaking uncontrollably. It's worse than when our first-born died. Rudolph was her son, too. She treated him like he was human." He hoped Amak would understand her grief. "What's going on?"

Amak waited a moment, making certain that Santa was finished before he spoke. "I'm trying to figure out why anyone would want to kill Rudolph and then chop him up into meal-sized portions."

"I don't give a rat's ass about Rudolph. I want to know who the sonofabitch was that did it. Solve this problem or they'll be a new mayor by tomorrow. You'll be working full time making toys."

"Santa, I've already started trying to piece it together, but it might take some time." Stooped over, Santa supported himself on the table, and Amak thought it best to change the subject. "By the way, what are you planning to do to replace Rudolph?"

"Dammit! Forget Rudolph! Just tell the workers to rig up a spotlight on the sleigh, and let Peter figure out who he thinks should be put in the lead."

Amak understood that Santa was too distracted by his wife's ordeal to continue any rational discussion or questioning, and Mrs. Claus certainly could not be questioned in her current mental state. Loti and Dr. Skeen had been sitting with her for the past hour attempting to help her deal with Rudolph's murder. Amak remained confused—why would anyone want to upset Mrs. Claus? He assumed that was what the unknown individual had in mind. Whoever placed what was left of Rudolph in the freezer shed certainly knew Santa's wife would likely be the first person to discover the atrocity. Murdering Rudolph would not prevent the toys from being delivered next week. His shiny red nose was more symbolic than useful on Christmas Eve. What would be accomplished by scaring Mrs. Claus? Nothing would permanently change because of Rudolph's death; Santa had made that perfectly clear when he spoke of replacing him with a spotlight.

"I'll be back to update you whenever I hear or figure out anything of importance, but I have to leave to meet Erog. I'm hoping he can help discover some clue as to who did this."

"Find out who did this, Amak." Santa's face softened and this time he asked in a subdued voice, a request of a concerned husband and a tired old man, not a command from a ruler.

"I'll try."

Amak had already noticed the effects of Rudolph's demise on the workers. Rumors had immediately started about a possible connection between Amak's missing second-in-command, Norved, twelve days ago, the mutilation death of Knute Brulog, and now of Rudolph. Some elves thought a psychopathic killer was lurking in or near the village, maybe one of their own—but who? Three elves were worried enough to leave the village and two others sent their families away. Again, Amak tried to consider who might gain by such instability. Toy production was down, but no one would profit by that. Though overworked, the workers were not in bondage; they were always free to leave. But he had other concerns to worry about too. He still had to arrange either for someone or for himself to bring back the two elves beaten by the dwarfs, and then there was Loti. More than one worker had asked him what happened between Loti and Unata.

Nels entered the cottage without knocking, a privilege of being a member of the family, certainly not disrespect. He gently closed the door behind him and walked across the room to greet his uncle and Amak. "How's Aunt Becky?"

"No real change. Loti and Skeen are with her now." Santa kept his eyes fixed on the floor. Looking up, he continued, "Nels, I want you to help Amak figure out what's going on. I want to know who did this. There's too much going on. I'm confused. My head won't stop pounding. My heart races so fast I get dizzy. I'm used to the chaos associated with the season. What I'm not used to are elves being beaten by dwarfs, elves deserting in large numbers, elves being killed, production slowing down, Rudolph being mutilated, and someone trying to scare Becky half to death."

Santa turned and looked at the bedroom door. "I know I should be out there in uniform cheering on the troops, but not with Becky the way she is. I need to know who did this. I need to regain some type of order in my life. I don't have the time or the energy to combat all that's going on."

Nels listened to the self-catharsis and gently placed a supportive hand on his uncle's shoulder. "Why don't you go and sit with Aunt Becky. She needs you."

Santa responded by turning his back to both visitors to reenter the bedroom. Still facing away, he spoke, "Take care of everything." Neither Nels nor Amak knew who he had directed the request to.

He slowly opened the unpainted plank door not wishing to disturb his wife should she be asleep, but when the hinges squeaked she opened her eyes and turned towards him. Skeen was standing, looking out the window. Loti was sitting on the bed kneading Becky's fingers between her two smaller hands but released them when Santa entered.

Neither Loti nor Skeen had ever seen the inside of Santa's bedroom. Actually, Skeen had never been invited into Santa's home before today and on entering had at once been intimidated by the change in the scale of things. He was unaccustomed to furniture as large as he now encountered and had actually banged into the sides of two pieces, miscalculating the dimensions as he passed by. It had taken him a minute to understand what else seemed odd about the house—there were no seasonal decorations. After all, he realized, why tack stockings to the mantel or go to the trouble of transporting and putting up a tree when the person most would expect to deliver the presents on Christmas Eve was the owner and resident of the house.

When he and Loti were ushered into the bedroom, they found Mrs. Claus laying on her bed curled in a fetal position. Her eyes were squeezed close and her quiet sobs were occasionally interrupted by garbled, unintelligible conversation with some unknown individual. The room was as spacious as the outer living room and again Skeen seemed overwhelmed with the size of things. There were about a half a dozen photographs of the Claus's deceased children hung in a tight oval pattern. Portraits of Nels' and Matthew's families were on another wall—both pictures slightly askew. The largest picture in the room hung on the wall facing the bed. It was an amateurish oil painting of a heron plucking a fish from a swamp. Mrs. Claus was lying across a bed quilt that Loti recognized the elves had given her as a surprise birthday present last year.

"Mrs. Claus slept for about a half hour," she whispered to Santa. "I'm going back to my cottage to cook some food for the two of you and then I'll be back."

"Thanks, Loti. I'd appreciate that." He turned to Skeen, who was still looking out the window. "Doctor Skeen, how's she doing?"

Skeen valued the professional salutation conferred on him by a man who normally wouldn't accept any medical advice, but he realized Santa would do anything to ease his wife's suffering, even calling him Doctor in front of her. "She'll be okay. It was probably a delayed shock that caused her to pass out when you brought her back to the cottage. I have some tranquilizers left in the pharmacy from the last time Dr. Better was here. It wouldn't be a bad idea to keep her on the pills for a couple of days, but I think a real doctor should see her as soon as possible."

Santa appreciated the self-degradation.

"I'll drop the pills off at Loti's and she can bring them over, but I need to first visit Mrs. Brulog to see how she's doing."

Nels greeted Loti and Skeen as he entered and they left the

bedroom. This time the noisy hinges fully awakened his aunt. "Aunt Becky, how are you feeling?"

"Much better, Nels." She held out her hand for Santa and didn't continue talking until she had a firm grip. "Kris, what's going on? Who would want to kill my Rudolph?"

"I don't have the slightest idea." He paused, staring at her, trying to assess her condition before continuing. "Becky, Amak wanted me to ask you some questions. Are you up to it?"

"I still feel a little weak, but there's nothing to tell. I went to the shed to get some meat for your dinner and something fell from above, striking my shoulder before it hit the ground. When I realized what it was, I just lost it and started screaming. The next thing I remember was you carrying me back to the house. I didn't see or hear anything else while in the shed."

"When was the last time you were in the shed?"

"I was there two days ago, putting some food away."

"Did you notice the meat stacked high then?"

"No, it wasn't. I'm sure of it. At first I thought Nels had put some fresh meat on the pile." She squeezed her husband's hand and before she again spoke, tears welled up. "Does that mean someone killed Rudolph last night?"

"It must have been right before you went into the shed, Becky, because Peter fed the reindeer yesterday afternoon and swears he saw Rudolph in the corral eating with the rest of them. In fact, he must have been feeling pretty good because Peter said he was shouldering Prancer and Dancer away from their portions. Erog also said he saw Rudolph prancing around when he returned the dogs and the sled."

Nels interrupted the conversation, "I can't imagine anyone in the village being involved. I just don't know who would want to do such a thing."

"Do you think Knute Brulog's death and Rudolph's murder are related?"

"Why would you say that, Becky? Amak asked me the same question. Brulog was killed by a bear, and I don't know of any bear that could neatly package a reindeer in butcher paper."

"Kris!" Tears again accumulated in Rebecca's eyes as she envisioned the terrible scene of her favorite's death.

"I'm sorry, Becky, but I think everyone is beginning to catastrophize a little too much. I can't imagine any master plan that would tie these two events together."

"But, Kris, what about Norved? He's still missing."

"Aunt Becky, obviously someone, for some reason that we'll eventually find out, killed Rudolph, but I don't see any connection to a missing elf and one that was killed by a bear."

Santa nodded in agreement. "What puzzles me is that no strangers were seen in the village, and I can't believe anyone here would have done this."

Dr. Skeen left Santa's house after briefing Amak on Mrs. Claus' condition. Loti walked around the room straightening chairs, fluffing pillows, trying to look busy until she was alone with Amak.

"Amak, I'm surprised to see you here."

"Why, Loti, where else did you think I would be?"

"I figured you'd be investigating some footprint or polar bear turd. I didn't think you would be wasting your time coming to see Santa's wife. Why did you really come?"

"I came to report to Santa and to talk with you."

"About what?"

"About the other night. I think you are making too much of something that's not very important. How we make love should not have to be analyzed for symbolic or hidden reasons."

"I don't think a discussion of our lovemaking should take place in Santa's living room. In fact, we've had this discussion before and we've yet to agree on a mutual answer to the problem."

"That's just it. There isn't any problem. It's no big deal one way or the other."

"Kiss off, Amak. I have too much to do and you are wasting my time."

Loti grabbed her coat, stormed out of the cottage without fully buttoning the coat and before Amak could ask her about her fight with Unata.

"I understand you and Loti are at each other's throats again," Nels stated as he reentered the room.

"Who told you that?"

"Amak, first of all I don't need to tell you it's a small village, and second of all, it's not often that I see Danat looking so happy."

"Piss on Danat!"

Nels smiled broadly having evoked the desired reaction. "Ease up. I'm just fooling with you." Looking towards the closed bedroom door, he continued softly, "Come on outside. We have to talk."

"Becky, I told Amak and Nels to take over for the time being. For the next day or so, I'm going to stay here with you."

"Kris, I know you are concerned, but I feel all right. I think it was just the shock of the event. Nothing more. You can't take off these last few days before Christmas."

"I don't have to leave the house to check Amak's production lists, and I don't want to go to the workshop to give a speech to boost their morale. The less I am involved this year, the better I'll feel."

"I am all right. Believe me, I really am. You don't have to babysit me."

"What did you want to talk to me about, Nels?"

"It's my uncle. There's no way he can continue his duties the way he's reacting to all of this. Amak, I think you need to take over. I think you should assume the leadership role at the workshop. After all, you're the mayor of the village. You already have a leadership role and are obviously respected by the workers."

"Well enough, Nels, but do you remember the name of this village? It's "Santa's Village," and being mayor of this village means nothing. It is like being the King or Queen of England. All I have is a title while Santa has the power."

"But I don't think my uncle can be expected to continue in his role this year. I think someone has to temporarily take over while he gets his act back together."

"It should be you, Nels. I know Matthew is next in command, but by the time he could return, the village and the schedule would be a total mess. No, it has to be you. The elves expect a Santa to boss them around or at least a proxy of similar physical stature. I don't think they would react favorably to having one of their own assume a true leadership role. You must take charge. But that doesn't mean we shouldn't work and rule together.

"Nels, this goes back to our previous discussions. We need to persuade Santa to retire early. You, yourself, have brought it up. These last few seasons have been a terrible mess. We've been lucky to get as many toys produced and delivered as we have. Once this season is over, we need to approach others in the village about a replacement for Santa."

"That may be, Amak, but remember, my brother Matthew is in line to be the next Santa, and he certainly wouldn't institute any change."

"There's no written law that says who should become the next Santa. If we elves decide to follow you, then Matthew would have no choice but to bow to this pressure."

"Well, let's worry about that later. Right now, I'll agree with you to take over, but I will not wear that ridiculous red suit."

Nels turned when he thought he heard Santa's front door open but soon realized it was just the wind mimicking the sound. And true to his reputation of clumsiness, when he turning back, he almost slipped and fell.

They spoke a while longer as to exactly what needed to be accomplished, the best way to do it, and then Amak left to meet Erog.

chapter 16

"Amak, wait a second." The shout from one of the elves was barely audible over the wind gust.

"What's up, Sponson?"

"Erog asked me to tell you that he's going to be tied up for about an hour and that he'd still meet you at Santa's freezer."

"Where's he now?"

"Hey, I don't babysit the man. I've no idea where he's at. He just said if I see you to give you the message."

"Thanks," and because he hadn't been there today, Amak asked, "By the way, how's everything at the workshop?"

"I'm hearing and seeing a lot of worried elves. I think it's the confusion of these last few days that's upsetting everyone. No one can figure out what's going on. I mean who would want to kill Rudolph and scare Mrs. Claus?"

"I'd like to know the answer myself," Amak replied. "What about you? What do you think is going on?"

"Who knows? All I know is that the more elves that don't show up for work, the more I'm expected to do. Isn't there any way we can recruit some workers from the other villages for these last few days?"

"Maybe there is a way. I'm going to Haulvit to bring Sven and Hans home and I'll try to convince some of those villagers to return with me."

"I've heard a little about the attack."

"A pack of dwarfs attacked and almost killed them."

"When did this happen?"

"Three days ago. Anyway, someone has to bring the pair back, and I figure I'll go. I certainly don't want to take anyone else out of the workshop."

"Do you know why the attack took place?"

"We're talking about dwarfs here. We're talking about creatures that would rather kill than eat. They don't need a reason to attack one of us. They just do it."

"There's sure a lot of crap going on: Norved, Knute, Rudolph, Sven, and Hans. Do you think it's all related?"

"Don't start any great conspiracy theory, Sponson. We have enough worried elves as is."

"But so much happening in so short a time, I think . . ."

"I don't need you to guess. The facts will come out soon enough. In the meantime, let's not spook anyone with your ideas about conspiracies."

They talked a short time more, each unsuccessfully trying to derive answers to questions that they realized might not require explanations. Sponson told Amak he had to leave but not before he made Amak promise to keep him informed. Finished, he continued his journey to the other side of the village, to his cottage tucked in between the schoolhouse and one of the many supply sheds.

Ice crystals grew in the frigid air and the rising wind helped create a fresh, white coating on a land of infinite whiteness. The crystals bombarded Amak's exposed face. He prided himself that he had not adopted the outlander's ways, but slowly even he had allowed their foreign civilization to corrupt him. Sterile electricity in his home now replaced the pungent smell of burning whale oil. Indoor plumbing replaced the treacherous and sometimes embarrassing excursions outside—too many village children had caught him relieving himself in the open. He'd built the cottage to house only him, and for this reason, he'd kept the size small even by village standards. He assumed, should he ever marry Loti, they would have to move into her larger home. To stay here was to subject both to likely claustrophobia. His Spartan dwelling served him well, but Loti refused to ever spend the night there saying its starkness and loneliness depressed her too much. She often blamed Amak's attitude and moods on the type of home he lived in. Of course, all these potential problems and decisions might be academic now that they were arguing with greater frequency and intensity.

Amak delayed his entry into the cottage and went to the side of the building where he located scattered pieces of scrap wood and other articles he had previously discarded as junk. He picked up and studied four different sized sticks before selecting one that met his needs. And spent an additional few minutes to find three smaller sticks also required for his project. He walked around to the front door and carefully brushed the snow off both himself and the wood he carried.

The light bulb appeared brighter glowing against the winter darkness. The small, rectangular room lacked any of the color of Loti's dwelling. Here, animal skins hung on the walls supplanted the photographs and pictures on Loti's. A white polar bear pelt partially covered a thin, obviously lumpy mattress on a wooden bed frame. The monotony of color did not bother Amak. He had never lived outside the northern reaches of the Arctic and this unvarying white was quite normal to him.

Amak placed the sticks on the square wooden table that sat alone in the middle of the room, then removed and threw his coat over the chair by his bed. He stood next to the table in a trance-like state straining to recall the location of the needed tools. Remembering, he walked to the shelves next to the bathroom. A musty odor lofted from dust blanketing the lower shelf and mixed with the heavy smell from a pile of unwashed clothes. He pushed the soiled shirts and underwear aside and retrieved a box filled with various tools discarded by workshop employees. A small piece of cord, a piece of walrus tusk, and two feathers from a snowy owl completed his requirements. He'd found the feathers, undigested, in the stomach of a recently killed polar bear.

Amak grabbed his coat from the chair and threw it onto to bed before sliding the chair to the table. He sat and began to fabricate his weapon. The atlatl is an adjunct to the customary spear or harpoon used by most Arctic natives, that is before many hunters changed to the rifle with telescopic sights and high-powered bullets. By artificially extending the user's arm, the atlatl allowed the hunter to achieve greater throwing force and distance. The construction was easy enough. He had made these weapons before, but he had to admit he was never proficient in its use. He tied three leather loops, used as finger grips, to one end of the two-foot stick, carved the other end to fit into a hollowed out section in the butt of the spear, tipped the five-foot spear with a sharpened walrus tusk, and completed the project by attaching two feathers needed to stabilize the spear's flight.

He'd decided to carry this weapon instead of a rifle when retrieving the two wounded elves. Dwarfs respected traditional weapons and might actually back down more readily against the atlatl than against a rifle. All was completed in about forty-five minutes, and Amak still wanted to go outside to test his construction prowess before meeting Erog.

Amak had not used an atlatl for many months—maybe, he thought, even a year—and was not surprised when the spear did not travel as far as he thought he could throw it. The toss, if not performed frequently, was a skill soon lost. He carried out three differently weighed spears, but when launched, all traveled about the same distance.

"You're flipping your arm too hard."

Amak turned. "Erog, I thought I was supposed to meet you at Santa's freezer."

"Actually, I was on my way there when I saw a spear wobble across the sky and figured it could only be an idiot like you practicing with such a primitive weapon instead of a rifle." He walked over, picked up the spears that had landed close by and carried them to where Amak stood. "Either the spears are too heavy or you are flipping your arm too much. The butt of the spear is dipping down. That's why you are not getting any distance from the throw."

"I haven't used an atlatl in a long time. Maybe I should have joined your recent lessons."

"Watching you throw, I'd have to agree."

"How do you know so much about the atlatl? Even most old-timers don't use it. They'd rather use a rifle."

"Do I have to remind you again that you're older than me? Anyway, my grandfather taught me the skill, and when bored, I like to practice using it. But for an invalid like me, a rifle is better and safer."

Amak took the spears from his friend and tried additional tosses using a more overhand arm motion. He aimed the end of the even, sweeping arc directly at a small snow mound far across the field. Two of the three spears pierced the target and the third landed no more than a foot away.

"Two out of three isn't bad, but when you have a large, pissed-off polar bear charging at you full speed, I think having a rifle with you might be a little smarter."

"I'm not concerned about polar bears," Amak answered. "I'm bringing these along in case I meet up with the dwarfs who attacked Hans and Sven."

Erog stared at him for a few seconds. "You really hate dwarfs, don't you? Most of us could live without them, but you hate them. Why?"

"Because they exist."

"A really intelligent answer, Amak." Erog rolled his eyes. "Is it because of tradition—a tradition that an elf is supposed to hate a dwarf? Or is it because you're jealous that dwarfs have not changed their ways the way elves have? Sometimes I think that you have more in common with the dwarfs than with your own kind."

"I hate them because they beat and kill for no reason! I hate them because they're illiterate! I hate them because they have six toes!"

"Six toes. You hate them and you want to kill them because they have six toes. Amak, sometimes you're a real asshole. I think there are times that you say things just to convince yourself there's a legitimate reason for one of your dumbass thoughts or actions. I agree that most elves hate dwarfs and most dwarfs despise elves, but they do have common ground. Think about it for a minute—dwarfs and elves have a universal enemy, but it's not each other. It's the outlanders and that includes Santa Claus."

"Santa and his kind are just a temporary problem, Erog. Dwarfs have been our problem forever. There's no reasoning with them. We could never unite to kick the outlanders back to where they came from. We elves can do that job alone. In the meantime, if a hairy dwarf gets in my way, I'll drive my atlatl up his ass."

Erog lowered his voice, spoke slowly and distinctly, but Amak still had to lean closer to understand. "Be careful, my friend. You are isolating and alienating yourself from too many people. Like our animal friends, we must adapt to survive. I, too, believe in tradition, but I'm beginning to think that compromise occasionally is necessary."

"It may be easier, but it certainly isn't necessary. Come on, let's check out Santa's freezer."

Even in the dim, yellowish light of the outer lamp, Amak was able to see a glut of tracks in and out of Santa's shed. Trying to discern anything abnormal out here would be a waste of time. He felt the same was probably true inside.

The shed was not just a storage area for foodstuff. It was originally used by Santa's family to shelter the only generator in the village. Eventually, additional sheds were used to contain the bigger generators needed to produce the electric current now used by Santa, the elves in the workshop, and by other villagers who desired the comforts that electricity brought to their homes. Santa had long ago moved the working generator outside the shed and used the building as a general storage area. One side of the structure had shelves stocked with food supplies wrapped and still stacked neatly in small columns. The opposite wall also had shelves, but those held tools, broken electrical equipment, and worn blankets and pelts undoubtedly used by Santa for assorted coverings. Pegs on the back wall supported a mismatched assortment of snowshoes, three leather sleigh harnesses, shovels, and two deflated rubber inner tubes. When younger, Santa's nephews, and now their children, had used the tubes to slide and tumble down the snow mounds surrounding the village. A small electric generator secured in Japan by Santa last year remained uncrated in the far corner of the shed. The wooden stepping stool used by Mrs. Claus to reach to the top shelves lay overturned beneath the food shelves.

Amak noted the large accumulation of worthless, broken,

miscellaneous items that one would expect to find leaning against the walls of a shed, and he decided this clutter offered the best place to begin any search for potential clues. He chose to examine the area near the overturned stool, while Erog, not wishing to be jammed against his investigative partner in such tight quarters, began his inspection below the tools on the other side of the shed.

It was obvious that other elves had previously searched the area. Rebecca Claus would never tolerate the disheveled appearance of even these discarded and broken items. Amak haphazardly pushed objects aside. He picked some up to examine them more closely, but more often than not, he studied them out of curiosity, trying to understand why Santa would want to save these seemingly worthless artifacts. He wasn't looking for any particular item; instead, he tried to clear his mind against such a probe. When tracking, Amak learned the best method was to let his eyes and mind flutter over the landscape. Inevitably, something foreign to the scene would leap to the forefront.

Amak rummaged through a tangled clump of discarded sticks and poles. He tossed each layer aside, unconcerned with the neatness of the new pile. "Whoa! Look at this."

Erog turned.

"Look what I found." Amak stood and displayed a rifle partially hidden by a worn blanket.

"What the hell is that doing here?" Erog asked. "As far as I know neither Santa nor his nephews hunt."

Amak unwrapped and studied the rifle. "No, I doubt this is for hunting. There's no scope."

"Maybe it's just a relic from a past Santa."

"I don't think so. It looks new."

Erog approached and caressed the rifle barrel. "Do you think someone was trying to hide it or do you think someone threw it in the corner because they had no use for it?"

"Who knows? I guess I could ask Santa, but you know what, Erog? In the big scheme of things, I don't see where it would make a difference with our current problem."

"I guess you're right, but I'm still curious if Santa even knows there's a rifle in his shed."

The two continued their search for a few more minutes before giving up.

"I wish I could figure out why someone killed Rudolph in the first place. Then maybe we would have an idea of what's going on and who might have done it."

"I can't figure it out either. It just doesn't make sense," Erog added. He reached for his walking stick, pushed down and stood. "Look, why don't I go back to where they found Brulog's body. Maybe all this talk about some connection between these recent events is true. Let me search the area again and perhaps I will find some new clue."

"I'd appreciate that, although I really do think we checked the area over well enough. I hate to see you make an unnecessary trip."

"There's not much else for me to do. I'm just trying to be helpful."

Amak's guilt was instantaneous. "Sure, Erog, go ahead. Knowing me, I probably did miss something important." And in an attempt to bolster his friend's ego, he added, "If you don't mind, I'm going to tell Santa you are handling the investigation while I'm away from the village."

"No problem. I just hope I'll have some worthwhile new information to give you on your return. And don't worry; I won't tell Santa or anybody anything until I talk to you first. You'll get all the credit," Erog said with a broad smile.

"Yes, and all the blame when you don't find anything."

They switched off the light and left the shed making sure to secure the wooden throw latch on the door. They didn't want the wind to blow the door open and expose the shed's contents to the weather, the curious elf, or a scavenger.

"Before I leave, I better go home and let Unata know where I'm going. When are you going to leave?"

"I wanted to start today, but it's getting a little too late to begin the long trip. I still have to pack the sled and talk to Nels again. He's agreed to take over until either Santa feels he can continue with his duties or until Matthew returns."

"I heard Santa is taking the season off," Erog replied. "Still, I'm surprised. Although, with all that's going on, I guess I shouldn't be."

"I don't know if Santa actually called it quits, but for now, he wants to spend his time with his wife. You can't fault him for that."

"No, I guess not," said Erog. "Still, Nels should have things screwed up in no time flat."

"I agree. That's why I'd hoped to leave today, so I could get back before too much damage has been done."

chapter 17

Amak was on his way to meet Santa when intercepted by Danat.

"Hey, Amak!"

"What now, Danat?"

"I'll tell you what's now! Now is when I plan to pound your face in. This fight figures to be a little fairer since no one is holding me down."

Amak moved to walk around this annoying obstacle. "I've got no time for this crap."

"Make time, you chickenshit." Danat's voice was somewhat garbled because of his recently fractured teeth and still swollen lips. "You're history, Amak. I'll be in charge again by the end of the week. They're already talking about replacing you. Unsolved killings, elves deserting daily, Santa in a daze, and the final joke is that you said I was worthless. I think that statement needs rethinking. Why don't you and your slut leave the village and take up residence on some far away ice floe?"

Amak stepped forward to confront Danat and was met with a further verbal attack.

"Oh excuse me. I forgot. Rumor has it that Loti may be having thoughts about dumping you. She may be easy but I guess she's not as stupid as I thought. No one wants to be stuck with a loser."

"Give it up, Danat. I told you I have no time for this."

"Sure, Amak, slink over to your master. Make sure you tell the fat man everything is going great and that you have everything under control."

Ironically, that was what Amak had planned on doing, but now two courses of actions confronted him. He could stay and allow the argument to progress to an inevitable new fight or leave before he no longer had a choice. He decided on the latter and walked away allowing Danat to continue to berate him with louder and more descriptive obscenities. Actually, Amak thought, some were pretty good, and he hoped to remember them for some future verbal sparring with someone other than Danat.

Erog did not go directly home as he had told Amak. Instead, he headed towards the dog compound. No one individual owned the dogs. They were the property of the village. While everyone had the right to use the dogs as needed, it was an unwritten rule that the user should first check with either Amak or Peter to make sure no one needed the animals for a more important purpose.

Erog approached the reindeer corral and noted two elves hard at work on Santa's sleigh. They had moved it out of the confines of the storage shed, and as per Santa's instructions, were in the process of wiring two outrigger halogen lamps on either side of the massive form.

One of the workers looked up at the passing figure. "Hey, Erog, got a second? Come over here. We need a third set of hands."

Although in a hurry, Erog stopped to help.

"What's up?"

"I have to crawl under the sleigh to check the wiring to the other lamp while Monde makes the connections on this side, and we need someone to hold the lamp before we bolt it to the sleigh."

The task seemed easy enough and Erog estimated that it would not delay his own needs. So, without protesting, he grabbed the lamp from the cardboard box. Even though blessed with their night vision, the intricate wiring required a source of artificial light, and, with his free hand, Erog directed a flashlight beam back and forth between the two work areas. Once wired and bolted in place, Monde switched the lamps on and adjusted the beams to focus approximately forty feet in front of the sleigh. The idea being that this forward glow would curb any anxiety of the Rudolphless reindeer team.

Erog asked what other changes Santa had requested, and the workers told him they were also going to install a small radar device. Santa had expressed a desire for one a few years ago after narrowly missing a cloud-covered mountaintop over Colorado but had held back in deference to traditional ways and Rebecca's opinion that such a device would belittle her ward, Rudolph. She'd said that Rudolph would sense its presence and it might adversely affect his psyche. Now with Rudolph no longer in the lead, Santa saw an opportunity to install some needed changes without much protest. The new equipment meant extra weight and, therefore, less toy capacity, but the elves had assured Santa that they would keep the needed material as light as possible and that a row of ultra-light lithium batteries would be sufficient to power both the lights and the radar. At the most, maybe twenty or thirty toys would be displaced from delivery.

Erog laughed at the idea of radar and lights on Santa's sled. "What, no GPS?"

"I guess there are limits," one of the elves answered.

Santa, Peter, and many of the elves were involved in arranging for the great Christmas Eve trek. Donner and Blitzen would become the co-leaders. Usually harnessed right behind Rudolph, they were accustomed to being near the front of the line of reindeer. Actually, they were the first to initiate the sled's movement. Rudolph's takeoff was just a signal for the others to begin their pull.

It would be at least a year or two until Rudolph's son would grow enough to take his father's place. His nose had not even begun to glow. Breeding the flying reindeer was important and Peter maintained a strict schedule of propagation, but no one could have foreseen the recent tragedy. Allowances were thus going to have to be made this year and perhaps even next.

Erog walked around the sleigh inspecting the improvements, asked a few questions, and then left to prepare a sled for his own trip.

Amak's only friend was uncertain as to which of the five dogs he had chosen to pull his small sled might be the best leader. Erog decided to place the largest and loudest one in front and harnessing the others in a single line connecting back to the sled.

Danat was still wandering aimlessly around the village when he spied Erog at work in the dog compound. He watched as the cripple laboriously gathered some blankets and a whip and tossed them on the back of the sled. He knew Erog rarely left the village by himself, and Danat wondered if Amak was sending him on some secret mission. Asking would be useless, so there was no choice but to secretly follow. He also realized there would be an initial problem how to equip his own sled before losing Erog's trail. He had no choice but to wait until Erog left and then attempt to follow the tracks in the fresh blanket of snow.

He remained hidden behind one of the adjacent buildings while Erog completed his tasks and began his trip with a loud command to the dogs. Danat watched as the sled turned into the village instead of taking the path leading out and was pleasantly surprised when he saw Erog disembark in front of his nearby cottage. Danat would have the time to ready his own sled.

"Unata, are you home." No one answered from the darkened cottage. Danat entered and the smell from last night's unwashed dinner dishes still piled in the kitchen sink unceremoniously greeted him. He moved a large metal skillet teetering on a stack of filthy washrags next to the stove and walked into the bedroom. His calls for his wife remained unanswered. Dirty clothes heaped behind the door prevented him from opening it fully. The bed was unmade and its blanket draped onto the dusty floor. The footprints in the dust reminded him of tracks made in the snow.

Erog returned to the kitchen where he lathered fish spread onto stale bread. He supplemented the small meal with a piece of equally stale chocolate cake he found beneath a dishtowel. Unable to find anything to drink in the refrigerator, he filled a glass with water from the tap. Lunch was finished in less than ten minutes, and not wanting to waste any additional time, Erog just added his glass and plate to those already waiting for someone who would eventually clean them.

Amak watched as the five dogs strung in a straight line struggled to pull Erog's small sled from the village. The dogs were a poor team. All wanted to be leaders. Erog had chosen unwisely.

Danat was able to stay undiscovered during the trip by keeping far enough behind to remain out of sight. The fresh trail made by the dogs and sled was easy to follow. The direction of the trip puzzled him, however. Erog did not appear destined for any nearby village. Nothing but plains and hills of snow lay ahead.

Almost an hour passed before both travelers entered an area of abnormally high hummocks. Danat feared losing the trail of his quarry on the icy ground and decided to stop following so he could climb atop one of the elevations in order to see what direction Erog was traveling. The climb was easy and he was soon gratified to note that he had made the proper decision. Erog had stopped in an open area just on the other side of the hummock Danat had scaled. The dogs were already lying down, curled up in five tight balls of fur faced away from the wind, and Erog was leaning against the sled staring into the clearing sky.

The engine noise preceded the helicopter's appearance by at least two minutes. Danat had never seen one in person but had seen and worked on enough toy models to know that this was not a military machine. The white and yellow markings on the side of the pale blue fuselage indicated it was owned by COLLINS TOY MANUFACTURING. A large caricature of an outlander boy and girl tossing a multicolored ball completed the artwork.

Erog's sled dogs tugged against the sled's snow hook, but they could not escape the noise from the descending airship. The roar from the engines stopped well before the blades ceased rotating. The artificial wind created its own snow squall making it impossible for Danat to see what was taking place below. The area surrounding the landed craft remained bathed in the helicopter's lights, and until the snow finally settled, the scene was that of a summer whiteout. He was grateful that the helicopter had approached from the opposite direction and the passengers had probably not seen him or his dog sled. His luck was holding out. Minutes passed before the door to the helicopter opened and someone lowered a metal ladder. All but one light, that shining onto Erog's position, had been turned off. Erog did not move from his space and appeared nonchalant about the current events. This was certainly not the case with Danat whose heart raced with excitement and—though he would not have admitted it if he were asked—fear. An outlander backed from the door and carefully descended the ladder. Erog didn't say anything to the tall stranger until his descent was completed and he had turned to face his visitor.

"Erog, so nice to see you again."

"Collins, nice to see you too."

The conversation had begun slowly. Like most outlanders, Collins had difficulty deciphering elves' and dwarfs' accents, and he was often forced to ask Erog to repeat himself.

Danat crept forward hoping to better hear the conversation. The man he heard Erog call Collins was tall even for an outlander, well over six feet. A blond, well-groomed beard protected the lower part of his tanned face. And though his head was unprotected, his thick wavy hair did not move in the stiffening breeze. Danat wondered if this outlander was so vain as to use that much hair spray or mousse. But it was the outlander's eyes that kept Danat's attention. The blue irises remained intently focused on Erog, never wavering while the two individuals spoke. Even when the ice rumbled, he never looked to his side. *Is he so stupid as to not be concerned about possible danger or maybe it's only because he has trouble seeing in the winter darkness?* Collins' straight-backed posture reminded Danat of pictures he had seen of a military man speaking to his troops. The outlander kept speaking as he reached back to pull the parka's hood forward. The Arctic cold wears down even the bravest or most macho. Danat found it interesting that Collins had walked to Erog and not the reverse. Erog definitely was not the one in charge of this meeting, yet he certainly was not intimidated.

"Have you been waiting long?"

"No. I arrived only a few minutes ago. As always, you're right on time."

"Let's venture inside the helicopter. I'm freezing my ass off out here. If you're hungry, I've brought some food."

"No, I'm not hungry, and I've told you before that I feel more comfortable out here. Mechanical objects that large scare me."

"I doubt that anything scares you, Erog." Collins shuffled his feet either in disgust or because he was cold. He embraced himself as he continued, "Anything new?"

"What could be new? This entire project of yours could have been over and finished weeks ago if you had let me do it my way."

"Maybe so, but I really think my way is better. Uncertainty and confusion works best in small doses."

"Your way might be better if you have time to waste, but I'm the one stuck in Santa's Village. You're not."

"Haste makes waste."

Erog rolled his eyes in disbelief. *Why did I ever agree to work with this imbecile?* He was certain that the desired results could have been accomplished faster and better with his plan.

"Let me explain the situation again, Erog."

"I already know the situation. You don't have to explain anything."

Collins disregarded Erog's remark and continued. "I want to control the toy industry. Buying out other manufacturers is easy. I have the money to do that. But to create my desired monopoly, I must stop Santa from supplying free toys every Christmas.

"I've offered him a chance to escape from this hell hole and I've offered him wealth. He's accepted neither. I had to beg just to meet with him this year, and other times I had to talk through mediators. To proceed too fast would alert others that an outsider was involved. The eventual disruption of Santa's system must come from within."

Maybe, Erog thought, Collins' rehash was nothing more than an attempt to control the conversation. He certainly didn't offer anything new.

"I'll take over. The outcome is already determined. I have no doubt about that, but I'll have to progress slowly. Ironically, it will be the children of the world who'll be the ones to solidify my position. First, I'll change the workshop's output to include only traditional toys—you know, dolls and baseball mitts. Today's children won't accept this for long. Electronic toys are what they want, and they won't find them under the tree unless their parents were smart enough to shop early at stores—my stores and my toys. Soon I won't need a Santa to deliver them on Christmas Eve. In time, the children will say that Santa was just another myth, another child-rearing technique propagated by their parents so they would have to be good all the time."

Erog looked at the outlander with distain. "I've heard the speech before, Collins, and I still think it could have been accomplished just as well and even faster if I got rid of Santa. I'm a dwarf, so you know I'm not against killing elves. I've already done that twice. So why not kill Santa?"

"Again, I don't think you ever grasped the entire plan. Santa's nephew, Matthew, would just take over and nothing would be gained. A murder of that magnitude produces fear, and fear, Erog, tends to bring people together, whereas anxiety of the unknown isolates them. Of all the animals on Earth, man, and in this case that includes elves, is the most prone to anxiety because of his brain's capacity to anticipate events. The elves won't know who they can trust or even who they can associate with. I need to make conditions so miserable for Santa that he wants out and sells me the operation." Collins began shuffling his feet again.

Erog thought a moment about what he knew, which he had assumed was a lot, and thought about what he might not know, which he now realized might be a lot.

"How did Santa react to Rudolph being killed? I assume you completed that task without problem."

"Yes, Santa won't have a shiny red-nose leading the sleigh this year. What surprised me, however, was that Santa gave a shit less about Rudolph, but seemed more concerned that his wife was so upset when she discovered the dead freak reindeer. I have to say that was a good idea you had to place it where she would be the first to find it."

Collins was shivering now, chilled to the bone. It was not so much from the frigid blasts of air that bludgeoned his exposed face as it was from the thought that he might have to spend an extended amount of time outside in conversation. "Erog, I have to get inside. I'm freezing my butt off. Come on in and let me show you around."

"I'm dressed for the outside, not the inside."

"Don't be an ass. Come in with me."

Erog had met with Collins six times now, and each time the toy manufacturer had wanted him to see the inside of the giant airship. At first, he did not trust that Collins hadn't set some type of trap for him. Later, he just felt it better to have Collins meet on his playing field.

The ladder's steps were spaced for an outlander, not a dwarf, and Erog had some trouble negotiating the climb. His legs strained to reach the next step. He slipped on the ice that had formed on the next to last rung, and only because his arm caught between the metal bars, he did not fall to the ground. "Screw this," he said softly to himself.

Danat watched the two conspirators enter the massive airship. He guessed it had to be close to one-hundred feet long. It had twin sets of horizontally fixed rotors, one over the cockpit area and one over the tail. He could see only one side of the craft, but he assumed that the opposite side also had what appeared to be a jet engine mounted beneath the rear rotor. It certainly would beat travel with a dog sled or on foot.

Once inside, the opulence of the helicopter's interior immediately awed Erog. He expected a large, empty cargo area, but he was met by a thick shag carpet, oak furniture including a medium sized conference table, and multiple video screens on the walls—some displaying views from outside the craft and others displaying news channels and financial data, none of which made sense to Erog.

"Do me a favor and pull the door shut. There's no point in heating the outside." Erog turned and filled the request. "How do you like it in here?"

"Adequate," Erog replied. "More than I need or want. Not much here that would ensure survival in a winter storm. To each their own, I guess."

"This helicopter cost me a pretty penny. It's loaded with some top-secret military equipment. My government gave or sold it to Israel. Knowing my leaders, they gave it away. Anyway, the Israelis promptly sold it to South Africa in exchange for some uranium, and I secretly purchased it for an obscene amount of cash."

Erog did not move far from the doorway. Instead, he allowed Collins to move from object to object to continue his guided tour but after a few minutes, he interrupted the outlander. "Where's the crew?"

"The pilot and the copilot are up front." He pointed towards a closed door at one end of the large cabin. "There're usually two stewardesses and an assistant or two who accompany me on trips, but I figure the less people who have knowledge of this particular business deal, the better. Actually, I could fly this by myself, but why take the chance."

Collins spent the next few seconds in thought, all the while jingling the coins in his pocket. He asked if Erog wanted to see the rest of the helicopter but his guest declined. Bedrooms, kitchens, bathrooms, and such held no interest. Erog remained standing while

Collins unbuttoned his down-filled parka and plopped into a deep cushioned chair. The seating, as all else, was designed for someone quite a bit taller than an dwarf, and Erog, afraid that he would look too foolish sitting in a chair that would not allow his feet to touch the ground, decided to stand when Collins offered the chair next to his. A small, soggy patch was forming beneath Erog's feet as the heat from an air duct directly behind him began to melt the ice and snow that had hitched a ride on his clothes.

"How's your wife, Erog? Still giving you trouble?"

"Yes."

"I've only met Unata twice before and to be honest, she seemed to have a good head on her shoulders. She seemed to understand the problem and how best to attack it." His tone changed to that of a doctor questioning his patient. "Does our current project have anything to do with your marital discord?"

Erog was reluctant to discuss his private life with this outlander and so gave the simple answer, "Sometimes."

"Sometimes? What do you mean by that?"

"I mean sometimes we fight about being stuck here and sometimes we argue about other things."

"What other things? Unata seems like the type of woman who would give in just to avoid prolonged arguments. She seems so passive."

"Passive my ass! I can show you scars and bruises inflicted by my passive wife. Just last week she wielded a skillet that just missed my head."

Collins laughed, picturing the scene just described. He stood and walked to the bar at the rear of the room, pushed aside one of the oak barstools and reached for a glass decanter filled with a pale yellow-brown fluid. "Are you sure you don't want something to drink? Maybe something to eat?"

"No."

He poured himself a drink and dropped in three ice cubes he had retrieved from a nearby clear acrylic bucket. "Look, Erog, whether or not Unata is passive is not the question. She's been thrust into a situation that I'm sure is quite unpleasant. Living a lie is tough enough, but living a lie in a hostile environment is doubly tough. You're the only one she can complain to. I'm sure that minor conflicts have had a way of escalating into skillet wielding episodes." He took a sip from his drink and pursed his lips as if he really wasn't enjoying the beverage. "All I'm saying is that it will all be over in a few weeks, if not days. The plan is working. First, we had you infiltrate Santa's Village. That was easy enough. All you had to do to look like an elf was hide your sixth toe, and I'm sure you haven't taken too many showers with any of the villagers lately."

Erog stood for a moment, lips compressed, before he replied. "It sounds easy enough but you try to walk in shoes designed to look like those that enclose five instead of six toes. It's no wonder that my feet hurt and that I'm at the point that, more often than not, the cane has become a necessity." The dwarf was quickly losing patience with his coconspirator. "As far as complaining..."

Collins again began his rehash of the grand scheme. "Second, we had you befriend the village mayor, Amak. You gained his confidence so you could guide his actions. Finally, you created havoc and anxiety and disrupted the normal flow of events. A missing elf here, a murdered elf there, and then coup d' grace—a shiny red nose perched on a package of venison.

"Now the process has become self-propagating. From what you've told me, elves are leaving the village every day. Amak is under attack. Even the number of Santa's critics is growing."

Erog's face twitched with exasperation. "Look, Collins, you may have supreme confidence in your plan, but I don't. There are only a few days left before Christmas and things are still going too slowly."

† †

To avoid detection, it had taken Danat five minutes to sneak down the steep slope of the ice hummock. He assumed the two conspirators would come back outside, and he wanted to be closer if they continued their conversation. Still, he felt he had enough information to return to the village and announce that he had solved the mysteries of the past weeks. He knew he didn't fully understand the why and the how, but he had enough circumstantial evidence to name the who, and that would be sufficient to elevate his status among the other elves. Yes, Amak's days were numbered.

Danat had no idea when the clandestine meeting would end, but now he realized that he had best return to his sled before Erog left, or it and he would be discovered. He looked behind him trying to decide the best route back up the hummock and recognized that the path traveled down would not be the best path back up. He'd have to begin his upward return by starting at a crevice about ten feet from his current hiding place. The helicopter door was closed, and he couldn't see anyone through the small round windows. It was as safe as it was going to get.

"What was that?"

"What did you see?" asked Collins. They were now staring up at the video monitor that displayed the exterior landscape across from the doorway.

"I thought I saw someone moving at the base of the hummock."

Both stepped closer to the screen. Even though the spotlight bathed the area, Collins could barely discern any image.

"It's Danat!"

"Who's Danat?"

"I've told you about him. He's the one Amak replaced," Erog

replied. "How the hell did he find us here?" Erog answered his own question. "He must have suspected something and followed me."

"We can't let him screw things up now." Collins moved to the window and squinted to better see.

"Get the hell away from the window! He might see us." Collins stepped back quickly. "Is there another exit?" Erog asked.

"Yes, I had an emergency hatch built into the floor behind the cockpit wall."

Erog was already moving forward. "Tell your pilot to start the engines and I'll drop down. The blowing snow will mask Danat's view while I run across the field. I'll try and make my way up behind him."

The enormous rotor blades started turning, creating whooshing sounds that startled Danat's dog team hidden behind the hummock. But Danat was sure their barking couldn't be heard inside the helicopter. He was surprised that Erog stayed in the helicopter. What was he planning to do with the dogs and the sled? The churning, loose snow quickly turned into a blinding squall. He would use this artificial storm to his advantage to conceal his retreat to the sled.

The familiar smell of their current master quieted the dogs. Danat stopped short of the sled to sort out what he had seen. Obviously, Erog was not what he appeared to be. The frail elf seemed to be walking and climbing without any problem. Danat had been able to hear only snippets of the conversation. What did the toy manufacturer, Collins, have to do with Erog? They appeared to know each other well. Certainly, it was not a first meeting. Whatever was going on, he, and not Amak, had discovered it.

The dogs were standing now, shaking off the snowy blankets that had insulated them during their wait. The largest one pranced, looking towards the top of the adjacent hummock. The hair on

177

the back of his neck stood on end and his loud barks turned into growls.

"Shut up, you bag of shit." Danat was having difficulty turning the sled in the narrow canyon that separated the tall mounds of ice and snow. The dogs showed no effort to cooperate by moving to the other side of the sled, and it did not take long for the dogs, Danat, and the sled to tangle into a confusing mess. All the dogs were barking now. The hummocks would suppress the sound from traveling to the helicopter site, but Danat wanted to leave as soon as possible, and he became even more frustrated as he again was unsuccessful in straightening the sled and dogs.

He stopped his pushing and pulling and bent down to retrieve a blanket that had fallen from the sled and, therefore, did not see the attacker as it leaped upon his back. He first felt the attacker's hot breath on his neck and then the sharp pain as teeth penetrated his exposed skin. In the instant before his death, he thought it strange that the only thing that concerned him was that he would never see his killer.

"Why did you bring the body back here?"

"I need you to get rid of it for me. I don't have any time to cut it up and feed it to the bears."

"I don't see why you can't just leave it right here. No one will ever find him."

"Maybe not, but the Arctic is just one big icebox and nothing rots here. It might be months, weeks, or days until someone accidentally discovers Danat, and I don't want to take the chance that the discovery will be tomorrow or the next day."

"What's the big deal? So what if someone finds another dead elf? It will just stir things up even more."

"The problem is they'll see he died the same way that Brulog did, and it won't take them long to figure out that they didn't die from some polar bear attack. Next comes an investigation and somebody just might be lucky enough to point their finger at me—all this, right before Christmas, before we play out the final part of the plan."

"Just what do you expect me to do with the corpse? I suppose you want me to land the helicopter at my factory and ask the maintenance crew to throw any garbage or bodies they might find into the dumpster?"

"Use some of your creativity, Collins. Halfway home dump the body out over some open spot in the water."

They discussed future meeting places and times and went over the timetable of the conspiracy before Collins went forward to keep the crew distracted while Erog tied a rope hitch under Danat's armpits and pulled him up the ladder into the helicopter. Collins returned and told Erog to prop the body up next to the door. He realized he would have to travel with the dead elf for two hours, but worse yet, later, he'd have to touch the corpse to push it out. The thought made his stomach produce one of those internal squirts he was encountering more and more lately and which he knew would eventually produce one hell of an ulcer. It could be worse, he realized; it could have been a warm human body instead of a hairy, pointed-eared, worthless mass. Touching it might not be pleasant, but at least he wouldn't feel any sorrow when it plunged into the icy water. Collins calculated that, when he opened the door in flight, he could use his feet to manipulate and kick Danat out.

"What are you going to do with the dog sled?"

"I'll break off one of the skids and leave the sled behind. If someone finds it, they'll assume it was abandoned when no longer serviceable, but the dogs aren't expendable. I'll hitch them to my sled and bring them back to Santa's Village.

"I know what I have to do, Collins. Don't you worry your outlander ass over it. Just make sure you don't get too fidgety flying home with a body and dump it too soon. And by the way, don't start your goddamn engines until I'm well clear. Last time, I almost got blown across to the other side of the Arctic."

Collins assured Erog that he was not fidgety or nervous and that he could certainly handle his part. After again checking Danat's position, Erog backed out the door and clumsily descended the ladder to the snow-packed surface below. Collins watched his coconspirator walk away from the helicopter. He contemplated the arrogance of the dwarf and felt better knowing there was part of the plan that Erog didn't know.

The snow blew into Erog's nostrils restricting his breathing. "That sonofabitch!" The helicopter momentarily hovered over the sled before taking off in the direction of the open sea.

The closer Erog's dogs got to Danat's team, the less interested in each other they became. Their howls ceased when the two groups recognized each other. He didn't have a long enough lead rope for a single or double train, so he had to harness the dogs in a fan-shaped pattern. The dogs thus secured, Erog focused his attention on destroying the sled in a way to make it look as if it were accidentally broken and left behind by some unlucky traveler. He jumped on the overturned sled and easily snapped a skid into three pieces. Erog removed the middle piece and threw it beyond an adjacent hummock.

Boarding his own sled, he set off for his return to the village and a chance to begin a new rumor of another elf's disappearance. Besides, he had been mulling over his own ideas on how to end this intrigue.

Collins paced the area in front of the dead elf. The would-be leading toy manufacturer/distributor had made Erog place a plastic tablecloth beneath the body before he had disembarked the helicopter. And it was good that Collins had insisted, because the blood continued to ooze from the gaping neck wound.

Why did I agree to take the body on board? What are the chances anyone would come across it in this god-forsaken place?

The helicopter suddenly lurched to one side, but just as quickly regained proper alignment to the ground below. The shift caused the corpse to collapse on its side. Collins leaped backwards convinced that the elf had come alive. "Damnit!" He reached for the intercom attached to the bulkhead wall and pushed the button connecting him to the pilot.

"Sam, I have a slight problem here. No, you don't have to come back. I can handle it myself. But I need you to lower the craft and hover over the first opening in the ice that you see."

He looked at Danat's body and wanted the current situation to immediately end.

"I need to dump something that our visitor brought on board. I think he's trying to con me into smuggling illegal drugs back into the country . . . I have no idea where he'd get them here in the Arctic, but I don't want to take any chances with the authorities when we land."

Static masked Collins next remark and the pilot asked him to repeat what he said. Collins cut the pilot off, this time not with a polite request, but with a demand of a boss to his subordinate employee. "Never mind what I said. Just do what I asked. Find an area of open water, lower the craft to a few feet, and I'll do the rest."

It was ten minutes before the intercom buzzed and the pilot said they were approaching a break in the ice and he soon would start lowering the helicopter.

Collins cautiously approached the body, paced again, and then stood staring at Danat while contemplating what to do next. He was annoyed, not only because of the dead elf, but more so because the situation didn't allow him to remain in charge. He wasn't used to others telling him what to do. Now, a dwarf had put him into a position where he had not decided the course of action, and Collins didn't like it.

"Mr. Collins, we're over the opening." The continued static made it mandatory for Collins to concentrate on the message before acting.

He chose two towels from the bar area to substitute for gloves. Wrapped around his hands they provided a sufficient barrier when Collins grabbed and up righted Danat. An alarm sounded when he opened the outer door and even though he had been apprised of the forthcoming activity, the pilot voiced his concern over the intercom. A gust of wind jerked the helicopter sideways and Collins watched as Danat tumbled out the door.

"Shit!" The corpse had fallen not into the open water, but onto the surrounding ice floe. "Shit!"

Collins had little time to decide what to do. A new wind gust, greater than the last, again slammed against the airship knocking him to the floor. He carefully crawled to the doorway and looked out. Danat was no longer lying on the ice, the wind had driven him into the water. The body bobbed on the surface and Collins could tell it was slowly sinking. It took two minutes before it disappeared, time enough to curse Erog many times over and to decide that something had to be done to repay the dwarf.

chapter 18

Santa slouched against the light pole outside the cottage. Amak had never seen Santa like this: head drooped, arms hanging heavily at his sides, eyes glazed over. Santa, the eternal optimist, had given up. Amak gently touched Santa's elbow, "I'll handle things at the workshop. You just stay with Mrs. Claus and make sure she's okay." He was sure Santa hadn't heard anything he'd said during the past few minutes.

Only Amak turned to look when the cottage door opened. Nels appeared and was forced to speak to the back of Santa's head. "Aunt Becky is awake again, Uncle. She seems to be feeling better and wants me to ask Loti to prepare some food for both of you." He paused, waiting for his uncle to acknowledge his presence, which did not come. "I'd say it's a good sign that she's both hungry and concerned with your shrinking waistline. I don't think she wants to have to sew any more stuffing into your red suit." The poor attempt at humor was wasted on both Amak and Santa.

"Thanks for staying with her, Nels. Please tell Loti about the food, but if I remember, and at this point, I don't know if I remember anything right, she already volunteered to cook for us." He finally turned, but still didn't look at his nephew; instead, he stared into the black sky before beginning his reentry into the cottage. His arm reached for the door latch, but it stopped, remaining suspended in midair while he again stared blankly. The silence broke when he suddenly kicked out, soundly striking the wooden door. His blow narrowly missed his nephew who had just stepped aside to allow Santa's entry.

"Shit!" Amak and Nels stared in disbelief. They never had heard Santa use any profanity. "Amak, take care of those other things." Without facing his companions, he delivered another short expletive before going inside.

"I've never seen him like this. I can't believe Santa even knew that kind of language. This incident with Aunt Becky has emotionally strained him." Amak nodded in agreement. "By the way, what were the other things that he wants you to take care of?"

"Nothing really. Your uncle wants to be sure that everything is running well at the workshop."

"That's it?"

"No. I also promised him that I would find an explanation for what's been going on."

"Any ideas yet?"

"No. All I can say is that someone is trying to disrupt the normal flow at the time of the year that we can least afford it."

"But who, Amak? No one has anything to gain. No one has any kind of grudge to settle with Uncle."

"Hey, if I had any idea, I'd be acting on it instead of squashing rumors and trying to keep the workers from spending all their time huddled in discussions."

He was about to mention that Erog was out helping him by again investigating the scene of Knute's death when he saw his friend returning with his sled and large train of dogs. He would have to make time to talk to Erog before leaving on his trip.

"I'm going to Haulvit tomorrow. I have to bring Sven and Hans back but plan to return late tomorrow or the following morning. Hopefully, then, I can get organized and start sorting things out."

Erog unleashed the dogs as rapidly as possible. The other villagers knew he was no fool and certainly would not have secured so many dogs for a short trip. No easy explanation could be made. If caught and questioned Erog had decided that he would feign a fear of becoming a traveler crippled by both insufficient dog power and by physical dysfunction. One by one, he unhitched the dogs, walked them into the compound, and leashed them to their posts. Each trip into the pen increased the intensity and volume of the barking and thus increased the danger of someone coming to investigate. He worked rapidly and soon had the last dog secured, thankfully, without anybody appearing.

Erog dragged the small sled to the storage shed and leaned it against the outside wall. He entered the building, hung the reigns in place on the wall, and replaced the blankets on a shelf. No one would miss Danat's sled. The village children routinely confiscated these smaller sleds for their own enjoyment. Sled races down the taller hummocks were an acceptable form of entertainment; they kept the children busy while their parents worked overtime at the workshop. Common, too, was the destruction of the sleds as they crashed against an icy finish line. It mattered little that no child would admit to taking the missing sled. They never did. The sleds were easy to make.

Erog limped towards his home. There were times when the limp was bogus, performed for his audience. Not now, however; his feet throbbed in pain. He waved to a few of the elves he saw and chatted with others.

"Where have you been?" Unata asked

"Business with Collins," Erog answered matter-of-factly.

The cottage was still slovenly. The dishes, pots and pans remained piled in the sink. Paper and clothes were haphazardly strewn over various pieces of furniture.

"For someone who claims he has no use for outlanders, you sure spend a lot of time with them. I sometimes think you arrange these meetings just to spend time away from me," she added bitterly.

His wife was small even by dwarf standards. There was never any true physical beauty, but since arriving at Santa's village, she made no effort at all to maintain her appearance. Her long, black hair was frequently dirty and matted, her clothes perpetually wrinkled, and the body weight she once prided herself on easily controlling had crept up to near behemoth proportions.

Many of their friends, their dwarf friends, had been surprised when she and Erog announced that they were going to marry. She, the intellectual radical, and he, the militant radical, rarely agreed on anything in public. In time, Erog had realized that her convoluted plans to restore the dwarfs to power in the North had more chance for success than his more direct militant methods. The elves might have softened over the decades of subservience to Santa, but there were still enough traditionalists like Amak who could rally a better equipped force to defeat the dwarfs. He had soon understood a Trojan horse approach was best.

Unata had been content with Erog's rise in the other dwarfs' esteem. She had remained the consummate plotter—Rasputin hidden behind the pedestal of the public figure but with a whispered voice that the leader leaned to hear. Jealousy had eventually entered into the relationship. Not because of another woman, but because of Erog's growing independence and of the growing reverence the other dwarfs had showed him. They were her ideas that he mouthed in public. She had always been the ventriloquist, but through repetition, the dummy seemed to have learned to talk on his own, and the audience, who was never aware of her input, had now regarded her as excess baggage. He'd created plans on his own. He had begun to think rather than act and soon was firmly entrenched as leader in the movement. Maybe it was because of this that Unata had decided to meet with Collins, who had been attempting to form a union with the dwarfs—one he pledged would benefit both. Unata had no delusions that Collins had any real plans to share any rewards of deposing Santa, but in the game of intrigue, it was each conspirator's responsibility to protect himself. First, get rid of Santa and then Collins. She had her own plans, and by bringing Collins into the picture, she hoped to dilute Erog's imperium.

Unata had readily agreed to accompany Erog in this mission to destroy Santa. It was an idea that all those involved thought would eventually diminish the economic and political status enjoyed by the elves. Originally designed as a one-year campaign, it was now into the second year, and Unata complained daily that there was a need for a different plan. This from the person who thought the mind was always mightier than the sword. Anything to return home sooner.

One expected isolation in the Arctic. Most senses were eternally deprived. Darkness during the sun's winter vacation to the South impeded easy vision. The frigid cold retarded decay and growth and their associated smells. The noise of the Arctic became redundant. There were degrees of wind, but after time the natives tended to lump all these air currents under a single term—wind. And although there were some twenty different terms for different types of snow, these were eventually coalesced into the single descriptive noun— snow. Though a tolerance to the cold was innate for dwarfs and elves, even they required extra coverings in the extreme low temperatures. The result was a loss of the intimacy with whatever one held. The weight and shape of the carried object remained recognizable, but the texture, the sense of touch was lost. The isolation was expected and, therefore, tolerated by all who chose to live in the Arctic.

What Unata didn't choose to tolerate was the isolation from her own kind.

"Stop the bullshit, Unata. You know I can't stand Collins any more than I can stand the elves, and unless I'm mistaken, it was your idea to bring him into this."

"And it was a good idea. You originally wanted to lead a war party into Santa's village and kill all the inhabitants. All that would have accomplished was the elevation of a new Santa and a new group of subservient elves working for him. Both more rigid in their ways."

"Well, if it was your great master plan, why bitch so much? Why do you make life so miserable for me?" Erog asked.

"For you!" Unata launched herself from her chair. "Miserable for you! What about me? You've dragged this crap out to three times the length of time it should have taken. Two years of wearing tight shoes to hide the width of a foot with an extra toe. Two years of hobbling about because within an hour of standing the pain was unbearable. Two years of village assholes taunting us because we have no children. No pregnancy, no birth because a newborn dwarf would be hard to explain to a midwife.

"You sonofabitch. Erog, you don't give a damn about me and I sometimes think you don't give a damn about the dwarfs. This intrigue has become a big game to you and you're enjoying it too much."

Erog stepped closer to her. Lately, he had taken to slapping her across the face after such outbursts, but he recognized it was wrong. Not wrong to hit his wife, but wrong because it was ineffective. The outbursts had become more frequent and more boisterous.

"Go ahead, hit me again, you bastard! Hit me and I'll scream so loud that every elf in the village will come running and see a barefoot six-toed dwarf running from her repulsive, six-toed husband."

Erog smiled. It amused him to contemplate the elves' reaction on learning that the old man and his wife were members of the dreaded enemy.

"What the hell is so funny?"

"Enough, Unata. It's almost over. In less than a week, Santa will be history. In less than a month, Amak will be history. We'll be home in less than two months, with our friends and family, and most importantly, in power."

Erog sat on the chair Unata had vacated and began the arduous contest of removing the boots from his swollen feet.

"How can you just sit there and not show me any compassion, Erog?"

Even after loosening the laces all the way to the last hole, the boot would not come off. Competing against this tug-of-war, his calf muscles began to cramp.

"I'm going home," she continued. "I can't take this any longer."

He kneaded the back of his legs until the spasms disappeared and then slowly increased the pull on the boot. Finally, with a slight twist of the boot, it came free.

"Don't you care if I leave?"

Erog put his boot down. "No, I don't. Do what you want to do, but don't screw up what we're about to accomplish."

"To be honest, I don't care anymore if the elves run around claiming they're better than us. As long as they don't bother us, and they haven't in decades. Who cares what they say?"

"Because, Unata, eventually they'll stop talking and begin listening to people like Amak. Then our enemies will think they are powerful enough to not only push us further into the forests, but powerful enough to destroy our race."

"You know I've finally figured out why you spend so much time with Amak. It's not because you want to learn his plans or to steer him onto a wrong path of action. No, it's because you and he are so much alike. You both like this frozen wasteland. You're both unable to change. Only traditional means of solving problems make any sense to both of you."

The second boot came off more easily. "There's nothing wrong with tradition. It's kept us alive for centuries."

"So would electricity and snowmobiles. So would moving away from the Arctic. Why not leave it to the elves? Let them suffer. Let them stagnate."

"Because we belong here. No matter where else we moved to we would be intruders. No people would accept us. If we were not battling the elves, it would be whose ever land we slinked into. Sure, they might allow us to live there, but we'd always be a minority. Always second class citizens."

"Which is worse? Second class citizens in the world community or masters of a land that no one else claims as home except other misfits of nature and a fat recluse born from criminals?"

"Different does not mean misfits. We are what we are because we've adapted to the Arctic cold. The same way other races have adapted to the heat of the tropics." Erog moved to the sink looking for a clean plate among those lying about. He knew there wouldn't be any in the cupboard.

Unata responded to his thoughts. "Why don't you clean one yourself instead of wondering why I don't wash the dishes and clean the cottage?" Her voice was steadily rising. "I'll tell you why I don't. It's because I'm trying to make it as uncomfortable for you to remain here as it is for me. I'm serious, Erog. I'm leaving!"

"No, you won't! You leave now and I'll have to waste time making the villagers think I cared. I don't have the time to spend in mock mourning. It's going to end within a few days and each future minute has already been accounted for. I won't change my plan just so you can leave a few weeks earlier."

Unata pushed past him on her way to the bedroom. "Tough shit! I'm packing my bag and leaving right now."

Erog reacted quickly. He reached for the large skillet in the sink, took two strides to catch Unata, and swung the flat of the pan against the back of her head.

He heard the skull fracture. It reminded him of the sometimes muffled sounds ice movements make. Blood mixed with the grease dislodged from the pan and the two combined to form a paste that slowly tamponed the bleeding scalp.

Unata fell against the bedroom door and rapidly slid onto the floor. A second cracking sound accompanied the fall as the bony tectonic plates of the skull thrust over each other. Her back arched off the floor at the same time her arms and legs went rigid. The hands closed into tight fists and turned awkwardly inward. Erog watched as Unata's back again collapsed to the floor and a heavy labored breathing produced a froth of air and saliva. Her body shook uncontrollably and then, just as suddenly, all movement stopped. The heavy breathing was replaced with a slow shallow breath that soon ceased. His wife of three years was dead.

Erog's pulse had remained steady throughout.

The problem of Unata's unexplained disappearance from the village, which he had just violently protested, was now a reality he had created. First, there would be a disposal problem. That he figured he could take care of in the usual way, but he still had to have a valid explanation as to Unata's whereabouts.

First things first.

He dragged his dead wife out the back door. This side of the house faced the open field north of the village and was a direction few traveled to or returned from. Besides, a mound of snow partially blocked the view of any uninvited villager.

Erog reentered the cottage and took a nervous minute to locate his axe among the mess in the bedroom closet. He supplemented this equipment with two cloth sacks and a sharp knife. Before exiting again, he turned off all the lights. Lights meant someone was home and this was no time for any visitors.

The cold ground did not bother Erog's bare feet. It actually was soothing to his still aching toes.

He laid Unata spread eagled on the snow and commenced the butchering process with his knife. He followed by detaching any thick ligament or bone joint with a single heavy blow from the axe. Through previous experience, he was getting quite good at this and, in less than an hour, he had his wife's legs, arms, and head separated from her torso and stuffed neatly into the two sacks.

Again, the harnessing of a sled and exiting the village was not a problem. This was the one time of year that traveling in and out of the village was commonplace. He even waved and briefly spoke to a neighbor.

Erog stopped the sled after a two-mile southward journey. The rest of the trip would be on foot. He had stopped here because he had recently heard of evidence of a polar bear roaming in the vicinity. Erog walked towards a nearby ridge of snow mounds and was soon rewarded when he discovered the opening to a bear's den. He was not about to enter to see who was at home but felt confident to hide behind another mound and toss snowballs at the opening. The first ball splattered next to the entrance, but the second one ricocheted off the side and into the hole.

The den's resident lumbered out to investigate and was greeted by a sack flung at his feet. The second sack struck the ground nearby. The bear growled and backed away from these assaults. When the objects didn't return any hostile action, the smell of fresh meat overcame any lingering fear the bear might have entertained. He ripped open the first sack and began his feast.

The Arctic's answer to civilization's electric garbage disposal, Erog thought as he watched.

The massive animal quickly ravaged the contents of the sack and was about to begin on the second course when a loud cracking sound in the ice floe startled both Erog and the bear, which dropped the leg he had just begun to devour. The bear rose on his hind feet to survey the area, and finding nothing to fear, used his canine teeth to pierce the sack and carry it away. Neither Erog nor the bear noted Unata's abandoned leg and a section of her left arm that had fallen out of the cloth container.

DECEMBER 23rd

chapter 19

The trip to Haulvit was trouble-free. Even though Amak had never been there before, Sprog's directions were easy to follow. The weather cooperated. It was cold, of course, but there was no wind or new snowfall. The terrain was, for the most part, flat and Amak easily circumnavigated those hummocks he encountered without losing much time. Still, the trip took almost six hours counting the two stops Amak needed to rest the dogs.

Haulvit was home to twenty-eight elves, sometimes a few more and sometimes a few less. Half the inhabitants worked directly for Santa. The others refused to conform to the "civilized ways" and survived by hunting walrus and selling the ivory tusks to outlanders. It was against the law to sell the tusks, but the elves felt that breaking an outlander law was like not breaking any law at all. Those employed by Santa lectured their comrades on conservation and the need to preserve all species. Actually, it mattered little since the hunters used atlatls, not rifles, and their kills did little to diminish the planet's walrus population. The ivory sold was only that for which the hunters had no use.

There was no social structure in such small villages and the leader tended to be the strongest and not necessarily the most respected.

197

One hundred and fifty years ago and hundreds of miles further south, this same village would have been the prototypical Wild West outpost.

The structured life of Santa's village was in marked contrast to Haulvit. One's initial impression of the village would likely be that the populace had deserted years ago. Abandoned cottages were scattered about. On closer inspection, it was evident that the current inhabitants of the village had scavenged the dilapidated buildings whenever they required materials for their own damaged homes. The elves had built their homes in a haphazard fashion. There were no straight-lined paths between the buildings. No attempt had ever been made to resemble a planned, physically organized village, and while there was no official main structure, one building did seem a bit larger and more important than the others. Two roof vents spewed clouds of smoke and a large woodpile was stacked neatly next to a side door.

Amak noted the snow leading to the building was well trampled. He was about to enter when someone from behind called out. "Who's that? Is that you, Krog?"

He turned to face his questioner who, when confronted with an unfamiliar face, stopped his approach.

"Who are you? What are you doing here?"

"It's me, Amak, mayor of Santa's village. I came to see how Sven and Hans are doing."

The Haulvit native still did not move. "I don't know you. Nobody told me anyone was coming. How did you hear about the attack?"

"Someone from your village radioed Santa, and he sent . . . and I volunteered to bring them home."

"Good luck with that." Stelgard introduced himself and stepped around Amak to open the door to the village workshop, meeting place and currently a makeshift infirmary. They entered a small vestibule and while removing their coats, Stelgard apprised Amak of Sven's and Han's injuries. Both had broken legs. Sven's arm had been severely smashed with a club. Both had sustained head injuries and Hans would probably lose an eye due to a puncture from a spear. A cursory examination of Hans had revealed part of his right calf muscle had been chewed off during the carnage. The subcontinent of India had its infamous *berserkers*—here they were called dwarfs.

"Sven and Hans really had the shit knocked out of them. It was lucky an outlander came across them and brought them in. No way could they have survived on their own. Dwarfs attacked them, a hunting party I would assume, and beat them for no other reason but they're elves. Beat to shit, they were."

Stelgard was two or three inches taller than Amak. Four of his front teeth were decayed to the gum line. His left hand had only three full fingers and half of another. The missing digits most likely lost to frostbite. The odor circling his body indicated a lack of bathing for at least a few weeks.

They left the vestibule and entered a cluttered room. "They're in here. We tried to make them comfortable but none of us are doctors, and a doctor is what is what they need. I've never seen that many broken bones, not even when one of the villagers made the mistake of taking shelter in a bear's den with the bear still inside." He stopped speaking to roll his eyes. "What a stupid asshole!"

Stelgard stopped walking and grabbed Amak's arm. "When are we going to stop taking all the crap Santa shovels on us, and when are we going to take charge of our own lives? What we really need is someone to lead us in a final battle against the dwarfs."

"Stelgard, the time will come when we will bust heads, but that time is not now."

"Sure. I just hope that when the time comes, it's not the day after I've been mugged by a band of dwarfs. I'd like to be able to walk into battle and not be carried in on a litter."

† †

Three elves were busy at work fabricating rag dolls and did not look up when the door opened. It was almost as cold inside as outside, but at least there was no accompanying wind. Dolls of all sizes and colors were arbitrarily piled in a corner next to the worktable. The opposite corner seemed a mess, too, but when the mess moaned, Amak realized the rags were covering Sven.

"Sven, damn, you look like shit!"

A blood-soaked cloth wrapped his right knee and another encircled his forehead. Blood-tinged saliva dripped from the corner of Sven's mouth as he tried to respond. The gross shift of his lower face indicated an obvious jaw fracture and that combined with the nasal tone that resulted from a broken nose filled with dried blood, made understanding him a monumental task. Amak leaned closer to try to read Sven's lips, but he still could not decipher more than an occasional word.

"Okay." Amak turned around and asked Stelgard where Hans was. It was Sven, however, who answered with a groan and pointed to a crumbled mass on a rope cot. Again, Amak's first impression was that the mass was just rags tossed aside by the elves working to meet Santa's Christmas deadline.

A quick inspection of Hans revealed the serious nature of his injuries: shallow, labored breathing; a pinpoint pupil and glazed eye; his left eye invisible beneath severely lacerated and swollen eyelids; legs and arms in splints. This was a wasted trip. Neither Hans nor Sven were in any condition to travel. The problem was they couldn't receive proper treatment if left in Haulvit.

Amak spent the next few minutes explaining to Sven that he'd have to return to Santa's Village, get Dr. Skeen, and return tomorrow. In the meantime, the villagers here would have to care for him and Hans. Sven nodded his agreement.

200

Stelgard and Amak left the building. The combination of increased wind and falling temperature made standing still uncomfortable even for these lifelong Arctic residents. Neither wished to be the one to complain and, consequently, an unspoken compromise was reached when in unison, they turned their backs to the wind.

"Stelgard, tell me again what they told you about the attack?"

"Hans told me nothing. He hasn't talked since he was brought here and I already told you what Sven had to say." He stopped talking to take a note pad out of his pocket. "I figured I might forget something important so I wrote down everything they said." He flipped through the pages to see if he had left anything out and paused when he found something he had indeed failed to mention, something quizzical and maybe something important. "Sven did mention that he overheard the dwarfs bragging after they finished beating him."

"What did they say?"

"They were standing over Sven and Hans, who by this time were both beaten to a pulp, and one of them told the others to stop. The dwarf said that they didn't want them dead. That he was sure this would get you down here. This would keep you busy."

"They really mentioned my name, not just saying someone would have to come from Santa's Village? Are you sure that's what Sven remembered?"

"Actually, they said they hoped you would come. Do you think they only mugged them to get you to leave Santa's Village? I'm confused. Why would they want to do that?"

"Damn, this is getting too complicated!"

"What do you mean by that? Has something else happened?"

"I guess you wouldn't have heard. There've been some of the normal desertions from the village; there's been a gruesome mauling by a bear; and yesterday somebody killed Rudolph. Chopped him up and packaged him so Mrs. Claus might serve him to Santa."

"Holy shit!"

"Even the circumstances surrounding the bear attack appear suspect. For some reason someone seems to be trying to bring about disorder in the village. I can't figure out what's going on. All I know is, each day something occurs that screws things up a little more. I guess you're right, that the beatings Sven and Hans took weren't just accidental." Erog continued. "I guess it's all tied together, but I don't understand how."

They walked back to the cottage intending to question Sven further, but he was asleep when they entered and they felt he needed his rest. Stelgard gave the notepad to Amak who stuffed it into his parka's outer pocket.

The storm began suddenly. Two miles from home, the steady wind with a minimum of fresh snow changed to a rampaging blizzard and forced Amak to slow his pace. He could no longer be sure of his location. His sense of direction, innate to all Arctic inhabitants, had enabled him to continue this far. The storm precluded navigating by the stars; he was a traveler without a map. Two of the dogs rebelled against the strong head wind by attempting to steer the sled in the opposite direction. Verbal threats had no effect, and Amak was forced to leave the sled to walk alongside the malcontents. Within minutes, it was impossible to see any further than four to six feet. He could barely make out the sled dragging behind the last pair of dogs. The whiteout created an impenetrable envelope. Depth of vision was reduced to feet, sometimes inches.

One hour later and less than a mile closer to his destination, the storm stopped and a relieved Amak decided to rest the dogs and himself behind the protection of a natural windbreak formed by a large row of hummocks. The dogs immediately fell to the ground, curled themselves tight, and slept. As usual, they kept their heads tucked under their front legs to impart the smallest target possible to any assailing icy wind. Amak opened his food pouch, removed a small piece of meat, and ate his first meal of the day. The dogs probably could have continued the trip, but Amak was utterly exhausted from walking most of the past hour and felt he deserved a short rest. He walked back to the sled, collapsed onto the flat surface, and retreated under two bearskin blankets.

The howling woke him. Completely covered by the blankets, he wasn't sure if the noise he heard was from the dogs or if it was from the wind, which had once again heightened. He pulled the covering from his head and another blanket presented itself, this one white. Thirty-mile-an-hour wind gusts had kicked up the thin layer of snow and visibility was again limited to just a few feet. Amak could barely see the dogs that were standing ready to continue their journey. He forced himself from the comforts of the sled, afraid that the gusts were the precursors of worsening conditions. He feared possible imprisonment in a jail fabricated by the weather.

Something other than the wind was bothering the dogs. Snarls and growls replaced the cacophony of howls as they tugged at the tethers holding them to the sled. Something lurking behind the hummocks was rousing the dogs. The wind had again subsided, and he stood silent, straining his senses to help with the identification. Perhaps it was a noise he had unconsciously heard or an odor he unconsciously smelled, but he, too, felt a presence of something hidden behind the hummocks. He walked to the back of the sled to check that the snow hook was secure before reaching down under the blankets for his atlatl. As he pulled the weapon from under its cover, the spears slipped back deeper into the pocket of blankets. The temporary loss of his defense against a possible foe caused a rush of adrenaline to surge through his body. His motions became erratic leading to additional panic, but when he finally relocated the spears, calmness and composure quickly returned.

He cuffed his hands behind his ears trying to block the noise from the dogs and sniffed the air trying to discern a foreign smell. But he was unsuccessful with both endeavors. The dogs at the rear of the team strained at the weight of the sled and jerked it forward a few feet. Now the full team tugged and the hook that anchored the sled and them to the spot lurched loose. The lead dogs suddenly stopped pulling, turned around, and crashed into the remaining pack.

The six hundred pound polar bear charged within ten yards of the dogs before rearing up on his hind legs. Amak reacted instinctively and launched his spear at the exposed underbelly of the beast. The spear fell short and to the right of its target, but the missile's impact was enough to startle the bear, which turned and began to run away. With the bravery of knowing they were no longer in danger, the dogs took off after the fleeing predator, taking the sled with them.

"Whoa! Whoa! You damn sonsofbitches! Stop! Whoa!" But the dogs kept up the pursuit. The snow fell faster and heavier and the wind blew stronger, making it difficult for the pursuers to see their quarry. The distance between the members of the chain of elf, dogs and bear increased with each stride. Amak could now only hear the dogs. Visible contact was impossible. He continued his dash towards the disappearing sounds. His shouts to the team to stop were ineffective. Soon he had to stop his chase. Expending energy in a nonproductive task can be deadly in the Arctic. His lungs felt like they were on fire. A steady, dry cough began, not from any newborn infection but from the super-chilled air that tortured his lungs as he breathed.

Unable to see clearly through the snowfall, he stumbled on in a direction that he hoped was towards the village. He strained his eyes, searching for some natural barrier against the wind and cold. With his arms outstretched in front of him, he looked like a child playing blind man's bluff, but this was no game. This was a search for survival.

† †

The storm again abated, and although he could again see clearly in all directions, there was nothing to see. The dogs and the sled carrying all the survival gear remained invisible. He realized the dogs also must have eventually stopped and perhaps were no more than a few hundred feet away covered with a few inches of snow. The animals, however, did not respond to Amak's calls.

He re-established his direction and slowly plodded ahead.

The skin on his exposed face felt as if a barrage of pins and needles were poking at its surface. Amak knew to rub the area with his gloved hands and the generated warmth returned the veneer of skin to its normal sensation. He pulled the drawstrings of his parka's hood tighter, attempting to decrease the vulnerability to his face, and continued to stagger on, chin lowered to his chest and shoulders hunched. The cold continued its journey through his coat and underlying sweater and shirt.

Inside a few minutes the pins and needles returned, now accompanied by a numbness of his toes and fingers. He made a fist with his hand to satisfy his fear that the fingers were only numb but were still able to move. He had to watch them since he could not feel their motion against the gloves.

He needed shelter from the cold.

The wind continued to increase and a strong, unexpected gust propelled Amak's head against a mound of snow. Dizziness followed and minutes passed before he could rise to his knees. He attempted to dig out a shelter, but the combination of frozen, hard snow and an inability to coordinate his numb hands made the task impossible.

Fighting for breaths became more difficult. The air was sucked away each time he faced into the wind. He remained on his hands and knees, dropped to a crawl by his worsening physical condition. His body had no energy left to combat the cold. Fatigue, he realized, is hypothermia's inlet to the body. His conscious efforts to avoid the coming danger were useless now. The brain and the rest of the body systems were already automatically fighting their battle. The heart rate increased and the blood vessels in the arms and legs were instructed to redirect warm blood away from the cold area. Limbs could be sacrificed in order to save the more vital organs. The body began converting glycogen stored in tissues into glucose, with the result that the muscles began to twitch and shiver. It was a movement programmed to ferment heat, but the shivering would only last until the energy stores were depleted.

He was crawling now. The dogs had disappeared more than two hours ago. He fought the panic and fear that had engulfed and settled deep within him. He had urinated spontaneously and the liquid quickly froze against the side of his thigh, cementing it with the inner layer of his pants. Skin, liquid, cloth became one layer, and whenever he moved his leg, the cloth would pull at the skin, ripping it from the underlying tissue layer.

He kept crawling, looking for some type of shelter.

He knew he must not panic. It would speed the process of hypothermia even faster.

Amak tried to concentrate on anything but the cold, but even when he tried to think analytically, the cold entered his thoughts. He remembered when he was much younger, the elders telling him that at ninety-eight point six to ninety-five degrees body temperature, the first observable signs of shivering occur. Heart and respiratory rate increase. Urination may occur. That stage had passed.

Ninety-five to ninety-one point four degrees core temperature and your consciousness clouds up. Restricted blood flow results in decreased dexterity. He was working his way through stage two.

His arms and legs could no longer support his body weight. He fell, striking his head against two oddly shaped objects on the ground. Amak lifted his head and he was able to see through the icicles that now hung from his eyebrows. One of the objects was straight and about ten inches long, while the other was L-shaped and seemed to have multiple appendages attached to one end. It was a foot, a foot with six toes, and deep within the tissue of the ankle he thought he saw a gold ring.

What was a severed dwarf's foot doing in the middle of nowhere?

That was not his problem now. *Tissue will burn.* He had matches in his pocket, but it would be useless to attempt a fire in the open. He must find shelter.

Fifteen minutes elapsed while he crawled another twenty feet. He pushed the two body parts ahead of him with his forearm, not having the strength to pick them up.

The wind borne snow was slowing again. He could distinguish a dark circle just few feet ahead. It was an opening in a snow bank. Probably a bear den, but he had no choice. He was certain to die if he stayed outside but realized that he might also die if the den was currently inhabited. The thought of safety and warmth propelled his body forward at a rate faster than he thought physically possible. Once inside the den, he knew he was alone. If he wasn't, he would have been dead by now.

Even though the enclosure was large enough to house and protect three or four more travelers, he felt claustrophobic. Luckily, the wind was blowing away from the opening and the decrease in noise momentarily made him think he had gone deaf until he heard the sound of his own breath. The moisture froze as it left his mouth and made a sound like the firecrackers set off by the children of the village. He embraced himself trying to return the circulation to his arms and rubbed his gloved hands together trying to force heat to his fingers. The most he could feel was an occasional prickling sensation in his fingers. He pulled the gloves off with his teeth and again rubbed his fingers.

It took all of his fading concentration to direct his hand into his parka's pocket to retrieve the tin of waterproof matches. He accomplished the task more by sight than by feel. The small note pad Stelgard had given him tumbled out with the tin. Again, he directed his fingers with his eyes as he ripped the papers from the spiral binding and crumpled them in a heap by his side. He knew the most difficult task was to come.

The flame from the first match he struck died out when his shivering arms agitated the delicate glow through the air. The second match broke in two when he struck it against the gritty undersurface of the tin. The third match caught, but by the time the paper caught fire, the tips of the fingers holding the match also acted as kindling. It mattered little; he could not feel the pain. The tiny fire grew as he reached in his pockets for any flammable object. A pencil, a handkerchief, a leather pouch, all were tossed upon the red-yellow flame. *Tissue will burn.* He pushed aside the severed foot, threw the smaller body part onto the fire, and watched as the skin darkened then slowly burned through to the underlying layers. The fat soon sizzled and popped as deeper layers were exposed. The smell of burning flesh did not offend him. It actually calmed and made him feel good. The heat felt even better.

Amak tried to curl around the fire. He wanted all parts of his body to benefit. In time, he thought he could feel his fingers again. The fatigue remained, but he was afraid to sleep. He was afraid that he might not wake, but he also knew that his body required rest. The growing heat felt good against his exposed face. He clutched the remaining six-toed foot against his chest. The weight of the warming air within the den pushed the lids of his eyes close.

Before sleep overcame him, he dreamt about the six-toes, he dreamt about a print in the snow where Brulog was discovered, he dreamt about Brulog's chewed neck and the similar missing tissue from Han's leg. He now knew a dwarf had killed the elf.

chapter 20

rog approached slowly. His feet hurt. "Sprog, have you seen
Amak?"

"No. He told me he was going to Haulvit to bring back
Sven and Hans. Did you hear what happened to them?"

"Yes. I heard." Erog looked towards the workshop. "Do you
know if he's returned?"

"I told you I haven't seen him."

"Have you been to the workshop?"

"I just left, and as far as I know, Amak hasn't been there today;
but then again, I didn't ask anyone." Sprog seemed annoyed with all
the questions. He watched as Erog switched his walking stick from
one side to the other, grimacing as he shifted his weight. "By the
way, where's Unata today?"

Erog's eyes widened. "Why do you ask?"

"I heard some of the women wondering why she didn't show up
for work. I guess the crunch is on and they need all the hands they
can get. Actually, I heard the same comments at the workshop. Any
chance you could help us out?"

"Sure, why not. I have a few things to do first, but then I don't
see any reason not to help."

"So what about Unata?"

"She's not feeling well today. I was just on my way home to put some meals together. I hate to see her have to get out of bed."

"Boy does she have you whipped." They both chuckled knowing the absurdity of that statement. Sprog tugged his collar higher onto his neck and tried to position his back against the wind. "Where have you been?"

"I took the sled out to check out Knute's murder site."

"Murder site! What are you talking about? I saw the mangled body. It was a bear attack. Why are you talking about a murder?"

"I guess I shouldn't be spitting out wild statements like that. You're probably right about the bear attack. I came to the same conclusion; but lately, I've been thinking that there have been too many strange happenings over the past few days and they just may be related. That's why I went back out."

"Speaking of an accumulation of strange events, you can add another to your list—Danat is missing."

"Oh?"

Sprog seemed somewhat surprised that Erog did not react more to the news. "Somebody saw him skulking behind one of the cottages this morning. Now he's nowhere to be found. He was supposed to be in charge of crating yesterday's toys, but he never showed up for work."

"This is getting bizarre. I don't know. Maybe Danat decided to find the upside to the beating he took from Amak. Maybe he's just milking it. Goofing off 'til after Christmas."

"I don't think so," Sprog replied. "First, if he was faking it, he wouldn't be walking around where he could be seen. Secondly, if you recall, except for Amak's kick to the face, Danat was doing pretty good and seemed to be getting the best of it."

"Hey, I thought Amak was your buddy. How come you're saying it was Danat who won the fight? Seems like you're changing sides."

Erog paused while he again switched the cane to his other hand. "I respect Amak for trying to control Santa, but there are times I think he is running in the wrong gear. Slow when he should press the issue and fast when he should compromise. He asks for advice, but he won't listen. Lately, he seems to feel that if it comes from his mouth, it must be right. He had no reason to kick Danat's face in. It was a case of Danat trying to show him up. I'm sure Amak felt his authority was being threatened."

"You know what, Erog, I think the fight was about Loti. Nothing more."

"Sure, Loti's name was involved, but it was Amak's command that was being questioned. For some reason Amak feels that authority once bestowed is irrevocable. I'm afraid that if we ever get out from under Santa's yoke, we'd have to be careful not to find ourselves under Amak's foot." Erog paused to allow Sprog's notoriously slow thought process to absorb all he had said before he continued. "Everybody knows that I consider Amak to be my best friend, but I must admit that some of his ideas seem to be self-serving. Sometimes, he's a little too quick to dismiss someone else's ideas and too quick starting a campaign to discredit them. Maybe this time he's taking it a little too far."

Sprog's gaze seemed to focus on some distant object. Erog was sure it was not that he was trying to formulate a reply, but instead, he was trying to assimilate what had just been said. The person who had last spoken to him often formed Sprog's latest opinion. Sprog was everybody's friend. He had no enemies and Erog knew that if he could get Sprog to be his voice to the village, maybe the change in the leadership would be less difficult.

Not that Erog cared, but maybe he could accomplish a peaceful coup. It was a method his late wife had always advocated, back when he cared about her opinion.

Sprog finally spoke. "Do you think Danat's disappearance has anything to do with Amak?"

"I think you may be jumping ahead too many squares. All I said was that I thought Amak didn't want his authority questioned. I didn't say that he would go so far as to try to eliminate his opposition."

"I guess you're right, but I thought . . ."

Erog looked pensively to the sky. "Actually, you might be right. It never occurred to me that Amak could go that far. Maybe he does have something to do with Danat's disappearance. Do you think all these events are somehow tied together?"

"Erog, are you saying that Amak might be behind everything? Norved? Knute? Rudolph? Danat?"

"I wonder if you are right."

Sprog was confused. Was it his idea or Erog's? No matter, he needed time to sift through, sort out these recent events, and decide if Amak really might be the culprit. If nothing else, he was now sure that Amak was not the leader he wished to follow. Maybe he should discuss his new ideas with some of the other elves. Maybe radical changes were now required. He bid goodbye to Erog and told him to seek him out whenever Amak returned.

The dogs nonchalantly dragged the overturned sled through the center of the village and came to a stop by the opening to the dog compound. Five of the dogs promptly lay down and curled themselves into a comfortable sleeping position. The younger, sixth dog was hungry, however. He had yet to experience any extended period without food. He strained against the weight of the sled and the resistance of the dormant members of the team in the hope that this would somehow reward him with a meal. Pulling on the harness accomplished little other than stretching the leashes connected to the other dogs. His repeated efforts were soon met with snarls from his mates who wished to be left to their sleep. Unable to produce the desired reaction, the young husky began staccato, throaty barks.

Peter's ears were used to the sounds of the dogs kept penned up next to his cottage. Without looking, he was usually able to identify the particular dog making the noise and determine from the type, pitch, and loudness of the sound, exactly what was bothering the animal. This dog's barks indicated more than hunger. Something else seemed to be bothering him. Peter looked out his window, but a small shed blocked his view of the source of the noise. There was no distress in the noise, but rather a combination of hunger and confusion. No other dogs had joined in the serenade. Investigating the problem could wait.

It was another ten minutes before Peter realized the barking had not stopped. The increased volume was what finally tweaked his attention again. Maybe one of the other dogs had attacked the barker. Peter thought it best that he pause work on his current project and examine the predicament. Next to the reindeer, the health of the sled dogs was of utmost importance during this busy season.

As he approached the compound and saw the abandoned sled, he knew that there was indeed a problem. The guilt of not having immediately come out to investigate propelled Peter into a trot towards the dogs and their riderless sled.

No one would just leave an unattended sled with the dogs still in harness. The only feasible explanation was that the rider had been tossed and the dogs had returned to their home alone. But who was the missing rider and where was he now?

Peter searched through the items still strapped on the sled and was able to identify a blanket wrapped around an ice knife he knew belonged to Amak. That answered the question as to who was missing, but Peter still had no clue as to where and why.

The first wave of the storm blew into the village during the formation of the search party. There was no sense leaving in the middle of a whiteout. If they left now, only more search parties would have to be formed to find these new lost travelers.

The storm lasted almost one hour, during which they agreed to search the possible paths Amak could have taken from Haulvit. All were concerned with the delay because it was evident since Amak had lost his ice knife, he had little or no chance to build a protective cover to outlast any storm.

"Amak knows how to take care of himself," one of the would-be rescuers said while harnessing a sled. But no one really believed that just because Amak probably knew more about surviving the Arctic necessarily meant he was still alive. They needed to find him without further delay.

Four teams of two left the village. Each team separated itself from the others by less than a tenth of a mile and traveled in zigzag lines crossing the usual paths taken by anybody traveling to Haulvit.

The workshop was the most electrified building in the village, needing seven gasoline generators working full time to supply the power to the countless lights and equipment. Long parallel rows of wooden tables stretched the length of the interior. Each table was responsible for the manufacture of a different category of toy or other present. Some categories, and thus some jobs, never changed. Within the last few years, Nels had radically altered the types of toys produced by the elves. Rumors had it that after this year's holiday season, Nels was going to experiment with automating some of the production. His excuse was there were fewer elves successfully recruited or volunteering to move to Santa's home base.

The building had no other function than the assemblage of Christmas presents. Elves performed the pre-manufacturing tasks in two smaller buildings. The term "workshop" was loosely used to represent any of these buildings, but to say you "worked in the workshop" was understood to mean that you worked in the largest of this group of structures.

The cold and sterile environment outside was mirrored with the environment inside the workshops. Hand painted signs were the only adornments on the walls. The signs were unvarying, each informing the workers that they must check the daily quota lists in the back of the shop.

The eight elves pulled from the workshop assembly line were not the reason for the marked slowdown in production. The remaining workers had just finished arguing the merits of Sprog's suggestion that Amak was somehow involved with the mysterious past events and now they learned that Amak was among the missing. Would the rescuers find him, as they had found Knute, in a mangled heap in some ice canyon?

Some elves stood alone, speaking in dialects only they knew. Groups of elves formed in the corners and against the walls of the workshop. In whispered voices, the concerns of the unexplained events provoked additional fears. Was one person behind everything? Who could be trusted? Was Amak really missing or was this part of his fiendish plan? If Amak really was missing, who was going to take charge? Lots of questions but no answers, and in the meantime, no toy production.

chapter 21

The knock on the door was soft, but its rapidity and persistence communicated a sense of urgency. Erog had no idea how long the visitor had been trying to get in. He had returned to his cottage intending to eat and to confirm there were no residual traces of the recent foul play. Instead, he had collapsed onto the bed and quickly had fallen asleep.

The knocking grew louder. Erog had no intention of answering. He was too tired and still needed to inspect the cottage. He lay motionless, listened to the knocking, and refused to answer.

"Erog! Erog, are you in there?" It was Loti.

He jumped from the bed and almost tripped while struggling to pull his boots on. "I'll be right there, Loti." He tried to sound relaxed and jovial. "You've caught me exposed."

The door was barely opened before she pushed her way through. "Loti, what's wrong? You look upset."

"Haven't you heard about Amak?"

He was perplexed and worried. Had she figured out that he was the origin of the new rumors about her lover? "No. What are you talking about?"

"The dogs dragged his empty sled into the village. No one knows where he is or what's happened to him. He was supposed to bring back those two workers from Haulvit, but the only thing that returned was his sled." She continued to pace even though she had finished speaking.

"First of all, how does anybody know it was Amak's sled?"

"They found his blanket and snow knife caught in the webbing."

"Okay, but did anybody radio Haulvit to ask if they knew anything?"

"They tried to, but didn't get any answer. From what I understand it's not unusual for their radio to be down." She stopped pacing and turned to face him. "I'm worried, Erog."

He embraced her with feigned sympathy. Both individuals derived their own, but different, comfort from the physical act. "I'll go and organize a search party. Don't worry. We'll find him. If nothing else, Amak knows how to survive the Arctic battle."

He didn't want to let go, but she pulled back and again nervously paced. "There already are search parties, but they were delayed by a storm."

"Well then, what exactly do you want me to do? You know I'll do anything to help, but if they're already organized . . ."

"Something else is going on, Erog," she interrupted. "All of a sudden there're rumors that Amak is somehow involved with Knute's death and Rudolph's murder. In the past hour, I must have had four or five people question me as to what Amak was up to." She continued with a statement spoken as if it were a question, "There's no way Amak could be involved with those events?"

He was relieved she didn't know the source of the rumors. Sprog was probably taking credit for these incisive accusations. Let him also take the blame if the scheme failed. "Loti, I know you care a great deal about Amak, and I know you must be terrified that something has happened to him, but trust me—it will be all right."

"Erog, I do care about Amak, but to be honest, lately, I just don't know if I care for him as deeply as I used to." She wondered why she was being so open. "We've been arguing about everything. I don't know if we are testing each other's commitment to our relationship or if we're trying to get the other person to say it's over. But all that doesn't matter right now. I am afraid for him. I don't trust those out searching for him. You're his closest friend, his only real friend. I want you to go out with me and try to find him."

"A school teacher raised in a city and a cripple are not what I would call the ideal Arctic rescuers. It's best if we leave the search to those who can function best."

"They may be able to function best, but right now I'm not sure if they really care about finding Amak."

While he listened, Erog calculated the possibilities. Certainly, if Amak wasn't found one of his major problems would be solved. By going with Loti, he could reinforce his image of being a loyal friend even if Amak was now possibly discredited. Being trustworthy in times of need and danger was a well looked upon character trait in this hostile environment. But it was the appearance of the crack in Loti's and Amak's relationship, which was the eventual reason Erog agreed to help. He told her that he would harness a dog team, get the necessary supplies for the journey and meet her at her cottage in twenty minutes.

Loti embraced him again and left.

The snow began blowing almost as soon as they left the village. Erog decided to head west, away from the path Amak probably had taken. He explained this route by telling Loti they would just be duplicating the other search party's pattern if they went south.

"Maybe Amak got caught in a storm and lost his bearings. We'll search in this direction for a while and then double back."

Loti pulled the bear skin up around her neck. Pellets of snow blew into her eyes, each new intrusion stinging mercilessly. Still, she strained to see ahead, hoping to spy any dark object against the sea of white.

The westerly wind abated and Loti could now see somewhat farther. There was something in the distance. She was sure of it. She pointed and shouted that she saw something to the right.

"Mush! Mush!"

"Hurry, Erog! Hurry them up! I think I see him."

"Mush, you lazy bastards!"

Fifty feet further, they realized she had seen only a small snow pack sculpted by the wind into the shape of an elf. Amak was still lost.

"Let's head back towards the other groups. Maybe somebody else had some luck."

The bogus discovery drained Loti. She slid back against the rear netting and covered part of her face so she used only one eye for reconnaissance. The cold intensified and her new, uncontrolled shaking was a combination of her body's reaction to the lower temperature and spent emotions.

Erog's occasional commands to the dog team were all that interrupted the din of the constant wind. Only the four-legged animals seemed impervious to the inhospitality.

"I can't see anything past the tip of the sled, Loti, and I have no idea what the dogs might be leading us into. It's best that we stop for a while and wait out the storm." They had traveled a mile from the false sighting, and in that short distance and the time it took to travel, the wind speed had risen well past the usual forty miles per hour peak. "I'd better build a shelter," continued Erog. "It may be a while before conditions let us continue."

Loti stayed bundled on the sled and the dogs quickly made themselves comfortable in the loose snow cover. Erog cautiously moved away from the area in search of a large mound of snow, one large enough to use for a shelter.

A bear must have once used the hummock he found. A cave-like hole was already present, but it wouldn't be large enough for both him and Loti. He could not have been more than a few dozen feet away, but when he turned his head, he couldn't see his fellow travelers. There was no time to waste. He climbed to the top of the snow embankment and tramped on it to compact the undersurface.

"Erog, are you still there?" Loti sounded frightened.

The wind carried her words away, making it difficult for Erog to hear, but that same wind made his reply seem as if he was standing right next to her. "Try to keep warm, Loti. I'll be through in a few minutes."

Alternating between his snow knife and his cupped, gloved hand, he enlarged the hole, which thankfully faced away from the prevailing wind direction. Erog continued to cut and scoop out the snow until a shell of compacted snow encompassed a cave five by six feet with a ceiling a little more than five feet from the floor. He continued using his knife to poke two ventilation holes through the dome. The shelter was completed in less than fifteen minutes.

Erog struggled against the wind to stay on his feet. He returned to the sled and told Loti to gather the bearskins while he set the snow hook firmly into the ground. He did not want the villagers to experience another riderless dog sled. Taking one of the bearskins from Loti, he wrapped the food and pieces of wood he had astutely packed for the trip. "Hold onto my coat, Loti, and stay close. The shelter is only a few yards away." She willingly followed Erog's instructions and let him lead her to sanctuary. "Set up house, Loti, while I make a door for our new home."

Pushing the bearskin ahead of her, she eagerly crawled through the opening. Erog followed her in and unraveled the skin carrying the food and wood. He pulled a match tin from his pocket and asked Loti to start a fire. "Only use two of the logs. I don't know how long we'll be here." Backing out of the enclosure, his head banged against the side of the opening and the blow knocked down some of the bordering snow.

"Don't bury us alive, Erog," she joked nervously.

He smiled while answering, "I just hope I didn't make the hole big enough to make it too inviting for some passing bear to come in out of the storm." From outside he continued, "I'll be right back." Erog wielded his long, snow knife against an adjacent hummock and dislodged a large, irregular chunk of ice. He finished his task by using the knife to carve the ice into the shape and size of the shelter's opening.

Backing through the doorway, he plugged the hole by pulling the snow block into position. "Let the wind blow all it wants. We're safe now. Be it ever so humble there's no place like home." He turned and was surprised to see Loti had spread one of the skins on the floor, lit a fire, and was already heating some food.

She recognized his expression. "Even those of us raised in electrified homes and villages know how to light a fire. We're not the helpless group you think we are."

The smoke lazily drifted up and filtered through the ventilation holes. The gray-white puffs converged above the fire into finger-like forms that seemed to grab and drag away what little heat there was. Loti was unable to acclimate to the cold and she asked Erog to give her one of the bearskins. He handed it to her and then knelt behind her to place the second one over her back.

"How long do you think the storm will last?"

"There's no way to predict something like that."

"I would have thought that you, much like Amak, someone who places so much emphasis on knowing the old ways, would be able to stick his finger in the air and determine the exact minute a storm would end."

He moved to sit next to her—the fire no longer in between. "Give me a break, Loti. I'm out in this miserable weather trying to help."

Silence followed, but only the silence of conversation. The muffled sound of the wind and the occasional whistling as the outside turbulence streaked over the ventilation holes was still audible. Loti remained motionless, staring into the fire's dwindling blue-yellow flame. Erog sat watching her. He had mistakenly supposed she would protest his suggestion that they postpone the search until after the storm. He was unsure if her compliance was because she was well aware of the danger of staying outside or if her concern for Amak's safety wasn't as genuine as it first appeared.

There were times in the past, many times, that Erog confessed to himself that he was very much enamored with her beauty and intelligence. He had also imagined that Loti might like him not because they were forced together as Amak's friends and confidants, but because Loti just liked him. Her flirtations directed toward him, he assumed they were just flirtations, had increased lately. He was never sure if her giggles and touches represented nothing, a true fondness, or just a female's ploy to keep her lover's interest piqued. Perhaps it was her plan to make Amak think there was competition, even if it was just Erog, so she might be able to manipulate and control him easier. But then there were times when Erog felt that it was more than flirtation, that she really was interested in what he was saying, and that just maybe she did have some feelings for him.

"You seemed to have calmed down since this afternoon."

Loti looked up slowly and observed him for a moment before replying. "I was just thinking the same thing and wondering whether I should be feeling guilty."

"Guilty about what?" He didn't allow her to answer, however. "We had to stop the search. No one could find their way through this storm. We could have gone on, been only yards away from Amak and still not have seen him."

She looked away, then again stared into the flame. "That's not the reason for the guilt." A few seconds passed. She appreciated Erog's not pursuing the conversation but felt obligated in some way to continue, to explain. "You and Amak are best of friends." He did not interrupt this misconception. "To watch the both of you together, I can see why you're probably each other's only real comrade. Amak and I talk, but we don't communicate. After a while, I'll start to babble. I've discovered that the absence of conversation makes it most difficult to think in words. He complains about this, I complain about that, but neither of us seems to care about the other's problems. Well, maybe caring is the wrong word, maybe it's just that we can't understand each other's problems."

She paused and again made eye contact with Erog. "I might be wrong, but I have the impression that might be your difficulty with Unata. Opposites may attract, but there's no physical law that says they have to exist harmoniously.

"I feel guilty because I'm not sure that I wouldn't have felt the same degree of pain if I had been told anyone else was missing. It just seems to me that I ran around screaming only because in the back of my mind I thought it was what I was supposed to feel and do and not because I really cared."

She leaned forward to hold his hand. "Am I saying it right? Do you understand, Erog?"

He did not want her to remove her hand. "I understand, Loti. It sounds like you intended to finally break off your relation with Amak, but the timing was bad. You didn't end it before his disappearance and now you're feeling like you must continue to be the dutiful girlfriend, worried about someone that you think should be the most important person in your life."

She slowly withdrew her hand. "It's funny, but he probably still is the most important person in my life." Then with a laugh she added, "That's not saying too much for my life, is it?"

"I know it's a cliché to say everyone needs somebody, Loti, but the fear of isolation pushes us into relationships with others."

"The fact is, Erog, that members of most animal species, including man, live in groups. Man, like other animals, is dependent on others."

"Not true. What about polar bears—'the lonely hunters'. Hell, male bears will eat their own offspring if they're hungry. One man's dependency creates another's responsibility, and that responsibility is often seen as a threat to one's freedom."

"Amak said something like that just last week, although he wasn't as eloquent."

"I guess I have to thank Unata for that. That's about the only thing I must give her credit for—teaching me to communicate."

"You and Amak certainly think alike. Perhaps he should live with you instead of asking me to move in with him."

Erog laughed, "I can't believe he asked you to live with him." Her eyes opened wide. He realized how that must have sounded and tried to correct any wrong perception by quickly adding, "No. I mean anyone would be a fool not to want to live with you, but I meant I can't believe he asked you to live with him without being married." Again, he realized he was not saying what he wanted to impart. "This is not coming out the way I mean it." Now she was smiling. "What I mean to say is not that I feel living together without being married is such a wicked thing, but we all know

Santa's view on the subject. The big man won't tolerate such a living arrangement in his village.

"It's funny that we're the natives and he and his past relatives are the immigrants," Erog continued. "Yet, we allowed him to change our social structure, our social rules. Why did we have to adapt to his foreign values and not the other way around? Why do they all hold Santa in such awe?"

"Erog, long ago Santa assumed his right to make binding requests on us. We gave him the authority because no one protested. The power resides not in the person, but rather in the position."

"Unata says I'm not a traditionalist, but rather a ritualist looking for a rebellion. I'm too stupid to see any difference—at least that's what she says."

"You aren't stupid, Erog." She imagined the henpecking Erog must endure from his mate.

"Well, I don't think I'm stupid either. I may not be able to put the words together as well as Unata can, but most often, the ideas she delivers are mine. She's just more expressive."

She didn't want to talk about Unata. She didn't want to have to discuss their altercation that took place three days ago. Loti felt it would either infuriate or embarrass him. "It's not the words that impress me, Erog. Amak's a good communicator and I don't always agree with some of his irrational ideas, but I do respect his commitment to what he believes."

He spoke to defend himself, not Amak. "Remember, Loti, that a man is considered irrational only by those who disagree with him. It's a matter of perspective. Is it wrong to believe that the outlander's ideas will end our civilization? Whose virtues are better? Whose are right? Is materialism to be so highly regarded and desired? Is it wrong to want to continue the traditions of our ancestors? Am I irrational just because I don't think we should be under Santa's control?"

Loti was not familiar with this Erog, one who waxed philosophical versus the inane conversations she observed between him and Amak. "No, Erog, you're not wrong, but for some reason when Amak says the same thing he seems to be preaching to me. Like a parent to a child. And like most children I find myself arguing with him even if I'm really in agreement."

Now, it was Erog who gazed into the fire before he continued. "I guess that's why I let others do all the talking. Let them take the heat. It's not easy to follow traditional ways."

Loti remembered the last time she and Amak made love and he insisted on a "traditional position."

Erog was so involved in his speech, that he did not realize when Loti had grasped his hand and was now gently caressing it with her thumb. Her action gave him the confidence to continue.

"Do you know who the outlander Collins is, Loti?"

"I think Amak mentioned him once. Isn't he that toy manufacturer who offered to buy out Santa?"

"Yes, that's him. A man like Collins likes to increase his holdings, to increase his power over those around him. He doesn't give one thought about people as long as he can buy them. Then, there's the benevolent dictator, Santa Claus, who likes to collect elves and hold sway over them. Finally, there are people like Amak, self-proclaimed celebrities, who like to hear the chorus of people repeat his name. All of them need us. They all need people to worship or fear them. Without us they'd be lost."

This was the first time Loti heard him say anything negative about Amak, but the opening was there and he intended to enter while he could. In time, he might have to justify his abandonment of his comrade's leadership, and he needed to set the foundation for such an action. Loti, for her part, was relieved to hear Amak's eternal flatterer confirm that not all was perfect. She, too, had entertained the thought that Amak wasn't the dedicated traditionalist he blazoned, but that he might be using the issue to replace Santa as the power figure. Loti looked away, needing time to compose her thoughts. Still not returning his questioning stare, she continued. "Does Unata understand? Is she as big a pain-in-the-ass to you as I am to Amak?"

"Don't place yourself in the same category as Unata." He placed his hand beneath her chin and gently raised her head so she had to meet his gaze. "She's a selfish pig I married when I was feeling sorry for myself and felt nobody else would accept a marriage proposal. I didn't want to live alone. I might be a traditionalist, but I'm not an isolationist.

"It's been a fight with Unata from day one. I married her thinking a mate would be good for my failing self-esteem, but before long, I realized that her constant belittling actually decreased whatever self-esteem I had left. I tried to maintain a decent relationship with her, but she made that impossible. She's not satisfied until she's hoarse from yelling at me. Only then, will her tirades stop. I thought having children might help. I would love to have children, but she refuses. She said I'm a cripple and she would have to do all the work raising them.

"I dread old age. I dread being alone."

Erog was uncertain if he was saying these things because he was beginning a cover-up for Unata's future unexplained disappearance or was telling these half-truths in hope of Loti's sympathy. In any case, he was euphoric when she again covered his hand and held her other hand against his cheek. They sat like this, neither having the courage to look in each other's eyes. He noted her slight tremble and asked if she was cold. Loti replied that she guessed so. Erog moved closer and brought his arms around her. The warmth from the embrace did not stop the trembling; indeed, it increased when he held her close.

Loti smoothed and arranged her hair, slowly crossed and uncrossed her legs, and caressed the inside of her thigh.

Loti could not be sure if it was he who kissed her or she who had initiated the act. Minutes of kissing, holding, and fondling advanced as Erog removed the bearskin blanket wrapped around her and both undressed each other in the near darkness of the dying fire. She lay back while he caressed her breast and gently kissed the erect nipple. He rolled on top and was about to enter her when she surprised him by gently pushing him off and saying she wasn't ready.

What had he done wrong? He could not understand what he was supposed to do before she would allow him to continue, but Loti didn't expect him to do anything more. She rolled onto her stomach, leaned forward on her elbows, and raised her hips. "Let's be traditional."

They lay beneath the bearskin. He was sleeping soundly on his back, occasionally moving his head whenever he snored and gasped for air. Loti awoke slowly and moved closer to Erog. She wanted to make love again but decided against waking him. The fire needed tending. Loti pushed the skin aside and sat up. She reached for two pieces of wood and placed them perpendicular to each other on the fire. The flames licked at the new fuel and the trapped air and moisture popped and crackled as the heat increased. Shadows flickering on the walls reminded her of tribal dances done to celebrate a new marriage.

Loti's nipples were again erect, but now it was because of the cold. Lying back down, she pulled on the disheveled cover and was amused when she saw she had exposed her feet. She looked to see if Erog's feet had also been exposed to the cold and gasped aloud when she saw each of his feet had six toes.

DECEMBER 24th

chapter 22

The voices woke him from a dream whose memory disappeared within seconds, though it left him with the idea that he had solved a puzzle. Amak struggled to retreat into his dream and rediscover the solution, but the voices wouldn't let him. His body was being manhandled. Somebody shook his shoulders while others tried to grapple something from his arms. Somehow he knew he should not release whatever it was he had wrapped his arms around, but his assailants were persistent and stronger, and he soon lost control of the cold, hard object.

Amak's eyes remained closed. He labored to decipher what the voices were saying.

"Amak! Amak! Wake up!"

There was more manhandling. "I think he's all right. Put some wood on that fire and get some blankets from the sled."

It was a matter of minutes before he felt the penetrating heat from the fire. Hands squeezed and kneaded his feet at a frantic pace. He felt encased in a plaster cast beneath which he could not move. Sensation had abandoned his skin and underlying tissues, and he was uncertain if his attempt to open his clinched hand was successful.

"Can you hear me, Amak? It's me, Sprog."

He watched the kaleidoscope of colors against the inside of his closed eyelids. The irritating voices would not leave him alone. He wanted to return to his dream.

A commanding voice boomed into his ear, "Open your eyes, Amak!"

He had no choice. He raised his protective eyelids but couldn't tolerate the light, so again shut his eyes. The voice repeated itself, this time accompanied by more abusive shoving and prodding of his body. "Open your eyes! How are you feeling?"

"How's he feeling?" another voice added. "Damn, he's frozen solid! How would you be feeling? He'll be all right once he warms up and we get some food into him."

The voices droned on and Amak felt the dream returning.

"Amak, wake up! Here, drink this." Someone raised his head and something hot was against his lips. This time he knew the dream was lost, and he opened his eyes. Once again, the dancing brilliance of the fire greeted him and it forced him to blink until his pupils acclimated.

He awoke inside a house made of snow, not the one he had crawled into sometime in the past. This one was man made. Ignoring the interruptions created by someone standing in his view, he studied the blocks of compacted snow, stacked atop each other, and was transfixed by the beauty and simplicity of a structure made of frozen liquid. His eyes followed the parallel lines the rows of blocks made around the circumference of the igloo.

"How are you feeling?"

He focused on the individual holding a steaming cup in front of his mouth. "I've been better, Sprog." He spied the second member of the search party kneeling in the entrance to the shelter. "Mikel, I see you're here too." And turning back to Sprog, Amak continued, "How long have I been here?"

"Drink this first, then I'll answer your questions."

The warmth of the drink cascaded from the back of his mouth, down his throat, and pooled in his stomach. It felt good. The heat radiated from this internal core and soon his limbs seemed to also benefit. By the time he finished his nourishment, he was able to hold the metal cup himself. "I feel better. Thanks, Sprog. Thanks for finding me. Let's get out of here and get back to the village."

Amak sat up, still supported by his rescuers. He waited a few minutes before slowly standing, now braced against the side of the ice walls.

"You don't look so good."

"Suddenly, I don't feel so good." Amak's fall to the ground was decidedly swifter than his rise.

The sled bounced over a rut and jostled Amak awake. He looked through the opening in the blanket. The winter sky seemed empty beyond the clouds. The few stars he was able to see appeared lonely and abandoned. Gradually sleep overcame him again.

With the return of consciousness came the introduction of pain. He looked down to see blisters had developed on his fingertips—a sure sign of frostbite. Patches of white, waxy skin encircled additional blisters on the back of his hands. The way his toes, nose, and ear lobes hurt, he was certain the same tissue destruction had occurred there as well.

"What happened to you?" Sprog asked. "Where are Hans and Sven? And where the hell did you get the dwarf's foot?"

Amak remembered fighting to keep hold of it. He sat up, found he was still weak, and pushed his arm against the mattress for support. "Where's the foot? Where is it?" He snapped his head from side to side, desperately searching for its location and just then realized he was in his own cottage. "Where is it, Sprog?" He tried to stand, but Sprog firmly pushed against his shoulders, keeping him from rising.

Mikel pleaded with him to put his hands into a basin of warm water, hoping the treatment would successfully curtail the tissue destruction.

"Stay calm, Amak. Don't try to stand. You're not in any shape yet."

"Where's the foot, Sprog? What did you do with it?"

"It's outside. The cottage is confining enough without sharing space with some dwarf's remains. How did you latch on to this trophy? Were you in a fight?"

While Mikel went outside to retrieve the foot, Amak explained the recent events to Sprog, who in turn reciprocated with events that took place up to the rescue.

"It looks like something sharp severed the foot." Mikel held the appendage away from his chest as if it were contagious. "No bear did this. It certainly doesn't look as if was chewed off. I don't understand. I never heard that dwarfs cut up their dead before leaving them."

"Let me see it, Mikel." Amak tried to examine what was left of his enemy but his eyes still had trouble focusing. Like elves, dwarfs just left their dead outside, away from the villages. The difficulty digging a burial site wasn't justified when one considered the blowing snow would soon mold a coffin around the corpse and the cold would keep putrescence from invading the body.

The light hanging from the ceiling reflected against the water droplets forming on the defrosting foot. White, diamond-shaped outlines sparkled from the surface as Amak turned the foot in examination. "I agree. I've never heard of dwarfs cutting up their own," he said as he deposited the foot on the table next to the bed.

His mind fought to interpret some translucent information in his dream. Something he'd heard or seen in his dream. No, it wasn't in his dream! He grabbed for the foot again. He remembered now. A glitter. Golden light coming from the foot. He examined a cut through the tissue surrounding the ankle and discovered a three-inch section of a gold ankle bracelet embedded in the opening. Folds of muscle almost completely covered it. He held the piece of bracelet closer to the light and wiped away some of the bloody debris from its surface.

"My god! It's Unata!"

"What are you talking about, Amak?"

"This foot—it's Unata's. This is her bracelet. I saw Erog make her one exactly like this. In fact, he's making a similar one for Loti. This is Unata's foot!" The epiphany jolted Amak alert.

"How can it be? This foot has six toes. It was attached to a dwarf, not Unata."

"I don't understand either, Mikel, but there is no way this bracelet should be on a dwarf's foot unless Unata gave it away." He put the section of the bracelet in his pocket and pushed himself up. "Let's go find her."

He remembered now. His thoughts were no longer those vague reflections of his dreams, but were now concrete, able to be analyzed: the strange print he thought he saw next to Knute's corpse, the one Erog accidentally trod upon; and now a bracelet made by Erog for his wife found on a dwarf's severed foot.

What else was there? He tried to shake off any residual stupor. He remembered more. Erog always asking and prying information about production, about Santa's plans, about Amak's own plans. He remembered events that occurred in a pattern obviously meant to disrupt. He realized there was someone trying to destroy Santa's village, someone who understood elves and had knowledge of theirs and Santa's needs.

Amak thought about all of this and by the time they reached

Erog's cottage, he realized he was about to enter the home of an enemy, not that of his best friend.

"Mikel, check around back, and while you're at it, ask Erog's neighbors if they have seen him or Unata."

Sprog entered the cottage before Amak completed his instructions. He recalled his conversation with Erog and still had reservations about Amak, but the bracelet on the dwarf's foot was confusing the issue. How would a dwarf get hold of Erog's gift to his wife?

The room that greeted Sprog was a mess. Clothes scattered across furniture, dishes piled in the sink, and dirt everywhere. All kinds of dirt. A layer of dust covered the floor and furniture. Crusted dirt caked the knives and forks. Clumps of dirt were strewed in front of the bedroom door. Unata was certainly not a fanatic housekeeper.

The red smudge on the floor drew him closer. Colors always received attention. He was about to bend down for a closer look when Mikel burst into the cottage. "Where's Amak?"

"What's wrong?"

"Where is he?"

"He's somewhere outside. He never came in. What's wrong?" Sprog asked.

Mikel never answered. Instead, he turned and left the cottage, leaving the door open. Sprog could hear Mikel shouting for Amak and Amak answering back. Seconds later the three elves converged in the back of Erog's home.

"Amak, look over there. Next to the back door. I think there's blood mixed in with the snow."

They crouched next to the area of pink snow. Amak scooped some of it up for a better view and noticed the underlying layer was deeper red in color. The warm blood must have seeped into a lower level before the cold had impeded its progress by freezing the intruding liquid. Amak fingered the colored snow hoping the

ALL I WANT FOR CHRISTMAS

intimacy would confirm the clinical visual diagnosis that it was blood and not some other fluid.

"Look at this, Amak." Sprog had continued to burrow into the area and was now holding up pieces of tissue for inspection. It looks like someone butchered something here. Do you think Unata or Erog just cut up some meat back here?"

"Nobody butchers meat outside their back door. No one's stupid enough to leave a scent close to their house that might attract a hungry bear."

"Maybe somebody cut themselves," Sprog continued.

"If someone lost this much blood they would've bled to death. Where the hell is the body, and why are there so many pieces of meat mixed in with the blood?"

They continued to search the area and found two more areas of blood-soaked snow with chunks of meat compacted beneath the surface. The investigation led them to believe that something had driven the tissue below, something sharp, something like an axe blade.

Finding little else, they entered the cottage to see if they could find any other bizarre anomalies.

Sprog immediately went to the red smudges in front of the bathroom floor. It must be blood he thought. What else could it be? "Amak, come look at this. I think I've found more blood. Someone must've cut himself awfully bad. Blood outside. Blood inside. It must've been some cut."

The elves circled the stain. Each in turn fingered the dried area, trying to decipher its meaning.

Amak was the first to stand. He scanned the room before he entered the bathroom. Although stark white, it seemed as dirty as the rest of the dwelling. Dirty towels, dirty clothes, and dust. The red drop on the porcelain sink leaped out at him. More blood. But whose was it?

He continued his inspection of the room, noting more disarrayed clothing and more dirt. The dust was so deep and slippery on the floor that his foot twisted beneath him as he turned to leave. Amak bent down to rub his ankle and as his eyes closed in on a break in the dust, he realized it was a footprint. It was not his footprint. This was made by someone not wearing boots. It was made by a person with six toes. It was made by a dwarf.

chapter 23

Loti grabbed the sweater, tossed aside last night, and stuffed the end of a sleeve into her mouth. A loud gasp might waken Erog. Each time she peeked at his six toes during the night, she felt a surge of vomit about to erupt. She needed time to think. Confusion and terror enveloped her. She swallowed hard, trying to force back the rising nausea.

Erog was a dwarf. It followed that he was involved in the recent mysterious events. She had just made love to somebody who most likely was responsible for Knute Brulog's and maybe other elves' deaths. She was lying next to the individual who probably was Rudolph's killer. *How could a dwarf's hatred of elves justify such acts of violence? What did he have to gain by driving Rebecca Claus into a catatonic state?*

Erog rolled onto his side. His face was only inches from hers. He yawned and Loti was quick to note that his mouth opened disproportionately—menacingly—wide.

She was lying next to a murderer and she had no doubt he wouldn't hesitate to kill her if he learned she knew his secret. Loti hooked her toes to the blanket's border and slowly manipulated it to again cover his exposed feet. With the task completed, she turned, and was startled to see his open eyes. She was certain the blood had drained from her face and prayed he didn't notice in the darkened environment. He rubbed his eyes. *Does he know what I've discovered?*

Erog scrutinized Loti for what seemed to her forever. "Now it's my turn to feel guilty," he said.

She dug her fingernails into her thighs.

"I've never enjoyed making love like that with Unata."

He doesn't suspect. She pushed her sweater aside and he took the act to signify an invitation. Erog rolled towards her and reached to hold her close, but his touch only made her shiver and jerk away.

"Are you cold?" he asked gently. "Let me stoke the fire." He started to push the blanket off but stopped when he realized the dilemma of exposing his naked feet. Instead, he pushed the blanket level with his waist and used the excuse of his own coldness to dress while remaining partially covered.

He turned to her again and kissed her face and neck while gently kneading her nipples between his fingers. She didn't have to remind herself that this was a killer who was attempting to arouse her. His foreplay continued for another minute; but, receiving no positive response, he stopped, stared at her for a short time, and then stood.

"Loti, I don't think we're going to find Amak by ourselves. I think it might be best if we returned to the village to see if there's been any news." He paused to listen for the storm. "I don't hear the wind anymore. Maybe it's over or just a break in the weather. In either event, we should leave now in case it decides to attack us again."

She had not spoken since awakening, and he surmised that it was the confusion of making love while on a rescue mission to find her lover. He bent down and kissed her again. His desire grew. He was about to begin her seduction anew when she interrupted him by speaking. "Yes, I think it would be best to see if anyone else found Amak."

Erog left and allowed the fire in the center of the shelter to smolder. There was no fear of sparks igniting an inferno in this land of frozen water. Loti dressed and folded the blanket and bearskins while Erog returned, gathered the other supplies, and loaded the sled.

The wind had stopped and only the cold remained. Loti pulled the bearskin over her face and pushed back against the sled's blanket folded behind her head. Under the protective isolation of the covering, she felt safe to again think of a course of action.

Erog had tried to engage in conversation when the return trip began, but he was now preoccupied with commanding and steering the dogs away from new drifts created by the storm.

Loti pulled the cover tighter around her head. *What should I do if Amak remains lost? Who can I tell about my discovery and suspicions? Are there any other dwarfs posing as elves? What if I confide in the wrong person? Should I tell Santa, and if so, would he know what to do?*

First things first. She had to maintain her charade with Erog. Sexual guilt would easily explain her abrupt change in attitude. She couldn't let him suspect that she knew his secret.

The trip seemed endless. Loti spoke of the storm, of Amak, of Santa. She didn't speak of the passion each had recently felt. Erog added little to the conversation, agreeing only when Loti said she was sure Amak would be found. In fact, he somehow hoped Amak had survived whatever peril he might have encountered. No one, including enemies, should die alone.

"If you don't mind, please drop me off at my cottage. I need to change."

"Let's first unhitch the sled and then try to find out if there's any news about Amak. We'll walk over to the workshop. Somebody's sure to know what's going on."

They approached the dog enclosure by circling the village rather than the more direct route through the village proper.

She thought of running when he left her to replace the harness in the shed, but who would she run to? She stood in the middle of the bedded dog teams thinking they might offer some safety.

Erog approached slowly. He didn't use his cane nor was he limping. The dogs didn't stir. He stopped in front of her, searched her eyes for a moment, and then looked at the ground. "You know, don't you?"

"Know what?"

His head snapped up. "Don't mess with me, Loti!"

"What are you talking about? I don't like your tone. You're not with the boys."

His cupped hand struck the side of her head. The pain from the ruptured eardrum, not the intensity of the blow, forced her to the ground. Only one ear was capable of detecting the now barking dogs. She intended to scream for help, but he was on top of her immediately, covering her mouth and speaking softly into her remaining good ear. "Keep quiet, woman." He continued slowly, without emotion. "We're getting up and going into the shed. Don't try running away and don't try shouting for help. Just get up and walk calmly into the shed." His serene behavior scared her. This was an individual accustomed to violence.

He pushed himself up, casually brushed the snow off his clothes, and extended his hand to help her rise. Loti stared at him in disbelief and demonstrated her refusal of his offer of assistance by instead rolling onto her stomach, pushing herself to a position where she could pull her knees forward, and then standing.

Blood dripped from her ear, creating an expanding, red circle on the shoulder of her parka. A low, shrill ringing joined the steady pain. Rubbing her ear did nothing to relieve the discomfort or stop the noise. She teetered to the side, and the dizziness forced her to grab onto Erog to prevent a fall. The blow to the ear had obviously affected her sense of balance, too.

She pushed herself away and slowly, deliberately walked to the shed. Erog stepped in front of her to open the door—a gentleman again. Loti entered and walked to the most distant corner of the small room. She was quick to note potential weapons everywhere. Harnesses and whips hung from the walls. Lengths of scrap wood were scattered about the floor. A broken atlatl and spear, still lethally tipped, rested against the lower shelf. An axe lay within feet of where she stood. But she was afraid to even give the impression that she was going to grab any of these objects. She didn't want to be struck again. Loti huddled in the corner, thankful for the darkness when he closed the door behind him.

"You know, don't you," he repeated.

She timidly confirmed his accusation.

"How did you figure it out? Did you know before we fucked?" No longer had they made love; now they had fucked.

She trembled and hugged herself.

When no immediate answer followed, Erog stepped closer. She spoke. "I saw your feet after we . . . you have six toes, damn it! You're a dwarf!"

He started back across the room, randomly picking up the equipment scattered on the floor. He worked at a leisurely pace and in silence.

Loti continued to press herself into the corner of the shack. Erog's silence and lack of attention intensified rather than quelled her fear. She watched as he calmly carried out his meaningless housekeeping task.

Finally, he turned and faced her. "I'd hoped you wouldn't learn until later, and then I hoped you'd understand."

"Understand what, Erog? Understand why you're probably a murderer. Understand why you're trying to disrupt Santa's work. You tell me, Erog. I'm too stupid to figure it out on my own. You tell me why you did the things you did."

"I did tell you, Loti. I explained it when we were trapped by the blizzard."

"I must have missed it. Explain it to me again."

Erog walked to the other side of the room, squatted, and sat cross-legged with his back against the door.

"Santa is an outlander. He doesn't belong here. Only we belong here. Dwarfs and elves. We may not get along, but we belong in this land.

"A few years ago an outlander, a toy manufacturer named Collins, came to my village. He wanted to recruit the dwarfs in his attempt to stop Santa's distribution of free toys. Collins's idea was to somehow unsettle Santa's village—enough that it could never return to normalcy.

"Unata and I revised his plan. We would infiltrate the village, disrupt production, and when Santa quit, take over. We don't want to take over manufacturing and giving away toys. Hell, Collins can have that if he wants. The outlanders corrupted the elves long ago. I doubt they can be saved. What we want is self-control of our Arctic. Our only wish is to return to the traditional ways, and only dwarfs know the way to do that.

"It's ironic. Amak is, or was, my biggest obstacle, yet his goal of removing Santa's authority was the same as mine."

"Why did you say he was your biggest obstacle? Did you do something to Amak? Erog, did you kill him?"

"No, as far as I know he's still lost in the blizzard."

Loti didn't believe him, but her main concern now was her own safety. *Keep him talking. Think of something to do.* "So what if Santa quits? He's always replaced. Matthew or Nels would take over."

"Matthew wants no part of being Santa. He doesn't want the responsibility. That's why he always volunteers for some task outside the village. Nels may want to be in charge, but no one respects or would listen to him. If he became the new Santa, it might delay the dwarf's takeover, but only temporarily. The elves would abandon him soon enough."

"It won't work. Santa isn't going to quit."

"I agree, and that's why I modified the plan once again. I hid a bomb on Santa's sleigh yesterday. It will detonate once he flies above five-hundred feet."

"You're going to kill Santa Claus!"

"Loti, understand it has to be done. The original plan has taken too long. There's no other way."

"And what about me, Erog? Are you going to kill me too? Where do I fit into this plan?"

Erog stood and massaged the calf muscles in his right leg to relieve a developing cramp. "Loti, I'd hoped that you'd want to leave with me. I plan on returning to my village tonight."

"What about Unata? I don't think she'd appreciate the additional baggage on the trip home."

"Unata's left me." Erog avoided the truth. It would be difficult trying to explain the killing of one of his own. Unata's death had nothing to do with his other actions. The original mission could justify those killings, not hers, however.

He stood and crossed the room.

She pushed back against the wall, expecting another blow. Erog raised his hand to her face, but this time he did not strike her. Instead, he gently caressed her neck and pulled her lips to his. The kiss was weak. Loti resisted the urge to turn her head. She needed more time to convince him to put an end to his scheme.

"I want you to go with me." He still held her by the back of her neck. "All I need to do is pick up some supplies at my cottage and we can leave now instead of waiting until tonight. I've arranged for some of my friends to meet us once we're well enough away from Santa's village. They'll bring us additional supplies. With any luck the trip can be made in two days."

"I can't go with you."

His grip tightened on her neck. "Because of Amak?"

"No, that's not it. Amak and I are through. But you can't expect me to change one unpleasant setting for another. I require a different kind of society and lifestyle than you and Amak want. I understand Amak and your beliefs, but those aren't mine. I need to live somewhere I don't have to worry about surviving the day should I wander a few miles from my home. I need to have conversations that will include topics other than somebody's constant daily hardships. I need to see people laugh on a regular basis. I need to get away from this monochromatic environment." She hoped this alternative explanation why she could not leave with him would be enough to convince Erog her refusal had nothing to do with him.

He released her neck and took her hand in his. "My village, my people are different from what you've been subjected to over these past years. Come with me and you'll see. Maybe our union will be the beginning of a new accord between our kinds. You can help bring about a peace in the Arctic."

"Just let me go, Erog, and you . . . you must try to convince Unata to take you back."

Erog pushed her away. "Unata is dead! Rudolph is dead! Brulog and two other elves are dead and I killed them! I killed them and I'm going to kill Santa." He looked at her menacingly. "And if you don't come with me, I must kill you."

Loti's scream was cut short when Erog's fist crushed against the side of her lower jaw, fracturing it in two.

chapter 24

I t was only minutes after he left, when Mikel burst through the door. "Peter just told me Erog hooked up a sled and that he and Loti were going to search for you."

"Loti doesn't know the danger she's in. We have to find them before he kills her too."

"Amak, you can't go looking for them. You shouldn't even have left your bed. Hell, two hours ago you couldn't stand without help. Now you want to lead yet another search party. Be smart, Amak, and go back to your cottage and lie down. I'll tell Santa what's been going on."

Amak shoved Mikel away from the door and left Erog's home. He didn't intend to allow others to take charge in the search for the dwarf and his hostage. Before harnessing a sled, he decided it would be prudent to check the schoolhouse, workshop, and Loti's cottage to ensure Mikel wasn't mistaken when he said Peter saw Erog and Loti leaving the village together.

Like most buildings in Santa's Village, there was no lock on the schoolhouse front door. Children were encouraged to enter and use any of the educational materials whenever they had free time. Amak heard voices when he entered the vestibule but was disappointed when he opened the inner door to discover the only inhabitants were children playing in the corner. He asked if any of them had seen their teacher and left when he received negative replies. He was not surprised.

A snow squall greeted him when he exited the building. His strength was slowly returning, although his frostbitten fingers had alternating areas of pain, numbness and tingling. The heavy gloves couldn't keep the cold out anymore. Amak hoped the legendary recuperative powers of the elves would prevent the loss of any of his fingers due to tissue death or Dr. Skeen's scalpel.

The recent storm had shattered the light bulb on the side of the school building and the darkness combined with blowing snow made vision difficult.

"Amak?"

He looked up and recognized one of the elves from one of the satellite villages staring at him. He could not remember his name so offered no greeting other than a nod of the head. The elf came no closer, apparently wanting a zone of safety between them.

"I just dropped off some toys at the workshop and they told me about all the strange goings on. Everyone seems to have their suspicion as to the who, what and why, but they all admit it's just a suspicion. Do you have any guesses?"

It was no longer a guess as to who was behind everything, but he didn't want to waste time discussing it now. He now understood that Erog's plan was to disrupt Santa's customary activities and to somehow dethrone Santa and to replace or destroy the elves.

Amak asked if the elf knew Erog, and when he replied that he did, Amak asked if he had seen him at the workshop. The elf answered that he had not and replied in same when asked about Loti. Amak excused himself with a few mumbles and proceeded on to Loti's home.

There was no answer when he knocked on the door. Again, he walked into an unlocked cottage. All seemed to be in place. The temperature inside matched the temperature outside, which meant Loti, who enjoyed warmth more than most of the inhabitants of the village, had probably not been here for most of the day. Like others in the village, one of the community generators supplied her electricity, but she preferred to heat her home with a fire constantly lit in a central hearth. Amak noted there wasn't any fire, just cold, gray ashes.

He checked the bedroom in case Loti was asleep, or worse—injured. He couldn't bring himself to think beyond injured. When he found only a tidy bed, he left.

They had told him that Erog was seen leaving on a sled traveling west. That would make sense, since all the disappearances and killings had occurred to the east and south, and Erog would want to draw attention away from these crime scenes. Amak decided to hitch a small dog sled and travel in a typical search pattern beginning a mile from the village.

He arrived back at his home, gathered the essential supplies, and grabbed a knife he used to butcher his quarry.

Exiting, he noted at once a dramatic change in the weather since he was inside. The storm had passed. The wind was nonexistent. The sky was clearing. The clouds would soon clear and allow the moon to illuminate the landscape.

Amak walked to his neighbor's home. He was one of the village's old-timers and Amak knew he had an atlatl. The neighbor asked why he needed to borrow the weapon since he knew Amak generally hunted with a rifle, but Amak gave no explanation. No additional questions were asked and Amak left with his request in hand. It was important to Amak that if he was to battle a traditional enemy, he was going to use a traditional weapon.

He was ten yards from the dog compound when he saw the figure. Whoever it was, he was carrying something large. The shadowy figure stopped next to a sled and gently placed his freight on the ground.

The dogs, already harnessed to the sled, barked in anticipation of a pull. Their bellows masked the sound of Amak's approach. His tired eyes strained to identify the elf by the sled. The clouds completed their journey across the moon, and, finally, the lunar glow allowed recognition. It was not an elf readying himself for travel—it was Erog—it was a dwarf.

Amak dropped the blanket and food supplies to his side and without taking time to aim, launched his spear.

Erog heard the whistle in the air and looked up in time to see Amak's weapon fall short and to the right of its intended target. Two feet further to the right and it would have embedded itself in Loti who was lying prone next to the sled. Erog saw Amak charging and realized he could use the spent missile against its original owner. He tried to grab the spear, but his hands slipped off the wet shaft.

Amak was upon him instantly, knocking him to the ground. Erog tried to rise, but he had landed with one leg trapped under his rear and had a difficult time establishing any leverage. Amak wasted no time continuing his attack and pummeled both sides of Erog's face.

He saw Loti lying motionless just to one side. "You sonofabitch! You're a damned dwarf! What did you do to Loti?" The punches did not stop; even if he wanted to answer, Erog wasn't given the chance.

Amak now directed the blows to the chest where the heavy clothing cushioned their force and damage. Erog rocked his supine body from side to side hoping to dislodge his assailant. The maneuver quickly had its desired effect as Amak toppled onto his side.

Erog jumped up and threw himself at his adversary. The dogs, which were at first spectators, were now caught up in the frenzy and tried to attack each other. The din of the barking masked Amak's shouts for assistance. It was now Erog's turn to pummel Amak. Heavy blows struck his assailant's head. Amak used his free hands to push up on Erog's chin trying to push him back and off. He forced the dwarf's head back in an acute angle, so much so, that all Erog could see was the sky. Erog's fists were no longer hitting their target because Amak's arms were longer and had pushed Erog back far enough that even with the widest arc, the blows were falling short.

Amak's one hand remained on Erog's chin, while the other hand changed position and now had a vise-like grip around his adversary's neck. Erog couldn't breathe. He tried to free himself, but the hand wouldn't let go. He flailed at the arm, but succeeded only in dislodging the hand under his chin. Amak's hand quickly returned to its original position, only this time, his fingers extended upwards towards Erog's mouth.

Even the noise from the sled dogs couldn't mask the howl of pain as Erog bit through two of Amak's fingers.

Erog made no attempt to spit out the separated appendages. Blood dripped from his mouth as he spoke. "Enough of this bullshit. I can't play with you any longer." Amak looked up into a cavernous opening where a mouth should have been. He knew, however, that it must be a mouth because his severed fingers remained impaled on two teeth. He tried to push Erog away, but his intact hand was pinned beneath a knee. The mouth was laughing now and approached him again. Amak swung his mangled hand at his attacker. One of the finger stumps poked Erog's eye and burst the globe. The combined shrieks of pain from the two combatants reached a crescendo that scared and bewildered the dogs to silence.

Erog's agony ended first. He was about to restart his attack when he felt a sudden searing pain in his side. He looked down and saw Amak's spear being withdrawn.

The elf was shouting at him. His words were somewhat garbled, but Erog understood. "You bastard! You killer! You fucking dwarf!"

Amak again plunged the tip of the spear into Erog's side, withdrew it a second time, and used two hands to plunge it into his chest. Blood spurted from the severed heart chambers and cascaded onto Amak and the snow. Erog fell backwards—dead. His mouth still unhinged and barbaric.

Before Amak collapsed to the ground, he looked down at the dead dwarf and gave a piercing war whoop.

He lay for minutes, silent until Loti awoke and spoke. "Amak, can I leave you? I have to get help." She held his head in her arms. "Let me get help. I'll be right back." The icy cold helped coagulate the blood from the severed fingers and Amak fought to sit up.

"No. Don't leave." The struggle had compressed and bruised his windpipe, and his voice was gravelly and barely audible. "I'll be all right. Just stay with me, Loti."

"Holy shit! What's happened here?" Loti turned to see Nels' towering figure walking toward them. He cradled a rifle in his arm. "I was at my uncle's house when Mikel came to tell him of your suspicions."

"He's hurt. Please get some help." Loti employed.

Nels looked at the lifeless body and asked, "Was it Erog? Was he the one causing all the trouble?"

"Yes, it was him," came the Amak's whispered answer. "He's a dwarf. But I still don't know why he did what he did."

"I know. He explained it all to me," Loti said.

"All of it?" questioned Nels.

Amak looked at Loti for an explanation, too.

"Remember that toy manufacturer, Collins? He's the one who's been asking Santa to join his company or at least to stop giving away free toys. Well, he convinced the dwarfs to disrupt Santa's production. Erog and Unata came here to carry out the plan. They set out to destroy Santa's authority, and when that failed, they tried to demoralize and frighten the workers. Erog must've known what would result when he killed Rudolph. Your uncle loves your aunt too much to continue his usual pre-Christmas routines."

"Well, their plan failed," said Amak. His voice was a bit stronger. "This will only bring the elves closer together. Collins will fail."

Loti interrupted Amak. "But they decided Santa must die. Erog placed a bomb in his sleigh." She realized that Santa still wouldn't know. "We must warn Santa! He must be getting ready to leave."

"No. That's not true. We weren't going to kill my uncle. That wasn't part of the plan." Loti and Amak both looked at Nels.

"How would you know, Nels?"

He stood, using his rifle as support. "That wasn't part of the plan. It took a long time for them to convince me that any murders were necessary, but there was never any mention of killing Santa—just some elves."

"My god! You're part of it?" Loti asked.

Nels disregarded Loti's question. He was confused too. No one ever talked about harming Santa. "My uncle's plan is to pass control to Matthew. What a joke. My brother has no idea how to be Santa. Santa has no idea how to be Santa! Collins and those manufacturers like him are the future. Children are tired of dolls and toy trains. They want computerized games. They want progress. Santa's too steeped in tradition. The only chance to perpetuate the institution of Santa Claus is to replace him. Matthew can't manage it. Only I can."

"They were going to kill your uncle, Nels!"

"No, they weren't. Collins told me everything. Erog was never told all. In fact, he didn't even know that I was involved. No they weren't going to kill Santa."

"Listen to me, Nels. Erog put a bomb in the sleigh. When it reaches five-hundred feet it'll explode."

"No! That wasn't part of the plan. Erog must have made that up."

Now it was Amak who spoke. "Nels, what makes you think that Collins told you everything? You said he didn't tell Erog everything."

Nels ignored Amak. To do otherwise was to admit that he was involved in a plot to kill his uncle. He shifted his weight from one side to another, likewise shifting ideas in his head. Finally, he settled into an upright, rigid posture. "Amak, I'm afraid you're right about one thing—the elves will rally behind you if they learn the truth. I'm sorry, Amak, but I can't allow you and Loti to tell your story. You've actually made it easy for me to continue the charade. The story's going to be that Erog killed both of you when you discovered he was a dwarf and I killed Erog."

He took a step back from the two elves and slipped. Amak hoped he would take his usual spill, but Nels used the rifle to regain his balance before Amak could rise.

Loti leaned over Amak trying to shield him as Nels' raised his rifle. The gun barrel looped in the air from side to side making a figure eight that arced on Loti and then came to rest on Amak.

"Give me the gun!" The voice boomed from around the shed. The newest entrant to the scene surprised the three combatants, who understandably were fixated on the gun's position. Santa appeared, his hand extended towards Nels. "Give me the gun, Nels. It's finished."

Nels turned swiftly and aimed the rifle at his uncle.

"Are you going to shoot me, too? How would you explain my death? Even if you could and you became the new Santa, it would be a Santa without a village. The elves would abandon the workshop before you ever put the "Red Coat" on." Santa again extended his hand and calmly continued. "Give me the gun."

"Santa, Erog planted a bomb on your sleigh."

"I know, Loti. Peter found and removed it during the routine preflight check."

Nels continued to point the gun at Santa.

"Give me the gun, son."

He lowered the rifle. Santa took a step towards his nephew, but he was too slow. Nels jammed the end of the barrel against his own chin, angled it backwards, and pulled the trigger.

epilogue

"The train will be stopping in front of the Welcome Center. We hope that you enjoyed this short ride from the airport. For those of you with reservations at the Amusement Park Hotel, please exit from the right side of the train. For those of you with reservations at the Santa's Workshop Hotel and Conference Center, please exit the train to the left. We ask that you remain seated until the train comes to a complete stop. Should you need any assistance, one of Santa's elves will be located the bottom of the escalators in the station."

The recorded message, heard over the speakers, was both soothing and enthusiastic.

"Mom! Mom! Look, there's Santa's Village!"

The twin domes looked like giant igloos rising up from a flat sea of snow. Beyond these massive metal structures lay the vast, austere wilderness of the subarctic. The monorail tracks dipped into a tunnel and the outside panorama went from white to black.

"Dad, can we go the amusement park first?"

"No. We're going to check into the hotel first, have some lunch, and then sit by the pool. We'll see the Workshop tomorrow and go to the amusement park on Thursday."

"Why can't we go to the park first?"

"If we go to the park first, you'll be too tired to see the Workshop. It cost too much to see only half of the Village."

The train stopped so gradually and smoothly that few of the passengers were aware that they had arrived.

The speakers came alive again. "Welcome to Santa's Village, brought to you by Collins' Toys. Santa's Helpers want to wish you all a pleasant stay."

The doors opened and children dashed in all directions. Parents tried to reach for luggage and small hands at the same time and were often unsuccessful with the latter.

"Dad, can we go on a dog sled ride?"

"We'll see." He turned to see his younger son exiting through the wrong door. "Thomas, wait up! Thomas, you're going the wrong way. Santa isn't going to bring you any present if you keep this up."

Santa and his reindeer had made their deliveries that past Christmas Eve. Millions of children were happy because of it. It wasn't just the toys, it was knowing that there really was a Santa bringing presents to those who had been good during the year—even to some who weren't so good. Knowing there was a Santa made those not so young feel good, too. It let them remember their uncomplicated youth—bounding down the stairs to see presents under the tree. They remembered the unabashed happiness.

Rebecca never fully recovered from the emotional stress heaped upon her. She became a recluse, no longer visiting the cabins of those elves stricken with some malady, no longer helping in the workshop or feeding the reindeer. Even Santa withdrew to his home, leaving the sanctuary only when necessary.

Two months after the tragic episode that took his nephew's life, Santa announced he was retiring. After much hesitation, a

259

committee of elves convinced Matthew to become the new Santa. He returned to the village the following month and assumed the mantel of the office—"The Red Coat".

Loti helped nurse Amak back to health. Dr. Skeen said that Erog probably saved Amak some additional surgery when he bit his frostbitten fingers off. Even so, two fingers from his other hand required amputation.

Amak realized Santa would resign even before Santa did but kept his campaign for change bridled in respect for this icon that had saved his and Loti's lives.

Whereas Amak had anticipated Santa's retirement, he did not anticipate or understand when Loti told him she was leaving. He had hoped the two of them would marry and someday replace the Claus family as the imperial family of the North.

Loti explained that she couldn't handle the isolation of this far outpost. She needed civilization. She needed to retreat to a habitat void of perpetual white.

Loti, and then Santa and Rebecca, left the village within a week of each other. With Santa's recommendation, Loti easily secured the job of head schoolmistress in the largest elf community in the Arctic. It was a village with more than two hundred inhabitants and included a good number of permanent outlanders in residence. Known as a trading center rather than an extended arm of Santa's workshop, travelers came and went. The culture was a mixture of elf and outlander. The desire to read and learn were traits not scorned.

Occasionally, Loti and Amak had the opportunity to speak to each other by ham radio. Amak even traveled to see her once. But they never really renewed their relationship. The radio conversations and letters eventually crept to a stop.

† †

Santa and Mrs. Claus, now known as Kris and Rebecca Kringle, returned to where they had first met, Rochester, New York. They sought anonymity and kept to themselves. During the winter, they'd walk hand-in-hand through the isolated, snow-covered parks, and in the warmer months, they would float lazily down the Genesee River in a rented canoe.

Rebecca died two years after the move. The following Christmas, Kris volunteered to dress as one of Santa's many surrogates and distribute presents in the children's wards of the local hospitals. He died, alone, soon after.

Matthew confirmed Nels' expectation that he could never really replace his uncle. He had neither the skill nor the desire. Little by little, he allowed Amak to become an equal and ultimately yielded all authority except "The Red Coat".

The workers never accepted Amak's new power. He had grossly misunderstood that tradition had bound them to Santa, not to another elf. The workers began to trickle away to return to their birth villages. As a consequence, those elves that remained had an increasingly difficult time meeting rising production quotas.

Discord between the elves, Amak, and the new Santa increased until Amak finally decided his plan for control was worthless in a dying village. He drifted further into traditional ways: refusing to use any electricity in his cottage, only using an atlatl to hunt, and rarely shaving. He woke one day, decided he had enough, and dissolved into the vast Arctic wilderness.

Collins bided his time. He realized there wasn't any way to gain control of Santa's production so he created a shell corporation to entice Matthew to relinquish any authority. One day, in early spring, a helicopter landed in the middle of Santa's Village. No one, including Matthew, had ever seen a helicopter before. The sham owner and his entourage stepped out and greeted the elves much as the early French and English explorers had greeted Native Americans. The toy tycoon's stand-in allowed tours of the flying machine and even gave the new Santa and some of the elves a fifteen minute ride over the area.

As expected, Matthew, tired of his responsibilities, was easily swayed to sign an agreement to stop producing and delivering free toys on Christmas Eve. He was obligated, however, during a short transition period, to dress in costume whenever any visitors arrived.

Two years later, Collins replaced Santa with a bulbous-nosed, recovered alcoholic and the elves with little-people, in his newly opened tourist site, "Collins Toys Presents Santa's Village." For fifteen hundred dollars, a family of four was flown to the Village, now relocated on the coast of James Bay, a mere six hundred miles north of Toronto. There they could spend three days with all the comforts of home.

TORONTO GAZETTE

U.S. TOY MANUFACTURER MURDERED

The world's largest toy manufacturer/distributor, Robert Collins, was murdered yesterday outside his recently opened theme park, "Santa's Village."

Witnesses to the crime originally assumed the killer had to be a child. "This little guy, about the size of a ten-year-old, came running from the crowd up to Collins as he exited his helicopter. The kid, I thought he was a kid, had what appeared to be a stick in his hand and, as he approached, he flicked his arm and the stick seemed to break in two." Mr. Andre Roget from Montreal continued to say that he later learned the killer used an atlatl, "Whatever that is. Anyway, the spear end of the weapon made a bull's eye hit into Collins' chest, and he immediately went down."

Later interviews with other witnesses said the killer wasn't a kid, or if he was, it was a kid with a heavy beard. They also said the attacker shouted what seemed to be multiple war whoops after he felled Collins

Ontario Provincial Policeman, Sgt. William Truss, said it was probably an elf or a dwarf, but he had no current explanation for the attack.

Whoever the attacker was, he disappeared during the confusion that ensued. The investigation is ongoing.

About the Author

Michael I Bresner tired of repeating the same bedtime stories to his children and grandchildren and decided to join revisionist authors in retelling classic myths, legends and fairy tales. He and his wife live in northern Virgina.

CPSIA information can be obtained at www.ICGtesting.com
Printed in the USA
BVOW07s0117151113

336322BV00001B/21/P